ATTEMPTING
Elizabeth

JESSICA GREY

For Jane,
thank you for writing stories that I want to jump into.

And for all of my fellow Indie Janeites,
thank you for encouraging me to tell this story.

CHAPTER
One

*"At such an assembly as
this..."*

"YOU NEED TO go with me to the party. I'm not taking no for an answer."

I didn't bother looking up from my novel to where my roommate, Tori, lounged against my doorjamb. "No."

"Yeah, see, I already told you I wasn't taking no for an answer, so you need to get your butt off the bed and get dressed. Showered too." She sounded bored; she was probably examining her cuticles.

I flipped a page. "No."

Tori abandoned her fake bored stance and plopped down on my bed. "Come on."

"Go away."

"Are you really going to let Jerkface ruin your entire social life?"

"I'm not discussing this." I flipped another page with a decisive motion.

"There's no way you just read that entire page. Give it up. You're just pretending so I'll leave you alone."

I sighed dramatically. "And yet, you don't seem to be getting the point."

She snatched the book out of my hands and waved it in front of my face. "Really babe, *Pride and Prejudice* again? This thing is going to warp your brain."

"It's not going to warp my brain."

"Hmm." She flipped through the book for a moment then looked up with a disturbingly evil glint in her blue eyes. "Let's go find you a real-life Mr. Darcy."

"I somehow highly doubt that Scott's party is going to have any real life Mr. Darcys at it."

"You never know. Besides, you don't need a forever Mr. Darcy, just a for the night Mr. Darcy." Tori waggled her eyebrows at me suggestively.

"Ew."

"Oh come on. Tall, dark, handsome; somebody to get your mind of Jerkface."

"Jordan was tall, dark, and handsome, and he turned out to be more of a Wickham than a Darcy," I pointed out. Just talking about Jordan made me feel slightly homicidal. He was hot as heck, but what the man knew about fidelity could apparently be written on the back of a postage stamp.

"Um, Jerkface was a skeeze. And you can sit and wallow here, in which case he wins, or you can come out with me and have a few drinks and dance with a few boys and have a good time, and then you win.

And I win, 'cause Charlie can't go and that leaves me dateless. I need you, Kelsey. Are you going to let me down in my hour of need?"

I pulled a pillow over my head and groaned. "Tor, really. Go away. I want to wallow. I don't want to go Mr. Darcy hunting. I only end up with Wickhams."

She pulled the pillow off my face and whacked me with it. "I've got it! Let's go Wickham hunting then— find you a cute, shallow playboy, and then you can treat him like dirt before he gets the chance to jerkface out on you!"

I considered that for a minute. "So, I, like, preemptively jerkface him?"

"Yes, it's brilliant. Like really. Sometimes I even impress myself. Do not even think about saying it," she warned as she popped off the bed and flung open my closet.

"I wasn't going to say anything," I lied through my teeth. As if I was so predictable that I couldn't let her Han Solo quote slide without answering with Leia's retort.

"Don't even pretend. You are such a nerd. I can see you *thinking* it." Tori flicked through the clothes-laden hangers and finally pulled out a short black dress and tossed it at me. "Wear that. Shave your legs."

"Argh!" I glared at the dress. "I don't want to."

"Wear the black boots. Seriously. Don't argue with me. If I don't hear the shower running in three minutes I'm coming back in here and forcibly throwing you in myself. I'm gonna go do my makeup." She turned, her long black hair flying out behind her, and sailed back out of my room.

"You suck!" I grumbled at her departing back.

"You love me," she shot back over her shoulder.

"Doubtful," I replied. She slammed the door and I gave in to the urge to shout after her. "'That doesn't sound too hard!'"

The door cracked back open and she stuck her head in, glaring at me. "Shut up. Shower." And then the door slammed again.

The party was loud and packed with people, just like I knew it would be. Scott Erickson, a friend of Tori's boyfriend Charlie, had rented out the entire top floor of a club in Long Beach. The drinks were flowing pretty freely, and the DJ was playing what passed for music, but I considered it more of a prosecution-worthy assault on the ears of the general public. I raised an eyebrow at Tori who was half-dancing along with the music as we pushed our way through the crowd near the door and toward the bar.

She caught my look and grinned. "Loosen up, babe!" she shouted over the driving beat. "Let's get a drink and find some cute boys to dance with!"

"I'll be sure to let Charlie know you were out trolling for cute boys," I shouted back. Her only response was an exaggerated eye roll as she sashayed ahead of me. I tugged on my skirt in a vain attempt to make it a little bit longer and tried to follow. Tori was several inches shorter than me. Tiny and petite, she managed to wend her way easily through the mass of writhing bodies blocking our way, whereas I felt like if I tried to push my way through, I'd probably end up injuring someone with the stiletto heels on the stupid boots she'd insisted I wear.

The nice thing about being 5'9 and in such high heels is I could see over most of the crowd. The bar was surrounded by several rows of people. Either people were thirsty, or there was something much more entertaining happening up there than just drinks being poured.

As we got closer I realized that almost the entire crowd around the bar was women.

"Good lord, what is going on, are they giving away free booze?" Tori wondered as we came up against the crowd. She stood on her tiptoes and tried to see over the heads in front of her.

I shrugged and searched in my purse for my wallet. I was going to need a seriously stiff drink to put up with this party for any amount of time. I could smell the hundreds of different perfumes from the group of women around the bar, sticking in the back of my throat and making me want to gag. That, coupled with the thrumming of the music, was brewing a headache at the base of my skull. I snagged a few bills out of my wallet, briefly contemplating ordering two drinks so I wouldn't have to stand in this line again, although I'm not sure standing around in my stiletto boots and mini skirt and holding two drinks was really the image I wanted to give off to this crowd. I'd already noticed a few guys eying the expanse of leg revealed between the top of my boots and my hemline.

"Did you see the guy over there checking you out? Is he Wickhamy enough for you?" Tori had leaned toward me, but she was still shouting so I could hear her over the music. I glanced in the direction she'd indicated and shuddered. The guy lounging against the far wall looked like he was interested in only one thing. What was the deal? Was every guy in the general area a leg man? I resisted the urge to tug my skirt down again.

"Yuck," I responded.

Tori giggled. "Okay, we'll try to find someone a little less obvious." We finally shuffled forward a few steps closer toward the bar. "What is with all these chicks?"

I glanced up as we moved forward. I could see over most of the overly styled heads in front of me now and I'd figured out the reason for the bevy of women in front of us.

There was a hot guy tending the bar. Not only was he hot, he was, as I'm sure most of the women bellying up to the bar had noticed, wearing a form fitting t-shirt. And the form it was fitting was extraordinary. Like maybe he supplemented his bartending income with construction work or filling in for Atlas and lugging the globe around.

He was totally *not* my type. As Tori had noted earlier, I preferred tall, dark, and handsome. While this guy had handsome in spades, he wasn't that much taller than me. In these boots, I may have actually been taller than him, but it was hard to tell for sure from this distance. He also had red hair. Curly red hair. Okay, it wasn't red exactly, more like a dark blond with a bit of red in it. I would have killed to get that shade from a bottle, but I didn't really like red-headed guys. However, I could see why the women were clamoring around the bar. Having all that muscle-bound goodness hand you a drink was probably a double bonus: it was like getting alcohol and a cheap thrill.

"There's a hottie tending bar," I informed Tori.

"Oh, is that what's going on?" She tried the tiptoe thing again, but there was no way she was going to get a peek until we were closer. She'd probably just tip over on her heels and break an ankle. "How hot are we talking?"

"Pretty hot. Bet he's making bank in tips." Right as I said it the bartender looked up right at me. There was no way he could have heard what I was talking about, but for some reason I felt my cheeks go pink. He looked at me for a heartbeat then turned back to the girl in front of him, laughing in response to something she was saying. I blew out a breath, feeling a little overheated. Yeah, bank in tips was probably an understatement.

We finally made our way to the front of the line. Tori leaned her elbows on the bar as if trying to get as close to the bartender as possible as she checked him out. I kept my arms off the bar; in fact, I was about half way behind Tori as if I was using her as a shield.

"What can I get you ladies?"

Oh god, he had an accent. A deep, lovely accent. I was horrible at identifying accents, but I was guessing Australian—all the vowels were wrong in all the right ways. I tried to ignore the shiver that ran up my spine and ordered my drink in as flat and uninteresting a voice as possible.

"Hey there," Tori drawled, and I resisted the urge to kick her. "I'll have a cosmopolitan."

He grinned at her. It didn't seem to be a flirty grin, just the smile of a guy who was used to women falling all over themselves. "No problem," he said as he turned and started our drinks.

Tori turned to me. "Oh my god, the accent!" she mouthed. I was pretty sure there was actual drool on her chin.

I steadfastly ignored her. When he handed us our drinks, I accepted my plastic cup without meeting his eye, but Tori made no attempt to hide her appreciation.

"Oh man, he was gorgeous. Too bad he's tending bar; makes it harder to ask him to dance," she pouted as we moved away from the bar.

"You think?" I asked.

"It's tragic, really. We will just have to find someone else for you to dance with."

I took a healthy swig of my drink. I didn't really want to dance with anyone. There wasn't anyone here that I knew very well, and I've always found dancing with strangers weird. The party had spilled out onto a patio and I gazed out longingly. It looked cool and fresh out there as opposed to the overheated, dimly lit interior of the club.

"Oh hey, look! There's Danny and Rick; you can dance with one of them. It won't be so bad if you start off with someone you know."

I reflected that it would probably be worse. I liked Danny and Rick. They were friends of Charlie's too, but it would kind of be like dancing with my brother. The mass of bodies on the dance floor were uncomfortably close to each other. I'm not sure I wanted to be that intimate with either guy. But Tori was on a mission, and sometimes it's best to just grit your teeth and go along, so I let myself be dragged over to the two guys.

"Hey guys!" Tori bounced up to Danny and Rick. "Which one of you is going to dance with Kelsey?"

I winced. The girl had all the subtlety of a sledge hammer. I wondered how fast I could get to the bottom of my drink—it seemed the only way to make the coming trial any more bearable.

"Hey Kels, looking hot." Danny eyed me with appreciation. He was relatively attractive, I supposed. On a scale of one to Hottie Bartender Guy, Danny was a solid six point five. If I hadn't been forced to walk around him and Charlie sprawled out in our living room eating pizza and watching football every Sunday for months, I might have even upped him to a seven.

"Don't even start," I warned him.

He gave me a look of mock outrage that was

ruined by his broad wink. "I'll dance with you. Somebody's got to do it. It might as well be me."

"Oh god," I groaned. "I'm a charity case."

"Just go!" Tori grabbed my drink and shoved me in the direction of the dance floor. I stumbled a bit on my high heels but managed to steady myself as Danny grabbed my hand and led me into the midst of the dancers.

I survived my dance with Danny. He was a bit of a flailer, but I was agile enough, even in the stilettos, to avoid any swinging limbs that came my way. After that I danced with Rick. I didn't know him as well as I knew Danny, but well enough to not be amused when the hands he had around my waist attempted to slide lower. Although crushing his instep with my heel was my gut reaction, I realized from the glazed look in his eyes that he was a step or two past inebriated, so I just shook my head and slipped out of his grasp.

As I turned around, still moving to the beat of the music and trying to dance my way away from Rick, I happened to glance up toward the bar. The crowd around it had thinned out a bit and reinforcements had apparently arrived because there was a second guy doling out drinks. The curly haired bartender was still there and I had the oddest feeling he was watching me. It was probably stupid to think so. There had to be forty or more people on the dance floor. He could have been looking at any of them.

Rick was somehow missing all of my silent signals and was still getting a bit grabby. I slapped his hand away a few more times and then gave up and stalked off the dance floor. I could see the large doors that opened out onto the patio and I made a beeline for them. It was too crowded, too loud, and I was done pretending to have fun on the dance floor. As soon as I walked out into the cool night air I felt the tension in my midsection ease. Even with the sounds of the city, traffic, and the voices drifting up from the sidewalk below, it was so much more quiet than inside. I could actually hear myself think. I took a deep breath of salty air and walked over to the ledge, leaning against it to take the weight off the balls of my feet. These shoes had been a spectacularly bad idea.

There were a few other people milling around the patio, laughing and talking and drinking. I closed my eyes for a moment.

"Hey!"

I almost jumped out of my skin, Tori's voice was startlingly close. I hadn't heard her come up.

"Are you trying to give me a heart attack?" I demanded.

"What are you doing out here? I thought the point was to have fun and dance." Tori handed me another drink. "I went back to the bar and Hottie is missing..." she trailed off, glancing over my shoulder. "Don't look now, but Hottie is right there. Oh my god, I think he is coming over here. Maybe he's gonna ask you to dance!"

I sighed. "Tor, I don't care. I don't want to dance with anyone, especially not some slacker who tends bar for a living. I don't care how hot everyone else thinks he is. I want to go home and take off these stupid shoes and go to bed."

Tori's eyes were getting wider and wider as I spoke, and I had a sudden sinking feeling. "He's right behind me isn't he?"

She nodded slowly. I was pretty sure her eyes couldn't possibly get any bigger without popping right off her face. I turned around, my mouth dry, and there he was, just a foot or so behind me. I didn't know if he had overheard what I'd said. I hoped he hadn't. He looked more vaguely amused than angry. There was a dimple playing around the edges of his mouth. At the sight of that dimple I felt suddenly weak in the knees. The thought occurred to me that there would be worse fates than spending some time on the dance floor with him.

"I'm sorry—" I started, just in case he had heard me.

"You're Tori Mansfield, yeah?" He ignored me completely and directed his question at my friend.

"Yes."

"Mark Barnes," he extended a hand, and Tori, after a brief pause, took it and shook it. "I didn't recognize you at first. You're Charlie's girlfriend, right?"

"Yes, how do you know Charlie...I mean...recognize me? I think I would have remembered meeting you." Tori blushed.

"I go to Charlie's poker games on Monday nights. I've seen your picture. I didn't realize it was you until I saw you talking with Danny. I was taking a break, so I just thought I'd come over and say hi."

He hadn't looked at me since he'd cut me off, but

as he said that, his dark eyes slid over to me with an amused glint.

Oh. My. God. He *had* heard me. And double oh my god—he's been in my apartment. Charlie uses our kitchen for his stupid poker games because neither Tori or I are home on Monday nights. Those pictures Hottie, er, Mark, had seen of Tori had most likely included me. They were hanging on the walls of our living room and stuck onto our fridge with "I Love Chocolate" and "Only Mr. Darcy Will Do" magnets.

"Well, it's so nice to meet you, Mark." Tori's voice sounded wrong. Was she...no, she couldn't possibly be flirting? "This is my friend, Kelsey."

"Hi," I managed.

"Nice to meet you." His voice was completely disinterested, and I noticed he didn't offer me a handshake like he had Tori.

Triple oh my god. Not only had he heard me, he was annoyed. I really hadn't meant anything by it. I was just cranky and tired and wanted to go home. But I'd managed to insult him and his profession all in his hearing 'cause I hadn't believed Tori that über Hottie was walking toward us. Although, she *had* been wrong, he wasn't coming to ask me to dance...'cause, well, right? I mean the skirt was working for me, but I doubt it was working quite that much.

I figured the best thing to do was just lapse back into silence. I wasn't really sure what to say in the situation. So I didn't say anything. Mark asked Tori some question, I didn't even really hear what it was because I was too busy trying not to look like the very awkward third wheel I was obviously becoming to this conversation. I caught Charlie's name in Tori's reply, so I'm guessing it had something to do with where he was for the evening.

It was cold, so I crossed my arms across my chest, balancing my drink in one hand. I tried not to glance at Mark's very well defined pectoral muscles as he chatted with Tori. But I failed. After a few minutes the conversation wrapped up and he turned to me with a small half smile and repeated his earlier "nice to meet you." I mumbled something in return and then he was gone.

As soon as he was out of earshot, Tori hit me with her purse. "What is wrong with you?" she hissed.

"I didn't realize he was right behind us!" I said defensively.

"Well that was bad enough. But then you just stood there with your arms crossed like you couldn't wait to be rid of him. Bitch central, babe!"

"I wasn't trying to be a bitch! It was cold! And he was obviously talking to you, not me, so I was just sort of awkward."

"Awkward is one word for it. Kels, I think you totally had a chance there and you blew it. He could have been your Wickham for the night. Come on! Did you see those arms? Don't you want those arms to do Wickhamesque things to you?"

I laughed in spite of myself. "I think maybe the Wickham hunt has gone to your head. All I really want to do is to go home and go to bed."

Tori grumbled something under her breath as we

moved toward the big doors leading back into the party. "Fine, we'll go home. Depressing. Wasting a perfectly good opportunity."

I nodded noncommittally. I wasn't sure how much of an opportunity I would have had with Mark and his arms. My guess is none. And even if I'd had the opportunity, I'm not really sure I was the rebound fling type. I was more the eat-twice-my-weight-in-chocolate-and-watch-sappy-movies type. I was just glad to be heading back home and if thoughts of what Wickhamesque things a certain Aussie could do to me with his spectacular arms kept popping into my mind, it was because of Tori's suggestion. And maybe the alcohol. Yeah, that's all it was.

CHAPTER
Two

"Well, I'm not saying I'd like
to build a summer home here,
but the trees are actually
quite lovely."

OKAY, IT WAS time to face it. Admit the truth and own up. Let the chips fall where they may.

I was obviously in the middle of some kind of life crisis. I'm only twenty-three. I can't even claim a quarter-life crisis for another two years. Well, maybe I can. Honestly, am I expecting to live to a hundred? Ninety doesn't even seem that plausible, so I can go right ahead and claim a quarter-life crisis.

Consider it claimed.

I have no idea what in the hell I am supposed to do with the rest of my life.

Here I am with a BA in literature. It's all pretty and shiny and cost me more than I'll likely make in the entirety of the rest of my twenties. Once I got out of college my options were: a) find a real job doing something that has nothing to do with my field of study, b) get a teaching degree and spend my days trying to get ninth graders to give a rip about Romeo and Juliet, or c) go to graduate school and spend more money for a newer, even shinier and more useless degree.

Of course I went with option c.

If there's one thing I excel at it's procrastination. A Masters of Arts in Literature is, in today's economy, the epitome of procrastination. Therefore, it's perfect for me! Just put off the real world for another day. I live my life like that song in *Les Mis*, except "one more day, one more dawn" isn't me hoping for revolution on the morrow, it's me shoving all important life decisions a bit farther into the future.

Someday I'm not going to be able to push them any later on the calendar. And that someday is May 5th of next year, when I walk up and get that piece of paper that represents the previous two years of my life and several tens of thousands of dollars.

So who am I to criticize a guy for bartending for a living? He at least was making a living. Something I had absolutely no idea how to do.

I groaned and rolled over, shoving another pillow over my head. All of this self-reflection was not the best start to a Saturday morning. But I couldn't turn off my brain. My poor, sad, addled brain that was slightly sore from my two drinks the night before. Two drinks—really, more like one and a half; I'd never gotten around to finishing the drink Tori had brought out to me. Seriously. I should have just gone

right ahead and called it a midlife crisis. I was
obviously old before my time if I could feel the effects
of two cocktails the next morning. Perhaps I could
blame the drinks for my nagging sense of guilt over
having dissed Hottie Bartender Guy.

I'd been a jerk.

"I *am* a jerk," I sadly addressed the pillow smashed
onto my face. "I spent too long with Jerkface Jordan
and now *I* am the Jerkface. Jerkface Jr. Jerkface II.
Baby Jerkface." I rolled back over, cautiously opening
an eyelid. The bright sun streaming in through my
window almost made me cry. Why in the heck hadn't
I closed the darn blinds. I literally had no forethought
or planning skills. None.

"It is possible I'm being a little too harsh on myself
this morning. Also, I'm talking to myself. Neither of
these are good signs."

Coffee. Coffee would fix all the world's problems.
Or at least all of my immediate problems.

I stuck my feet into my oversized Mickey Mouse
slippers and padded out to the kitchen without
bothering to stop by the bathroom first. Brushing
one's teeth is all well and good, but even personal
hygiene wasn't going to stand between me and my
beloved French press this morning.

Who cared anyway? The only one here was Tori
and maybe Charlie. I wasn't entirely sure what time it
was, but if the annoying brightness of the sun was
any indication, I'd slept away a good portion of the
morning.

Except, as I rounded the corner from the hallway

into the kitchen it became quickly apparent that Tori and Charlie weren't the only ones here. I froze in the doorway in shock. I don't know why I hadn't heard the voices. I was so out of it that I might not have noticed a bomb going off outside, but I should have heard four guys arguing and joking down the hall, right?

I almost turned to run back into my room, but it was too late. They'd seen me. Charlie, Danny and Rick, and...oh god, please don't let that be Hottie Bartender Guy. He was leaning over looking at a map that they had spread out on the kitchen table. All I could see was his blondish red hair. And his muscles, those were a bit hard to miss. The other guys were all gaping at me. I resisted the urge to pull my oversized t-shirt down—I had to be showing an indecent amount of leg—and looked up. His dark brown eyes assessed me for a minute. That dimple I remembered so well from last night flashed at the side of his mobile mouth, but to his credit he didn't smile or laugh. He also didn't look as, um, *appreciative* of my leg display as both Danny and Rick did. For some reason that mildly annoyed me. Not that I was parading around in a state of semi-undress to get complimentary stares from guys that I didn't even know were in my own kitchen.

My own damn kitchen.

"Morning, Kels," Tori said, turning around from where she'd been slicing something on the opposite counter. "We are gonna..." she broke off as she saw me standing in the doorway in all my messy hair, baggy t-shirt and ridiculously slippered glory.

"Can I...talk...to you for a minute, Tor? In my room?"

"Um, yeah," Tori's eyes slid guiltily from me to the group of guys, all of whom were still staring at me in wide-eyed silence. I must look a wreck. I turned as regally as possible and stalked back down the hall to my room. "If I'm not back in five, come in after me; I might not make it out alive," I heard Tori whisper to Charlie as she passed the table. I narrowed my eyes in rage. That girl was not helping her cause.

I waited just inside my door, arms crossed over my chest, until she came into my room looking guilty as sin.

"Tori Louise Mansfield." She winced at my emphasis on her hated middle name. "Why are there *men* in our kitchen on a Saturday morning?"

"In my defense, it's past noon," she began. I glared at her.

"I know you're upset. I probably should have come in to warn you or something, but I didn't want to wake you up. How was I supposed to know you'd come out in your pajamas?"

I rubbed my forehead, trying to push the headache out from behind my eyes where I could feel it starting. "I will forgive you if, and only if, you bring me a cup of coffee and tell me what in the heck that guy is doing here."

"Who?" She looked at me with wide, guileless eyes. I inhaled slowly, mentally calculating how many years any reasonable jury would give me for the murder of my roommate. If ever there was a case of justifiable homicide, this had to be it.

"Oh, Mark?" The innocence fairly dripped from her voice. I bet I could even argue it down to self-defense at this point, you know, if I got a good lawyer and wore light colored cardigans every day to court. Juries love cardigans. Cardigans scream "Innocent By Reason of a Very Annoying Roommate."

"Do you want to die?" I hissed between my teeth. "Like, slowly and in great pain?"

"Sorry, I shouldn't tease you before coffee. I'm a horrible person." The wicked gleam in her eye belied her contrite tone. She was having way too much fun at my expense. It was probably all my own fault. I was being punished by Tori and the gods of caffeine and awkward social situations for being unintentionally rude to a hot guy. "Actually, some of the guys from Charlie's poker group are going hiking up in Angeles National Forest. I'm going too. And I'd said I'd ask you if you wanted to go if you woke up before we left."

"Oh god," I groaned. "Please don't tell me that Rick asked you to ask me to go."

"Yeah, I think he was the one who suggested it. Why?"

I collapsed on my bed, and threw my arm over my face. "He totally grabbed my butt last night. I was hoping it was just the alcohol talking...or grabbing. Argh!"

"Ew, are you serious? Uncalled for. You don't have to go then." Her voice became thoughtful. "Although, and don't you ever tell Charlie I said this, it's probably worth the price of admission to watch Mark hike."

I peeled my arm off my eyes and squinted at her. "What?"

"He's wearing shorts," she informed me seriously. "They're kinda long, but they, um, fit well. And the t-shirt, well you've seen the t-shirt..." She gazed off into the distance with a slightly unfocused look.

"And you're seriously counting on me not to mention to Charlie that you're lusting after his friend when you've been so horribly mean to me this morning?"

"Hey, I'm not lusting. I'm just pointing out that you're single and there's no harm in enjoying the view."

"Uh-huh. Somehow it doesn't seem worth the physical exertion of hiking through a forest. A forest that's on a mountain."

"It's really more in the foothills."

"Go away, Tori." I covered my eyes again with my arm.

"The t-shirt, Kels. It's all soft and clingy and tight. But not like goonish tight, it's more like 'omg did you see those pecs?' tight. That is all I will say as I leave you to your lonely, hot-Australian-man-free Saturday."

I heard the door close and then a second later reopen.

"We're leaving in twenty. I suggest a ponytail because you don't have time to wash your hair, and babe, it's a mess."

"How did I let myself get talked into this?" I grumbled under my breath as I stared at the start of the trail. To my non-hiker eyes it looked like it went basically straight up. I was wearing my most comfortable shoes. I did horrible, evil things like Zumba at my local Y in them, but I doubted they were trail-worthy. Curse Tori and her suggestive...suggestions. Although I'd be drawn and quartered before I'd admit I'd allowed myself to be dragged along on what promised to be several hours of torture just so I could ogle a guy's chest, and/or other body parts.

Right now I couldn't see his chest at all. Mark was several yards in front of me, his very toned calves testifying to the fact that this was not his first hike. I vacillated between loathing at the ease with which he was striking out up the trail and admiration for his general hotness. I kind of hated him. And I was all sorts of awkward around him.

On the ride up here I'd been in Charlie's car with him (well, him, Charlie and Tori), and I'd managed to sit in the back seat, completely mute while he and the others joked and laughed. I was a total fifth wheel even though there were only four of us. Tori kept shooting me confused glances. Probably wondering what in the heck was wrong with me. I'm not a social butterfly, but I'm not entirely inept either. Usually.

Apparently, around Mark inept didn't even begin to cover it. I had no idea what to say to him. I felt bad about being Jerkface Jr. the night before, but I didn't know how to apologize. The sensible thing to do would be to just act normally, but I seemed to be having problems with that too.

"Hey, Kelsey."

"Rick," I replied from between gritted teeth as I started up the trail, Rick following after me like a lost puppy.

"How are you doing?"

"Fine, thanks."

"I, uh, I wanted to say sorry about last night."

I glanced over at him. His face was bright red. I hoped it was from embarrassment and not that he was going to have a heart attack before we were even a hundred feet up the trail.

"Okay."

Rick didn't look fully satisfied with my answer. "I just wanted you to know, I mean, I don't usually just grab girls' asses...I mean, not that you don't have a really nice—"

"Rick," I cut him off. "Apology accepted. There's really no need to discuss it further."

There was a low rumbling sound from in front of us and I narrowed my eyes suspiciously at Mark's broad back. Was he laughing? That's just what I needed. Him overhearing Rick's incredibly uncomfortable discussion of my butt and its grabable merits.

The day had started out crappy and was spiraling

quickly out of control.

I spent the next half hour in silence, darting suspicious glances at the trees. I was just waiting for a Rodent of Unusual Size to burst from the dense foliage and attack. If I even saw a hint of a whisker I was going to drop my backpack and run, screaming, back down the mountain. As far as I was concerned, everyone else could just fend for themselves.

Our destination turned out to be a little picnic area. Tori had packed sandwiches and carrot sticks in little baggies and doled them out before we headed up the trail so everyone was carrying their own sandwich weight. When we finally arrived at the flat, grassy picnic spot I was covered in sweat, probably an unbecoming shade of light purple, hungry, and grumpy. This had been a stupid idea. Even if I'd had a spectacular view of Mark's backside and calves all the way up the infernal mountain. It was not worth the price I was paying.

I sprawled down on the grass as soon as I realized we were stopping.

"I may never move again," I informed the brilliant blue sky above me. "Just leave me here to die."

"It might help if you stretched out a bit. If you just stop suddenly your muscles will tighten up." Mark's shadow partially blocked out the scorching sunlight, but I didn't bother to look over at him. I'd seen him a few minutes ago, looking calm, cool, and not out of breath in the slightest.

"I'd argue that I don't have muscles, but you can probably hear them screaming from there, so that'd be pointless."

Mark laughed. It sounded like warm honey. Okay, that's obviously stupid, and my brain had most likely been fried by the heat and the lack of oxygen at this elevation. But if warm honey had a sound, it would totally sound like Mark's laugh. In spite of the heat, I felt a not entirely unpleasant shiver race up my spine.

"I'm planning to die here, anyway. So it doesn't really matter if I die with cramped up muscles or not. Dead is dead."

"True. But Rick seems a chivalrous bloke. He might take it upon himself to carry you down the mountain if you're unable to walk."

I scrambled to my feet so quickly that I felt all of the blood leave my head in a rush and swayed in place.

This time Mark's laugh was full-bodied and loud as he grabbed my elbow and steadied me. "Easy there."

I was pretty sure he was laughing at me. I pulled my arm out of his large hand and rubbed my elbow as if he'd burned me. I'm not usually so sensitive, but this man made me feel completely off-kilter. I'd been in his presence only a few hours total and managed to always appear at my absolute worst. "I've got it, thanks," I said stiffly.

He shrugged, his face a mixture of confusion and mild annoyance. "Yeah, sure."

I made my way over to where Tori was spreading out a picnic blanket. I was going to stick to her like a burr the rest of the afternoon, using her to insulate me from the guys. Rick kept looking at me as if he was starving and I was a handy granola bar. It made me uncomfortable. Mark had resumed his nonchalant ignoring of me. It wasn't even like he was ignoring me. That implied effort. He just honestly didn't seem to notice my presence. For some reason that bothered me more than Rick's obvious staring. Even though being ignored was what I wanted. Why should I care if Mark didn't give two cents about me? I didn't give two cents about him. The non-caring was mutual...as evidenced by the fact that I spent the entire rest of the afternoon sneaking glances at him and wondering if he thought I was a total jerk, or if he was really just not thinking of me at all.

CHAPTER
Three

"Sorry about the mess."

FUN FACT ABOUT hiking: Going down the hill is so much easier than going up. Who knew? Another fun fact about hiking: It was not something I should participate in again. Ever. If someone had a gun to my head and ordered me to hike up another dusty, hot, steep trail again I would offer to take the gun from them and finish myself off so they could be spared the residual guilt and possible life sentence.

It seemed, however, that I was the only one in our party who was convinced that hiking was a tool of Satan. Everyone else was laughing and talking and looking like they'd done nothing more strenuous than take a leisurely stroll. I wanted to toss the lot of them off the nearest cliff. My feet hurt, my legs hurt, my head hurt, and all I wanted to do was see the parking lot and Charlie's stupid, ugly, yellow sedan. I'd probably kiss it. I might even be persuaded to marry it. If God had wanted us to walk straight up mountains he wouldn't have invented Henry Ford.

Rick and Charlie were walking in front of me and their conversation was getting louder and more animated. I glared at their backs.

Rick turned back to look at me with a smile. "What do you think, Kelsey?"

"About what?"

"*Star Wars*. Special Edition or not?"

I narrowed my eyes at him. They were not seriously trying to get me to discuss this now, were they?

"I don't know, Kels, I've been thinking about it and I'm wondering, why *not* watch the Special Edition." Charlie shot me an evil grin over his shoulder and I had the sudden urge to smack him. Hard. He had to know that my inner geek would not fail to rise up in protest at the thought that anyone would prefer that travesty of computer animated crap George Lucas had foisted on an unsuspecting movie-going public.

"Theatrical release. Only. The end," I managed to huff out.

"But if the director had a vision—a vision that couldn't be adequately met in 1977—why can't he go back and modify it? It's his piece of art, his call." Charlie was really doing his best to sound serious.

"Once a movie, or a book, or any piece of art has been part of society for that long, it's stupid to go back and modify it." I argued, knowing full well that he was baiting me. "Especially when you're changing the way a character behaves. Han Solo would never have let a bounty hunter get off a shot at him. The fact that Han shoots Greedo in the original with no warning demonstrates his character. In the Special Edition he's no longer sexy and swashbuckling, he's just careless enough to let a bounty hunter get off a shot at point blank range." I felt a little light-headed after this speech. It had taken a lot out of me.

"Exactly. Totally great points, Kelsey." Rick flashed me a smile that was a bit more warm than I preferred. I should have just kept my stupid mouth shut. I'd probably just cemented myself as Nerd Queen in his mind. I didn't want Rick harboring a geekery-induced crush on me.

From behind me I heard Tori say to Mark, "Kelsey has very strong opinions on the whole Han-shot-first controversy, but we love her anyway."

Mark laughed in response, and I gritted my teeth and turned my head to look up at them.

"It's Han-shot-*only*, not Han-shot-first," I said sweetly, hoping my eyes conveyed the "you are dead as soon as we get home, sister" message I was trying to send my traitor roommate.

Tori must have been completely missing the fact that her life was in imminent danger, because she winked up at Mark. "The only thing that would get her more riled up is a discussion of which actor is a better Mr. Darcy: Colin Firth or Matthew Macfadyen."

I wondered if there was something more dead than dead? Dead wasn't good enough for her. She needed to be deader. Like maybe I could kill her, then raise her in some horrific voodoo ceremony just so I could kill her again. It occurred to me that I'd been way more homicidal than usual today. I'm pretty sure I'd thought of killing Tori more times in the last six hours than in our entire fifteen-year friendship. The girl had no idea the kind of thin ice she was skating on. None.

Don't respond; don't respond; don't respond. "Firth, of course," I bit out and then wanted to smack myself. "What do you think, Mark?" I said quickly in an attempt to move the conversation back off myself.

"On Firth versus Macfadyen?"

"No. On Han versus. Greedo." Too late I saw the devilish twinkle in his eye. He'd known exactly what I was asking. I was beginning to come to the conclusion that this entire hiking experience had been orchestrated by the universe to put me in the worst possible light.

"I'm not sure it matters," he dismissed the topic with a shrug. "The essence of the movie is the same."

"But it changes the whole way the audience sees the character of Han Solo." I was indignant.

"But the movie isn't about Han Solo. People love him, especially women," he raised his eyebrow at me. "But it doesn't matter if Han is a little less sexy or dashing, because it's not his story, it's Luke's, yeah?"

I sputtered in outrage for a moment, searching for a reason why his argument had to be wrong. "But Han *is* a very important character. His character stands in opposition to Luke's earnestness, so when he finally changes in the end, it makes it that more epic."

"*Star Wars* is a typical Hero's Journey, written straight to Joseph Campbell. So Han's a great character, but he's a supporting one. Luke's journey isn't affected by who shoots first in the Cantina scene."

I almost tripped over my own feet. Had Hottie Bartender Guy just pulled a Joseph Campbell—the author of the definitive comparative mythology text—reference out of his back pocket?

"But," he continued. "I don't disagree that once a film has been out that long it becomes part of the broader cultural consciousness, and it's probably wisest not to tamper with it too much, even for the sake of—and in George Lucas's case I use this term loosely—broader artistic vision. I'm not sure it's quite worth getting worked up about, though."

I didn't even have to look at Tori to know she was trying not to collapse into hysterical laughter.

"Well, we all have things that push our buttons, I suppose," I said with as neutral an expression as possible. Such as hot guys with muscles, killer accents, and apparently brains, that managed to be both irritating and arousing. I couldn't decide which Mark was more of, but I was generally annoyed enough to side with irritation, even though his use of the term "cultural consciousness" had made me want to throw myself at him and beg him to let me have his babies. But he'd probably let those babies watch the Special Edition, and God forbid, maybe even the second trilogy. It would only end in acrimony and recriminations. And then I'd have to add him to my growing "To Murder" list, right after Tori.

Charlie and Rick started in on a new topic, and I

took the opportunity to lapse into a frustrated silence. Luckily the conversation had helped us cover the last quarter of the trail and it was only a few minutes before we were able to see the blessed sight of the parking lot. I was only too glad to have the end of the hike, and hopefully the entire day, within reach.

Why I'd let myself be dragged out for appetizers and drinks after the hiking excursion, I will never know. I was hot, sticky, in pain, and generally the worse for wear. I hadn't been aware that going to McKinney's Pub after was part of the deal, and Charlie would have had to drive back to the apartment to drop me off. I guess I didn't want to come off as that much of a spoilsport. Plus, McKinney's has these potato skins that are like a party in your mouth.

By the time said potato skins were deposited on our table, I was salivating. The sandwiches we'd eaten earlier had been good, but I'd worked up quite an appetite walking down the mountain. Stuffing my mouth full of potato, bacon, and cheesy goodness also meant I didn't have to participate as much in the conversation.

Which was probably good because whenever I opened my mouth around Mark, really stupid things seemed to pop out of their own accord.

"Hey, did that slacker Erickson pay you for saving

his butt last night?" Rick asked Mark. He turned to Charlie. "Dude, the bartender Scott hired didn't show up, but Barnes just jumped back there and ran the bar all night."

Charlie looked at Mark in appreciation. "I didn't know you were a bartender."

"Yeah. Earned some extra money when I was in uni that way. Been a while, but like riding a bike, I guess." Mark shrugged his broad shoulders. Had I mentioned his shoulders? I almost forgot to swallow the bite of potato skin in my mouth as I tried not to stare.

"That's awesome, I hope you at least made good tips."

Charlie had no idea. Good tips didn't even begin to cover it.

I blinked and tried to refocus my eyes somewhere other than Mark's shoulders.

"So, what do you do, if not bartend for a living, Mark? You're pretty good at it; my drink was amazing."

I could have kicked Tori, except she was sitting down the table from me. My legs are long, but not quite that long. Flirting with Mark right in front of Charlie was low. Although she was probably doing it more to get a rise out of me than out of Charlie, judging by the sly glances she was sending me.

"I teach history."

"Oh really?" Tori shot me another glance. I was too preoccupied with trying to look like I wasn't choking on a piece of potato to respond. I'd been mid-swallow when Mark had announced that he was a teacher. Hottie Bartender Guy was now Hottie Teacher Guy. Talk about jumping to conclusions about someone I'd never met. My eyes started to water, but I was still trying to act like nothing was wrong.

"Mark teaches at Whittier Prep," Charlie told Tori.

I was really choking now. The potato had made its way down but I still couldn't get any air. My face was probably turning bright purple. I reached for my drink, hoping that taking a sip would help.

Rick, who was, unfortunately, sitting right next to me, finally noticed my distress as I started coughing. "Kelsey, are you okay?" He reached over and thunked me on the back, causing me to gasp and splutter and spill daiquiri all over my shirt.

What was wrong with him? He obviously was not up on his CPR certification if he thought smacking a choking victim on the back was the way to go. Although, by that point I wasn't choking on anything but my own embarrassment, and the thought of Rick giving me the Heimlech actually made me break out in a cold sweat.

"Yes, thank you. I'm fine," I finally managed after taking a swig of my drink. I set it back down and grabbed my napkin, trying to sop up some of the liquid from the front of my shirt. Great, now in addition to smelling like sweat, I was going to smell like alcohol. That combo was sure to get more pleasant with time.

"Wow, that's cool. How long have you been teaching there?" Tori continued as if my little incident hadn't happened. Mark turned back to her, and I was grateful to her for reclaiming his attention.

"Coming up on a year," he answered.

"Kelsey went there. Just think, Kels, you could've had Mark for a teacher."

All eyes swung back toward me. The thought of Mark being a teacher of mine was making me feel vaguely sick to my stomach. My brief moment of gratefulness toward Tori evaporated. Was she on some kind of narcotic that made her suddenly witchy toward her basically harmless best friend?

"I graduated from high school almost *six* years ago, Tori. The same year you did."

Tori flashed Mark another smile. "I didn't go to Whit Prep though. Plain old public school for me."

"And me," Charlie grinned. "I don't know how I forgot you went there, Kels. Remember that dance I went with you to; what was that? The one right after you broke up with that football player."

"Junior formal." I muttered into what was left of my drink.

"Oh, yeah. How could I have forgotten that!"

I grimaced. "It was a pretty forgettable evening."

Luckily, Mark didn't seem interested in comparing people we may or may not know in common. The fact that he was probably colleagues with my former teachers was disconcerting. I was just hopeful that he'd never feel a need to go through any old year books.

"One of the pool tables is opening up. You guys want to play?" asked Danny. There was a mass exodus from the table. I didn't blame them, the conversation wasn't exactly sparkling. If I'd had opportunity to escape, I would have.

"Are you trying to torture me?" I asked Tori as soon as we were alone at the table. "He could have been my teacher? Seriously?"

"I was trying to involve you in the conversation," she defended herself. "What's up with you? You're not usually so standoffish. Is it because of what happened last night? Mark doesn't seem the type to hold a grudge."

"No, that's not it. I mean, only partly. I don't know, I just feel awkward."

"Well, you're certainly acting awkward."

"Um, thanks babe, real uplifting," I said sarcastically.

She arched an eyebrow at me. "I'm trying tough love. Something to break you out of this weird funk."

I sighed. "I don't know what to tell you."

Tori grabbed her bag. "Let's hit the ladies room. I have another shirt you can wear."

I stared at her, dumbfounded. "You have another shirt?"

"Well, yeah," she grinned. "Things happen when you're in nature; it's best to be prepared."

I followed her to the bathroom, studiously ignoring the guys at the pool table in the corner. When I finally surveyed the damage to my shirt, complimented by the tendrils of hair escaping my ponytail and sticking out wildly around my face, I actually laughed. "I look like a homeless person."

"It's not quite that bad," Tori grinned at me. "Close though."

I ducked into a stall and changed out of my smelly shirt and into Tori's black t-shirt. It was a little bit short on me, but as long as I didn't raise my arms, I wouldn't show any midriff. Wearing something that didn't smell like hiking trail and booze totally trumped not having freedom of movement.

I redid my ponytail and scrubbed my face with cool water before we went back out. I wasn't going to win any beauty contests, but I felt significantly better than I had before.

As we walked back into the pub, I glanced over toward the pool table. I stopped in surprise. There was a blonde in a very short dress leaning against the pool table, her head tilted toward Mark. Her body language was pretty darn aggressive. While I watched, she reached out and put a hand on his bicep.

Charlie was standing off to the side looking uncomfortable—he seemed to be scanning the crowd as if he was looking for someone. He caught sight of us and seemed relieved. He shook his head slightly at us.

"What's going on?" Tori asked me in a confused voice.

"I have no idea." I felt my jaw drop as the blonde tossed her hair over one shoulder, her face turning in our direction. Time slowed down and the room seemed to tilt a bit.

"Oh my god," I heard Tori breathe next to me.

Ashley Brandon. The bane of my college existence.

I'd know her anywhere. Finding her sucking face with my ex two months ago (which is how he'd achieved the status of ex) had burned her annoyingly perfect features permanently into my brain.

I was pretty sure I was going to throw up. The potato skins and daiquiri were churning around in my stomach in an entirely unpleasant way.

Ashley looked directly at me, her hand still on Mark's arm. Mark glanced up too. I must have looked like a crazy person, standing there, rooted to the floor, turning an unbecoming shade of red. Maybe if I'd been feeling less sick I would have noticed that he looked slightly uncomfortable at being manhandled by Ashley.

But I wasn't paying much attention to Mark's face. I was focused on Ashley and her perfectly manicured, bright red fingernails caressing his bicep. I'd seen those same fingers running through Jerkface Jordan's dark hair before he'd noticed me standing there in shock. The last I'd heard they were dating.

I had to get out of here. Before I did something dumb like cry.

"I'm going to the car," I said in an admirably even voice to Tori.

"I'll get Charlie's keys and meet you there." There was a grim determination in her voice that made me guess that she wasn't heading in the direction of the pool table just to retrieve the keys.

I couldn't bring myself to care. I turned on my heel and walked, slowly but steadily, out of the pub and to Charlie's car. I stood quietly and waited for her to come out to the parking lot. I was silent the entire ride home. Tori eyed me uneasily as she pulled up in front of our apartment.

"Do you want to talk about it?"

"No." I opened the door and climbed out. "I know you probably have to go back and get Charlie. It's okay. I'm fine."

"Are you sure?" She didn't look convinced.

"Yes. Fine. I'll see you when you get home." I made it all the way into the apartment and got the front door closed before I let myself cry.

CHAPTER
Four

*"You take the red pill—
you stay in Wonderland and I
show you how deep the
rabbit-hole goes."*

I FELT SLIGHTLY better after my crying jag. I'm not even sure why I was crying. I wasn't still crying over Jordan. I knew I was infinitely better off without him and his habit of subtly putting me down.

I wasn't really crying because of Ashley. I hated her, she hated me. It was a mutual thing. I had no idea how she knew it would bother me for her to be draping herself all over Mark. It could have been completely coincidental. I mean, he was hot. She probably couldn't help herself around someone that attractive. On the other hand, Charlie had been standing right there and she certainly knew who he was. Had she seen us all sitting at the table earlier and thought I liked Mark so she thought she'd make a move? Well, the joke was on her, because I didn't like Mark.

Okay, perhaps I was *slightly* attracted to him. Slightly might be a bit of an understatement. I hadn't been this attracted to a guy since Jerkface Jordan. And that certainly turned out well. But unlike Jordan, something about Mark annoyed me. I felt off-kilter and awkward around him. I'm not the smoothest person in the world, but so far, in my two days of knowing Mark, I'd yet to come across in anything approaching a good light.

"He's not my type anyway. I prefer tall, dark, and handsome, not short, red-headed, and snarky." I ignored the fact that tall, dark, and handsome obviously didn't prefer me, and that calling Mark short was patently unfair. Yeah, he wasn't towering over six feet, but there wasn't anything...lacking...about him physically. I pulled my mind back sharply from where it was wandering— not even wandering really, more like running full speed —down a very dangerous path.

The point was, I didn't like Mark.

There's really only one course of action after a sob fest of that magnitude. I changed into my rattiest and most comfortable sweatpants, pulled out *Pride and Prejudice*, poured myself a glass of wine, and stretched out on our living room couch for a date with some of my favorite characters.

I fell asleep reading. I hadn't started at the beginning of the book. I'd read it so many times that I knew the plot forward and backward. I could quote dialogue. I may or may not have read and written fan fiction. I admit nothing.

I do admit, however, that I'm not-so-secretly in love with Mr. Darcy. What's not to love about a handsome and rich man ("*ten thousand pounds a year!*") that falls so desperately in love with a woman that he is willing to examine his own prejudices and overcome his pride to be with her? Actually, it's even better than that, because Darcy changes not knowing if it will result in Lizzy falling in love with him. And he does, I think, a truly amazing and dashing thing, when he helps rescue her sister from certain ruin and wants no recognition for it. He saved her younger sister, Lydia, at great trouble and expense, just because he loved Elizabeth and didn't want to see her hurt. Sigh.

And yes, I know he is a fictional character; I'm still kind of in love with him. It's a pity that my own attempts at finding my own Mr. Darcy had turned into such debacles.

I had started reading at the first proposal scene. There is something so heartbreaking about Darcy's awkward attempt at a proposal. He so desperately doesn't want to love Elizabeth, and he makes it abundantly clear. The verbal smackdown she gives him is one of my favorite scenes in all of literature. I figured I'd read from first proposal, through Lizzy coming to love Darcy, and all the way to the happy ending.

I didn't make it to the end, though. I was so tired out from the ill-conceived hiking excursion and my crying jag that as soon as Darcy stormed out of Hunsford cottage after being soundly rejected, I felt my eyes getting heavier. I had barely made it through the letter Darcy gives Elizabeth the next day when I dropped off to sleep.

As my eyelids drifted shut, I felt like I was being pushed and pulled from all sides. There was a loud rushing sound in my ears. I opened my eyes, but I seemed to have trouble focusing. I could bring the scene in front of me into focus, briefly; then it got blurry again. It was bright, much brighter than my softly lit living room. After a moment or so of fighting to focus, my vision cleared. The strange sounds remained in my ears, like the sounds of waves pulling in and out.

I felt different. I looked down at my body. I was dressed in a pale muslin morning dress, holding a sampler as my hands—except they weren't my hands; they were much smaller and more delicate than my hands—were busily setting a series of small precise stitches into the fabric. I have never sewn in my life.

I looked around the room. It was lovely—filled with early afternoon sunlight from large multi-paned windows, decorated in a soft feminine style, and stocked with the most gorgeous antiques I had ever seen.

I became aware that someone was talking to me. There was a woman sitting on a small couch to my left. She was dressed in a Regency era dress just like I seemed to be and had a small lace cap on her head. It appeared she'd been speaking to me for some time, but her voice was just beginning to filter through the rushing in my ears.

The woman was dark-haired and petite and looked to be in her late thirties or early forties. She also sat with a sewing project in her lap, but unlike my hands, which were still busily working away, hers were gesturing in the air as she punctuated whatever point she was making. As her voice became clearer I became even more confused.

"...and I must say, he was paying you particular attention yesterday during our stroll. Did you not notice it? Such charming manners, and so handsome. Georgiana, are you attending me? You have quite a blank look on your face."

Georgiana? Who was she talking to? I turned my head slightly to each side, but there was no one in the room but the two of us. The woman looked at me in exasperation, but then laughed.

"I dare say you are daydreaming about a *certain* gentleman. You should do me the favor of attending when I am speaking of the very same gentleman," she teased.

I cleared my throat. "I'm sorry, I don't know who you are talking about." For some completely inexplicable reason my voice came out significantly higher and softer than my usual alto. And in an extremely refined sounding upper British class accent. I was so shocked I dropped my sewing sampler and it fell to the floor with a soft *whoosh*.

My companion looked surprised as well, but she recovered quickly with a patently fake-sounding laugh. "Oh my dear, what a dreadful tease you are turning into. Who else could we be speaking of? Do you have that many beaux that you are getting them confused?"

I continued to stare at her. The look on my face—I had a brief dumbfounded moment of realization that I had no idea what my face looked like; judging from the difference in the appearance of my hands and the tenor of my voice, it might look extremely different from my own—must have given her another moment's pause, because she furrowed her brow and said, "Why, Mr. Wickham of course."

If the surprise I felt at hearing my voice registered at about a nine out of ten on the shock scale, the mention of Wickham blew it right off the charts.

"Wickham?" My voice was now a frightfully high squeak, like a church mouse that inhaled helium and then was stomped on. I cleared my throat. My hands clutched at my skirts, frantically, as if by finding purchase on them I could somehow grab onto reality. My spine felt unnaturally straight. I don't think I'd ever sat up so straight in my life. My normal reaction would have been to jump up and pace about the room. I was kind of a fidgety person in general, but for some reason, other than the spastic movement of my hands, my body refused to move from its extremely still state.

I took a deep breath and tried again.

"Wickham? *George* Wickham?" I asked. My companion, clearly discomfited by my strange behavior, nodded vigorously. My brain, which had been feeling sluggish—maybe a byproduct of the strange rushing sounds that had been echoing inside my cranium—began to fit pieces together. "And...you're Mrs. Younge?"

She nodded again. "Miss Darcy, are you feeling quite well?"

Miss Darcy. *Georgiana Darcy.* Mr. Darcy's little sister. Which meant one of two things. I was dreaming or I was crazy. I closed my eyes briefly and ordered myself to wake up. Nothing happened. I peeled my eyelids open again to find Miss Darcy's paid companion, Mrs. Younge, still watching me.

Well, that still left crazy as an option.

"I feel, um, a little bit disoriented," I said truthfully. I was finally able to will myself to stand up. I was tiny! My eye line was completely different; it made everything look strange. I usually stood at 5'9, but I'd bet good money that I was now at least seven to eight inches shorter than that. I probably hadn't been this short since I was ten years old. I took a few steps, Mrs. Younge watching me the entire time. I would have said she looked concerned, but I had a poor opinion of her to start with. I knew she was complicit in trying to foist Wickham on poor, unsuspecting Georgiana, so I trusted her about as much as I'd trust a viper.

I glanced around the room. There wasn't a mirror, which was too bad because I was dying to find out what Georgiana Darcy looked like. I think that was the moment when it occurred to me that I might actually be in *Pride and Prejudice.* My brain somehow accepted that I was a different person—a character that I was familiar enough with to be curious about.

Likely I was a total nut case and had already been committed to a mental institution by concerned friends and family. My choice of hallucination seemed to be the pages of *Pride and Prejudice*, though why my poor, addled brain would pick Georgiana, I honestly had no idea.

I walked over to the window and looked out. We were on the first floor, and the sitting room window overlooked a cobblestone street, lined on either side with stately looking homes.

"We are in Ramsgate," I said out loud. I was mentally orienting myself in the novel's storyline. The seaside town of Ramsgate is where Georgiana Darcy had been seduced by Mr. Wickham into agreeing to elope with him. We were discussing Wickham, but Mrs. Younge hadn't acted as if he had already proposed to Georgiana—to *me*—I corrected myself.

"Yes, of course. Do you think you might need to retire? Mayhap if you lay down for a few moments. Mr. Wickham did promise to call today. We do not want him to see you in such a confused state."

"Don't we? I mean, do we not?" I tried to imitate Mrs. Younge's speaking pattern as I turned my head to look back at her. "And my brother, Mr. Darcy, we do not expect him?"

Mrs. Younge actually started at that and I smiled to myself. *Snake*, I thought. *It'd ruin all your plans if Darcy showed up right now. Although he manages to ruin them for you soon enough.* I wondered how long it would be until he did show up, wrecking Wickham's and Mrs. Younge's nefarious plans and swooping me off to

London. Would it be possible to stay crazy that long? Being crazy might be worth it if I got to see Mr. Darcy in the flesh. Although, I'd be his sister, which was kind of awkward and lame, but at least I'd get to see him.

I must be an incredibly sick cookie to be hoping to remain in a complete state of mental breakdown in order to see a hot fictional guy. I'm obviously *not* in a healthy place. Could it be that seeing Ashley with her paws all over Mark upset me more than I'd realized?

Mrs. Younge was now watching me with narrowed eyes. If she could have heard my thoughts, she would likely have run screaming from the room, but I could tell by her calculating look she was trying to figure out how to best question me about my contact with Darcy. She must want to know if all her best laid plans were about to be dashed.

"Your brother?" she asked in a sickly sweet voice. "Why no, I do not expect Mr. Darcy to visit. Unless you have heard from him that he is coming? I haven't noticed that you have received any letters from him in the last few days."

"Oh no, I have not heard from him. I thought, perhaps, that you had."

Mrs. Younge visibly relaxed. "Why no, my dear. I have not heard from him. As far as I know, he remains in London."

I almost snorted. Luckily for Georgiana, Darcy didn't feel the need to communicate his every move to Mrs. Younge. He would manage to take them all by surprise by showing up unannounced any day now.

"Do we expect Mr. Wickham soon?" I asked. I am not quite sure how I felt about meeting Wickham. I wondered if there was some way I could fast forward my hallucination and get to the Darcy part while conveniently skipping the agreeing to elope with Wickham part. I'd frankly had quite enough of skeezy weasel men. I didn't need to deal with literature's skeeziest of all weasels on top of dealing with my real life issues.

"Do sit down, Georgiana, you look quite pale. Mr. Wickham has been faithfully visiting us around two o'clock in the afternoon. I expect we shall see him then."

"Hmm." I resisted the urge to look at my wrist for the watch that I knew wasn't there and instead glanced at the clock in the corner of the room. It was 1:30 now, which meant I had a half hour to kill with this woman before Wickham made his appearance.

I walked back over to the settee, sat down, and picked up my sampler once again. Mrs. Younge continued to look at me suspiciously, as if she was waiting for me to pop out another head or something, but after a few moments she made an attempt to return to her sewing as well.

I stared at the sampler. It was quite intricate. A verse surrounded by a floral motif. I concentrated on trying to place a few stitches, and was rewarded by crooked stitches and a bleeding finger. I cursed silently and wondered why before, when I hadn't been thinking about it, my hands had seemed to move of their own volition.

Maybe that was the trick. I hadn't been thinking about it. I deliberately made my mind as blank as I could, trying for that sort of spacey feel you get when you're stuck on the freeway during a long drive and you let your mind wander and "come to" fifteen minutes later, only to realize you've driven yourself home without knowing it. You get home because it's routine. Your mind and body know what they're doing without you having to think too hard about it. I figured that Georgiana's hands must have some sort of muscle memory of stitching. If I could stop thinking so much as *Kelsey*, they'd resume their normal activities.

I stared off into space for a few moments. I'm sure I was making Mrs. Younge uncomfortable, but I really didn't care. After what felt like an age, I felt my hands moving: placing tiny, perfect stitches into the sampler. It was an extremely odd feeling letting my body do something that my mind *knew* I didn't know how to do. It took more effort to not concentrate on it than one would imagine.

I kept wanting to freak out about the body that I was in. It was strange to feel like I was me, but inside an entirely different body. A body that could do things like embroider without a thought. Every time I felt my mind veering off into panic I would reassure myself that I'd had a severe mental break. While this doesn't sound like it would be very reassuring, I found it oddly comforting to have an explanation. I figured that I was probably being taken care of by a crack team of specialists as well. I was just too fully involved in my hallucination to notice that I'd been strapped to a gurney in a nice hospital somewhere and, hopefully, fully medicated.

While I comforted myself with thoughts of my lunacy, my fingers continued sewing at a fast pace. Eventually Mrs. Younge seemed assured enough of my return to normal to pick back up where she left off, extolling the virtues of George Wickham. She spent a great deal of time on what a fine figure of a gentleman he had made in a new coat he had recently purchased, and added several references to how he had known me as a child and how surprised he must have been to find me quite grown up into a lady.

She didn't really seem to require much response. The conversation was entirely one-sided and obviously designed to promote Wickham's interests with Georgiana. I nodded a few times, and offered a "Yes, oh he did look quite fine," here and there, but the entire thirty minutes could have passed without one more word from me.

I was incredibly disappointed that the next half hour actually took a full thirty minutes to pass. I was really hopeful that, seeing as it was *my* hallucination after all, time would either speed up, or skip ahead, so I could get to the interesting parts. But, unfortunately, I was stuck there, the minutes ticking off at an annoyingly normal rate, for a full half hour before we heard a knock at the door.

CHAPTER
Five

"She was then but fifteen,
which must be her excuse..."

AT THE SOUND of the knock on the front door, Mrs.
Younge, started up eagerly, pinching her cheeks to
improve the color as she set her sewing aside. I
glanced at her speculatively. That was a whole theory
I had never considered before. Could Mrs. Younge
have been so invested in getting Wickham a rich wife
because she was interested in him herself? Maybe
once Georgiana was Mrs. Wickham and safely stashed
away at a country home, Mrs. Younge and Mr.
Wickham could live it up on her dowry. I'm not sure
if I was more shocked or amused by the thought of
the two of them together.

Mrs. Younge regained her composure as the butler
came in to announce Mr. Wickham. He was followed
into the room by Wickham himself. Mrs. Young and I
both stood and curtsied (something else that
Georgiana's body just did by itself without me

thinking about it) and Wickham bowed.

We all sat back down. Wickham sat next to me on the settee and looked at me earnestly. "I do hope you are feeling well today, Miss Darcy. I fear our walk yesterday was a bit long and damp. I had not a moment's rest last evening so concerned was I that you may have taken a chill."

I blinked for a moment, surveying him. How stupid did this guy think that Georgiana was? Apparently quite. Did this kind of syrupy flirting work with her? Then I remembered that Georgiana was only fifteen. I'd probably fallen for worse at fifteen. God, I'd probably fallen for worse up until two months ago with Jerkface Jordan.

Wickham was really attractive. I'm not sure what I'd expected him to look like. He's always decently handsome in the movies, and the book does say he has every manner and appearance of a gentleman. But somehow I'd expected something more obvious in his appearance to proclaim him a rake. Like a big red cursive R on his chest, kind of like Hester Prynne's A in the *Scarlet Letter*. This is why I focused on British Lit for my Masters. My fellow Americans can be so...literal.

Wickham had dark blond, slightly curly that was styled in such a way as to make him seem just a bit windblown, although I would bet it took at least an hour to achieve. He had light, silvery blue eyes, under rather heavy brows, a straight nose and a very sensual looking mouth. I was sure it was that mouth that had got him this far in life. His bottom lip was slightly fuller than the top one. He could probably get women to do whatever he wanted by just curling his lips slightly into a teasing smile. Which of course was set off perfectly by his dimples.

He wasn't extremely tall, but had broad enough shoulders, though he was generally slim. He looked great in a waistcoat and cravat. But then, I was partial to the whole cravat thing.

Everything about him screamed danger. But poor Georgiana—and really if you think about it, even Elizabeth and most definitely Lydia—was too young and inexperienced to know it. Being as I was unfortunately intimately familiar with his brand of smooth talker, I could smell the sleaze a mile away.

Mrs. Younge coughed discreetly and I suddenly realized that I'd been silent for too long. "Oh. Thank you for your concern, Mr. Wickham, but I do not find that I have developed a chill at all. I am quite well."

This seemed to satisfy him, though I did catch the questioning glance he shot Mrs. Younge who responded with a slight shrug of her shoulders. I folded my hands in my lap and attempted to appear properly interested in the man who was holding my fragile young heart in his dastardly grip.

"I hope our walk did not fatigue *you*, Mr. Wickham, although I doubt it could. You seem to be very strong and...robust." I batted my eyelashes—only twice, I didn't want to overdo it. I saw something flare in Wickham's eyes. Georgiana likely would have taken it for interest or desire, but I could see it for what it was. Victory.

"Thank you, my dear, for the compliment. I assure you I am not at all fatigued from our walk."

"That is good to hear, Mr. Wickham. I would hate to think that anything so trifling as our walk could fatigue a man such as you." I wondered if I'd pushed it too far, but neither Wickham nor Mrs. Younge expected Georgiana to have any knowledge of flirting or double entendres. It seemed I was safe.

"Perhaps then, Miss Darcy, as neither you nor Mr. Wickham seem the worse for yesterday's little stroll, we could take another one today. The weather is so fine." Mrs. Younge offered.

I turned to look at her with a smile. "Oh, Mrs. Younge, what a lovely idea. It is a perfect day for a walk, do you not agree, Mr. Wickham?"

"Any day that I could escort two such lovely ladies must be a perfect day. The weather would not dare refuse me such enjoyment."

I looked down at the fabric on the settee quickly, trying not to burst out laughing. I was hoping he read my move as a shy young girl being overwhelmed by such a compliment. And what a compliment it was. Did he always flirt quite so obviously? If I ever got out of crazytown (it could happen; they've developed some really great meds) I was going to have to reread *Pride and Prejudice* to see if he always talked like this or if he was just laying it on extra thick for Georgiana.

There was much hustle and bustle as Mrs. Younge called for our hats and parasols to be brought so we could prepare for our walk. It seemed like a lot of prep work for a short walk on a sunny day, but then the sun was the enemy of our delicate and pale English skin. I remembered Caroline Bingley's snide comment about Elizabeth's skin getting tanned while she travelled and had to suppress the urge to laugh. I wondered what would happen if I just set off for a walk without all the proper accoutrements. Or announced that in just a few hundred years tanned skin would be looked on favorably and that, in fact, people would pay good money to artificially turn their skin brown. I would bet that my current tan, still left over from those blessed few weeks over break when I'd had actual time away from school to hang out at the beach and lay mindlessly in the sand, was set off nicely by the straightjacket the doctors probably had me in. Assuming straight jackets were white. I'd only ever seen them in movies and they always seemed to be white.

Luckily, Georgiana's body remembered how to tie on a bonnet and the proper way to open and hold a parasol, and so, within a few minutes Mrs. Younge, Mr. Wickham, and I were out the door and on our way down the cobblestone street headed toward the seashore. Wickham had offered me his arm and we strolled together a few steps ahead of Mrs. Younge. I'm sure I wasn't supposed to notice as she fell farther and farther behind us, just like I wasn't supposed to notice the speaking looks she and Wickham had shared over my head as I was fiddling with my parasol.

They had decided between them that now was the best time to strike. I wondered if this is how it really went down, or if my extra bit of flirting had caused them to move up their scheduled seduction. I suddenly worried that I'd set things off too early and Darcy wouldn't reach us in time to save Georgiana. That could seriously mess up the whole novel. Georgiana would then be Mrs. Wickham, stuck with an unfaithful scoundrel of a husband who once he had his grubby paws on her thirty thousand pounds would likely never even look at her again. Darcy would never go to Netherfield, he'd be too distraught over his sister's elopement, and would likely take her back to Pemberley after he somehow paid off Wickham—unless of course, Wickham wanted to flaunt his power over Georgiana to Darcy and so kept her from her brother as much as possible. Of course Wickham would want to hurt Darcy anyway he could.

I tried not to hyperventilate. If Darcy never went to visit Bingley at Netherfield he would never meet Elizabeth Bennet. Literature's greatest couple would never get the chance to meet all because I'd batted my eyelashes a few times!

Wickham was saying something to me, but for the life of me I couldn't pay attention. I'd just ruined my favorite book of all time and I was sinking into a pit of despair.

"Miss Darcy? Are you well? You seem rather far off," Wickham's voice finally cut through my mind's frantic rambling. Miss Darcy. Wait a minute. I was not, in fact, Georgiana Darcy, but just a sad, overworked, and heartbroken grad student taking a slight vacation from reality. I had not ruined my favorite novel. I was merely insane.

I tilted my head up and flashed a sparkling smile at Wickham. "I am sorry. My mind did wander for a bit. I was just enjoying this lovely sunshine. It is quite beautiful today, is it not?"

"I do feel as though I am in the presence of great beauty today, though I confess I have not been paying attention to the sunshine."

I tried not to throw up. "Mr. Wickham, I am sorry to say I do not quite take your meaning." *'Cause you were so subtle*, I thought derisively as I tried once again for a slight eyelash flutter, *like a sledgehammer*.

We had reached a sort of walkway that ran right along the shoreline. The sea breeze was lovely and cool and it played with Wickham's tousled curls in a very appealing way. I wondered if he'd brought us down to the beach for just that very reason, so that he would appear young and carefree and edible. That would make him a hell of a set director, but I suppose all good actors secretly want to direct. I watched him turn slightly into the breeze and I realized that it *was* all staging. This was going to be it! I just knew this was going to be the moment.

I almost panicked and ran. Then I almost ruined the whole thing by laughing in his face as he looked down at me and proclaimed in a serious voice that he found himself to be quite in love with me and would I do him the great honor of becoming his wife.

"Uh," I swallowed. I was supposed to say yes. I just was having a hard time forming the words. This was my first proposal. And instead of coming from a man I loved and wanted to marry (and being directed actually at *me*), it was coming from a dirty, rotten, loser who only wanted money and revenge. I had compared my exes to Wickham and here I was with actual Wickham proposing to me.

It's okay, Kelsey, it's not really happening. Just say it.

"I am so flattered, I—" I cast my eyes downward. "Of course I shall marry you." I looked up through my lashes in time to see the exultant look cross his face before he rearranged his features back into something more appropriate for a happy lover. "How excited my brother will be when we tell him."

A muscle in Wickham's jaw ticked almost imperceptibly. "Yes, Darcy shall surely be happy that his childhood friend and his sister are making such a happy match of it. Just think of all the good times we shall have at Pemberley together, my dear."

"Oh, I cannot wait to tell him!" I gushed. "He will want us to be married at Pemberley. I have always dreamed of having a wedding there and now I shall! I daresay we should write to him immediately. Do let us turn back now so that we can write to him!" There was something perversely fun about not making this easy for him.

"What a splendid idea, my dear. Perhaps we should first share our joy with Mrs. Younge?"

"Mrs. Younge, of course, you should tell her, my… dear Wickham."

Wickham turned us around so that we could inform Mrs. Younge of our happy news. She had managed to end up several yards behind us. As a chaperone she sucked, however as co-conspirator for Wickham she was truly brilliant. She expressed her joy and happiness for us, and how she had always known this was just how it should be. That from the start she could tell we had been made for each other.

I'm sure at some point any decent person would have expressed concern over Georgiana's rather young age, the comparative age gap (I'm pretty sure it had to be about nine years, which at say, twenty and twenty-nine isn't too much of a big deal, but at fifteen and twenty-four it is kind of a different matter. In my day and age a prosecutable matter), and the fact that Wickham had most definitely not applied to her brother and her cousin who were co-guardians of Georgiana since the death of her parents, for her hand. But these were all apparently trifling matters that did not merit discussion.

As we headed back to the townhouse, Wickham played the devoted lover to the hilt, asking every few minutes if I was warm enough, complimenting me on the sparkle in my eye or the blush in my cheeks. I suppose if I was really a young, newly engaged girl, my head would have been turned by all of his nonsense, but to me it really did seem just like nonsense. He and Mrs. Younge still had to convince Georgiana that it was a brilliant plan to elope without informing her brother of her intentions and surprise Darcy with news of their marriage. I was actually very curious to find out how they were going to convince me. Even though she was young, parentless, and under the influence of an obviously unsuitable chaperone, with a handsome man paying attention to her as a woman for the first time, it still struck me as odd that she'd agree to run off with him. Elopements just did not happen in her class during this time period. And if they did they were severely looked down upon.

Darcy was a proud man. I can't believe he hadn't instilled in Georgiana the worth of her fortune or family. It could be that he just didn't believe her to be grown up enough to be the object of fortune hunters? That seemed like a huge lapse on his part. Fifteen is young, but nothing is off limits when the girl has a thirty thousand pound fortune. Even I knew that, and I was from a completely different century.

But then maybe I've just read more novels than Fitzwilliam Darcy.

We walked along with my only responses to Wickham's overly solicitous attitude being a few modest laughs and my almost perfected mock-innocent eyelash flutter thrown in here and there for good measure. I was still wrestling with Georgiana's naïveté. It was beginning to frustrate me. I realized I had no basis to guess how Wickham was going to manage to sway me to his will.

Austen just sort of skates over that part of the story. Actually, everything I was experiencing now didn't even happen as storyline in the novel. It's more like a flashback sequence. It was technically *before* the main storyline. This whole episode is just related to Elizabeth by Darcy in a few paragraphs of a letter. He was trying to lay out for her Wickham's true nature and felt that the only way was to tell the truth about what had happened to his young sister—trusting Elizabeth not to ruin Georgiana's reputation by spreading the story around. I'd always thought it showed a great deal of respect on Darcy's part for Lizzy's character and discretion, even though in that disastrous first proposal he made it clear he thought her family had no such discretion.

The letter. A light bulb went off in my head with a blinding flash. A very disconcerting, troubling, blinding flash.

I had been reading Darcy's letter to Elizabeth when I fell asleep last night. Or maybe it wasn't last night, maybe it was only about an hour or so ago—I'd been here for about that long. Tori had dropped me off after we'd seen Ashley at the pub, I'd cried myself silly, changed into my ratty sweats, had a glass of wine and started reading *Pride and Prejudice* at the first proposal scene and had drifted off during Darcy's explanation of the events in Ramsgate.

Which is where I now literally, physically was.

Okay, perhaps not physically. There was still the possibility that I really was nuts. Does the time in hallucinations run quite so linear? I couldn't speed it up by wishing. Having absolutely no previous experience with hallucinations, I had no idea if they were something that happened minute for actual minute or not.

But why pick to hallucinate as Georgiana? Why wouldn't my sad, scrambled little brain choose to be

Lizzy, as *she* was reading the letter? Even insane I'd have to prefer to be Lizzy. If I was honest I'd have to admit I'd wanted to be her for most of my life, ever since reading *Pride and Prejudice* for the first time when I was twelve.

And here was the kicker—the realization that I'd been reading Darcy's explanation of the aborted elopement right before I opened my eyes as Georgiana—I was starting to think it *wasn't* a hallucination. I'd opened my mind to the possibility, no matter how far removed and remote and impossible a possibility, that I had actually somehow jumped into the pages of my favorite novel. Into Darcy's letter.

I tightened my grip on Wickham's arm. His arm felt so real. He looked down at me and smiled and I felt my stomach turn. He was so dreadfully handsome and he looked absolutely nothing like any of the actors that had played this character in any of the movies or television productions. Mrs. Younge didn't look anything like the actresses that had played her either. Wouldn't I have used the likenesses of those actors in my hallucinations? Why would my brain go to the trouble of creating whole new faces? I'm just not that creative.

But what if this is what they *really* looked like? Okay, obviously they aren't real people, they are characters in a book. But what if this is what Austen had envisioned them as—how they appeared in the pages of the book?

What if this was all *real*?

We finally reached the steps leading up to the townhouse and I allowed Wickham to help me up the steps, leaning on his arm more heavily than I had been. I was beginning to feel lightheaded. I was cruising, at a very high rate of speed, toward a complete Austen fangirl meltdown.

I was in *Pride and Prejudice*.

Mrs. Younge and I dispensed with our bonnets and parasols, handing them to a maidservant, and Wickham guided me back over to the settee. I noticed he sat a lot closer to me this time, reaching forward and holding my hand earnestly.

"Darling, I have had a splendid idea! Oh what fun it would be!" Wickham began as he flashed his dimples at me once more.

I just bet he did. Let me guess: it has to do with Gretna Green, a quickie marriage, and his ultimate control over my money.

"What if, instead of writing to your brother directly, we surprised him with our good news?" Wickham continued.

"How would we do that?" I asked, furrowing my brow for good measure.

"How exciting would it be if we went to Gretna Green to be married, and then joined your brother in London and I could introduce you as my wife?"

"Gretna Green?" I allowed some shock to seep into my voice. "Do you mean elope? Oh no," I shook my head decisively, "I could never do that. I cannot think that Fitzwilliam would be pleased. He would want to be present for my wedding, surely?"

"But darling," and here Wickham lowered his voice seductively. "We would have to wait for so many months, there is so much to be done to prepare for a large wedding. I confess I am so entranced by you that I cannot stomach the idea of waiting so long —" he paused for effect, looking deeply into my eyes as he caressed my hand suggestively, "to make you my wife."

Hmm, outright seduction seemed like an obvious, but effective, ploy. He was so handsome, that even though I despised him as a person and character, I found myself momentarily entranced by the intensity in his eyes and voice. For her part, Mrs. Younge was busying herself with the sewing she hadn't been able to spare a minute for before Wickham arrived while he set out to seduce her charge right in front of her.

"I am not sure—" I started.

"But, sweet Georgiana, do you not want us to be man and wife as soon as possible?" Wickham's voice was now basically just a purr.

"Of course," I replied in little more than a whisper, "but I cannot hurt my brother like that."

Wickham actually surprised me by laughing. I could tell right away that he'd decided to change tactics. "Hurt him? Georgiana, surely you do not think it would be hurtful to him at all? He would likely be relieved to be free of the expense and tiresome duties of marrying you off. You cannot think a man his age is overly concerned about the romantic life of a younger sister. He would think it all a good joke, I assure you."

Even though I'd been expecting him to eventually change tactics when the seduction ploy failed, his abrupt change in demeanor took me aback.

"Somehow I doubt that," I commented drily. Too drily. I saw Wickham's eyebrows lift slightly.

Mrs. Younge looked up with a piercing stare, finally becoming involved in the conversation. "Miss Darcy, we cannot presume to understand the inclinations and pursuits of a young gentleman your brother's age. Things that seem very important to us women are only trifling matters to them."

"I think that Fitzwilliam would be concerned enough over an elopement not to find it a 'good joke,'" I said pulling my hand out of Wickham's and placing it back on my own lap.

He must have felt his prey slipping through his fingers. "I do not think, my dear, that you know your brother very well at all. You are, after all, much younger than him, whereas I have been his friend for years. We practically grew up together while you were still in the nursery."

For some reason this made me angry. I didn't really expect much from Wickham; in fact, what I expected was for him to be a complete and total tool and manipulate Georgiana mercilessly. I figured he would use whatever tactics seemed to work best, and it shouldn't have surprised me that he'd switch so quickly from seduction to trying to destroy the self-esteem of this poor fifteen-year-old girl and make her believe that the one person left in her immediate family not only didn't really care about her, but was completely beyond her understanding or comprehension because she was just a silly, young girl.

Maybe it was because these speeches were being given directly to me. Being present for the manipulation was a hell of a lot different than just sort of wondering, as a completely removed reader, why Georgiana had allowed herself to be swayed. As said reader, I knew that she was shy and often uncertain, and here was Wickham ruthlessly using those parts of her personality to get his own way. Manipulating bastards are frustrating enough (see Jordan as a case in point) but ones who prey on underage teenagers are the worst sort of creeps. I was suddenly filled with rage for fifteen-year-old girls everywhere (and, admittedly, the naïve awkward girl I had been at that age).

I didn't have to play along. I wasn't a real character in this little drama.

"Actually," I said imperiously as I stood up. "I think, my dear Mr. Wickham, that you are full of it."

Wickham gaped up at me. "I do not know what you mean," he sputtered.

"Don't you? Let me lay it out for you then." I abandoned all attempts at speaking with Regency diction as I picked up steam. "You're after Georgiana's, er, *my* money. Do you think I don't know that you've got no money of your own? And that you haven't spoken to my brother in years?"

I felt a thrill at the twin expressions of shock on Wickham and Mrs. Younge's faces. "I appreciate your attempts at deception here, truly I do. It must have been horrible to have to spend time convincing an innocent, unworldly teenager to fall in love with you and agree to hand over her freedom and her fortune to you. Well, sorry, Bud, that little fantasy ends here. I don't suppose it matters, because surprise! Fitzwilliam Darcy is going to show up here and ruin your little run away plot anyway, so there isn't really any point in getting me to agree to something so patently stupid and against my interests. You lose in the end, Wickham. So you might as well just go now and save me the trouble of pretending to be interested in this any longer."

Sometime during my speech Wickham had stood up as well, his cheeks were flushed dull red with anger. He opened his mouth, but before he could say anything I cut him off.

"Save it." I walked regally to the door of the sitting room. I had no idea where Georgiana's room was, but I figured either my feet would find it eventually or I could ask a servant. I was hoping I could lie down and sleep off the rest of this interesting little experience.

I was starting to doubt my earlier belief that I really was inside *Pride and Prejudice*. Mostly because that opened up a whole world of problems I wasn't ready to deal with. But if this was just a hallucination then it could only last for so long, right? I was suddenly very tired of playing along. As I reached the door, I turned my head and shot over my shoulder, "Oh, and Mrs. Younge? My brother will be firing you as soon as he gets here, so you might want to start packing."

With that I swept out of the room and into the hallway. I could hear the consternation I'd caused as the conspirators voices began to be raised, accusations over Georgiana's uncharacteristic behavior flying furiously. I couldn't really bring myself to care. I just wanted to be done with Wickham and the odious Mrs. Younge. And nice though I'm sure she was, I really wanted to be done being in Georgiana's body.

I was right, my feet knew exactly where to go. I entered Georgiana's room, done in soft pastels and cream, with a relieved sigh. I leaned against the door, glad to be away from other people. There was an open door on one wall of the room, and I was curious enough to investigate—it opened into a small dressing room, complete with vanity and mirror. I sat down on the padded stool in front of the vanity and stared into the mirror.

Georgiana stared back at me. Her thick dark hair was pulled back into a loose bun with a few curls framing her pale, thin face. She had overly large brown eyes ringed with thick lashes and high cheekbones. In my world she would probably be a high fashion model. In hers she probably was thought of as too thin and sallow. She was so, so very young. Her face and body still had that sort of coltish look that so many teen girls struggle through. You could see the beginnings of womanhood, but it hadn't been fully realized yet. Seeing for myself how young and innocent she was physically fired up my anger against Wickham even more. I muttered a curse under my breath and went back into the bedroom. Flinging myself onto the bed, I threw one arm over my eyes to block out the sunlight streaming in from the two windows that faced out toward the sea, and prayed that I would wake up soon. As myself.

CHAPTER
Six

*"Well, what if there is no
tomorrow? There wasn't
one today."*

MY SLEEP WAS restless. After hours of tossing and turning, the strange whooshing and sucking noise started again. This time I could almost feel it, like invisible waves pulling and tugging at my body.

Then I felt the warm sunlight on my face. I opened my eyes, blinking in confusion against the brightness.

"...and I must say, he was paying you particular attention yesterday during our stroll. Did you not notice it? Such charming manners, and so handsome."

Not only had I not gone to bed and awakened back at home, in my own body, I was right back in the sitting room on the settee with Mrs. Younge yammering to me about Wickham. I glared down at my sewing sampler in impotent rage and confusion. What. Was. Going. On?

It was time to face some facts. I had never before

exhibited any signs of mental illness. I would assume (not that I have anything beyond one general ed undergrad psychology class from which I remember less than nothing to base this assumption on) that such a complete psychotic break would have some sort of precursors or warnings. Like depression or moodiness or something, right?

It could be caused by a traumatic event. But honestly, though I'd cried after seeing Ashley at McKinney's, being cheated on by Jordan was less traumatic and shocking than one would hope. I felt a distinct lack of sadness over losing Jordan and was more just pissed off at being lied too. Could breaking up with someone that you secretly had already admitted to yourself that you didn't love involve enough trauma to send an otherwise steady and sound person into a complete tailspin two full months later?

So, if I were to rule out a complete break with reality that left me where? With this being reality? Was I actually physically in a fictional world created in the mind of a British woman two hundred years ago?

It wasn't like I could even claim I'd time travelled (and sadly, that seemed more probable to me than my current situation). Yes, this was Regency England— I'm guessing I was in 1810. Based on my understanding of the timeline of *Pride and Prejudice*, it mostly takes place in 1811 and Darcy says in his letter to Elizabeth that Georgiana's near elopement had taken place the summer before. I suppose if I'd known I was going to end up trapped between the pages of the book I'd have paid a bit more attention to details like dates.

But it wasn't really 1810. It was 1810 as written about in a novel by Jane Austen. A novel populated by fictional characters. And I was one of them. And apparently time hadn't moved forward at all, because this all felt very *déjà vu*.

I decided to test my "time has not moved forward" theory. "I was just thinking what a lovely walk we had yesterday with Mr. Wickham."

"Yes, it was quite a nice walk. Mr Wickham is such a great walker," she replied.

"Oh, er, yes," I answered cautiously. "It was quite a lovely walk, though perhaps the conversation was a bit, um, unusual."

Mrs. Younge looked at me with one eyebrow raised. "Was it? It seemed quite normal to me, although Mr. Wickham did pay you several pretty compliments."

"So then, you don't remember Mr. Wickham proposing marriage to me yesterday?"

"I—I—beg you your pardon?" Mrs. Younge sputtered. "Wickham...No, surely he would have—"

"Would have what, Mrs. Younge? Told you ahead of time? You're co-conspirators after all." My theory was correct. I was right back where I'd started. And I'd already blown my demure Georgiana act before I'd even gotten it started. "So is he supposed to propose today, then?"

Mrs. Younge took a deep breath and schooled her

features into a placid expression. "I do not understand," she said carefully, "what you are speaking of."

"Don't you?" I asked sarcastically. My sense of *déjà vu* was now so strong that I was secretly glancing around for a glitch in the Matrix. "Me. Wickham. Eloping. Thirty thousand pounds. Any of these ringing a bell?" I crossed my legs and leaned back against the settee in a very unladylike manner "What's in it for you? Is he paying you off with part of my dowry?" Mrs. Younge's pale blue eyes shifted to the side, refusing to meet my direct stare. "Or is he already paying you off, so to speak?"

A flush, whether of anger or embarrassment, I couldn't tell, infused Mrs. Younge's cheeks.

"Oh," I said knowingly. "He *is* already paying you, and not just in money." I wondered how much I could get away with...maybe if I was just totally as un-Georgiana as possible I would somehow jar myself out of this craziness. "So, is George good in bed?" There was a small gasp of shock from Mrs. Younge, but I was on a roll. "I've always wondered why so many women fall all over themselves for him. I mean Georgiana, um, me, I get, and even Lydia—she's young and stupid—but why would a woman like you hitch your wagon to that mess? You could have a real and respectable job doing this companion thing, or even the boarding house thing you do later, why waste all this effort on Wickham? Is the sex really that good?"

By this time Mrs. Younge was shaking with rage.

Her face had contorted, her lips curling into an unattractive snarl. "Be quiet! Stop it this moment."

"Hitting a little to close to home there, huh, Younge? I find myself kind of morbidly curious about you're sordid little affair with Wickham. How much younger is he than you do you think? Ten, fifteen years? Does he make you feel all young and desirable and all that?"

Mrs. Younge stood up quickly from her chair. "You little viper," she spat. "I thought you were just a spoiled, stupid girl but you are —"

"Yeah, yeah, appearances can be deceiving." I rolled my eyes with deliberate insolence. "Take you, for example. And now this is going to be all awkward —you storming around, alerting Wickham that the plan has gone horribly awry, *yadda yadda yadda*. I'm not spending the rest of the day hiding in my room again, so save us all the trouble and stay out of my way. Pack your bags and get out of town and all that, but I don't want to see you, okay?"

"You do not have the authority to fire me."

"Did I forget to mention that my brother is already on his way here? Oh, oops! Silly of me. Yeah, my brother is on his way here to throw you out on your ass, so might as well beat him to the punch. Have a nice life. Tell Wickham to go screw himself. I hear the Militia is hiring, he might want to get an actual job as the heiress stealing seems to not be working out."

I thought for a minute she was going to leap across the room and throttle me. Instead, she turned with a strangled scream of frustration and fled the sitting room.

I crossed my arms behind my head. It was really quite satisfying to verbally abuse her like that. I supposed that made me a horrible person, I'm sure she had circumstances in her life that I knew nothing about that had turned her into the person she was— every character has a backstory—but I didn't really care. She was about to throw a fifteen-year-old girl under the bus so she and her lover could benefit from said fifteen-year-old's money. And she was going to use her influence as a woman in authority over Georgiana to convince her to run away from her family and marry this guy. It basically amounted to child sex-trafficking in my mind. And I was not okay with child sex-trafficking. Especially when I was the child involved.

After a moment of basking in my bad-ass glory, I decided to investigate the rest of the bottom floor of the townhouse. I'd really only seen the sitting room, the short distance between that room and the front door, and the stairs that led up to the second floor where the bedrooms. I wandered from room to room taking in the gracious furnishings. I'm sure it was nothing compared to Pemberley, or even the townhouse Darcy kept in London, but to me it was pretty awe inspiring. Both of my parents worked and were relatively well off, but the kind of money this house spoke of was beyond my comprehension. And it wasn't ostentatious at all, nothing screamed *"Hey look at me; I cost lots of money!"* the way some houses did back home. The house and furnishings and fabrics just sort of whispered of the wealth that provided them. Obviously the Darcys had taste. Classy, moneyed taste.

Eventually I ran out of rooms to wander through. I hadn't heard much from Mrs. Younge, other than some crashing and banging upstairs and the occasional concerned looking maid running up and down the stairs. One could only hope it meant she was packing her stuff and getting the heck out of Dodge. I felt bad for the maids though. There seemed to be three of them, and they were all very young. Then there was the butler, Hodges, who I'd met before our little walk the day before.

I meandered back to the sitting room. Georgiana's sewing sampler was sitting on the settee where I'd dropped it during my verbal sparring match with Younge. None of the stitches that I'd set "yesterday" were placed. While I'd been sitting there for that half hour mindlessly letting Georgiana's hands work away on the sampler an entire row of small roses to the left of the verse had been filled in. Now, the pale pink thread that I'd used was threaded through the needle, but only two stitches had been set in that color.

I sighed. I didn't want to have to think through what was actually happening. My brain hurt.

It was time I face it. There was no other explanation. I was living some sort of freakish Austenesque redux of *Groundhog Day*. I was Bill Murray. But like a chick, Regency era version of Bill Murray. I couldn't remember for the life of me the name of his character in that movie...Phil something or other I think...just the fact that he had the hots for Andie McDowell, was stuck reliving the same day over and over, and that each morning was heralded by the musical stylings of *Sonny and Cher* singing *I've Got You Babe* on the radio. Well, I didn't have a radio, or any electricity at all, nor was I even allowed to "wake up" in the traditional sense, so I'd been spared *Sonny and Cher*. I suppose I should be thankful for small favors.

My strongest memories of *Groundhog Day* were all of the attempts of Bill Murray's character to kill himself as he relived the day over and over. I distinctly remembered him throwing a toaster in the bath (again, no electricity) and stepping in front of a truck (not gonna happen in 1810, but perhaps I could throw myself in front of a carriage or something). Killing himself hadn't worked for Phil Whatever-His-Name-Was, and there was no reason to assume it would work for me either. I mean, what if by killing off Georgiana I did somehow rend the fragile fabric between novel and reality and permanently alter *Pride and Prejudice*. I couldn't live with myself if I screwed up my favorite book! Or maybe I wouldn't have to live with myself, maybe if I killed myself here I'd be dead in real life too.

It could be that even now I was still lying asleep or comatose or something on the couch in my apartment. And if I walked down the street and drowned myself in the ocean, or climbed up to the roof and threw myself down to the cobblestones below, I'd die here *and* there. Tori would find my cold, lifeless body on the couch. Oh god, I was wearing my rattiest sweats when I fell asleep. How humiliating would it be to die in those? I didn't want the coroner or the crime scene people (I mean, they'd call out CSI right, a perfectly healthy twenty-three year old dying randomly on her couch seemed suspicious, didn't it?) to see me in those sweats. Pathetic.

I didn't realize I was clutching the sampler in a death grip until the needle poked my thumb viciously. I cursed and dropped the offending fabric, sticking my thumb into my mouth even though I knew that it was a stupid thing to do. Good, maybe Georgiana had some sort of horrific bacteria in her mouth and I'd get gangrene and die.

But I'd still be in those damn sweats. Why couldn't I have fallen asleep in a really flattering outfit? Even the jeans I'd had on earlier would have been preferable.

Stupid, stupid, stupid Kelsey.

Okay, I needed to get a grip. A serious grip. I wasn't sure that this same day was going to replay over and over *à la Groundhog Day*. All I knew for sure was that I'd gone to sleep twice now, once in the real world, and once in Georgiana's bed, and awakened in the sitting room at 1:30 p.m.

There was nothing that said I had to sit around and wait for tomorrow to come anyway. Killing myself was out, but why jump to that extreme? I hadn't killed myself to get into the book. I wouldn't have to kill myself to get out.

I hadn't, until just the moment, realized that my

brain had fully embraced the concept that I was, in fact, inside the pages of *Pride and Prejudice*. That I'd let go of the hallucination explanation (I fully admit the odds of me being certifiable were still good, but the odds of this just being a hallucination were seeming slimmer and slimmer with every moment that passed).

I'd fallen asleep...and then here I was. What if all I needed to do was fall back asleep to get out. But I'd fallen asleep last night...just in Georgiana's bed. At home I'd fallen asleep on the couch. Perhaps I needed to do that here.

I stretched out, sprawling in a very unladylike manner, across the settee, propping my dress-clad legs up on the armrest and laying my head on the opposite headrest. It was not entirely comfortable. I lay there for a few minutes, not feeling sleepy at all. I kicked off Georgiana's shoes. Pretty sure I'd had my shoes off when I fell asleep. It wasn't like I could go find a pair of ten-year-old fuzzy sweatpants here, so this was as close as I was going to get.

I stared up at the ceiling, praying for sleep. Nothing. It was the middle of the day and I wasn't exactly a nap kind of person. I counted backward from a hundred, then from a thousand. Nothing.

I got up and went in search of some alcohol. There had to be some somewhere, right? I'd had wine before I went to sleep, maybe that would help. I remembered a promising looking cabinet in another room. It was set up kind of like a study or office, with a desk and a few chairs. It was probably intended to be used by the man of the house. Though I doubted that Darcy visited Georgiana here in Ramsgate that often, I had a slight hope that it had at least been stocked in case he chose to visit.

Bingo. The cabinet had a lock, but the key was, handily, already inserted. I guess the staff didn't expect Georgiana to be pilfering her brother's liquor cabinet. There was a decanter of something, probably brandy. Not that I was extremely familiar with hard liquor. I usually only had it in mixed in fruity-tasting girly drinks. Like the daiquiri I'd managed to dump all over myself right in front of Mark yesterday, or two days ago, or whenever the heck it was. I scowled at the thought of Mark as I grabbed the decanter. If he started seeing Ashley I was going to have to tell Charlie he wasn't allowed to invite Mark over to our apartment. This assumed, of course, I ever managed to get back to reality.

There was a pair of gorgeous cut crystal glasses sitting next to the decanter, but I eyed them suspiciously. They were likely leaded, and frankly, lead poisoning seemed a really long, drawn out way to go. If I was going to opt for the dying, I'd rather do it quickly. I grabbed the decanter and took it with me back to the sitting room.

The thudding and thumping from upstairs had quieted. With any luck Mrs. Younge was done throwing her tantrum and packing and was getting ready to exit the premises.

I unstopped the decanter and took a swig, spluttering and gasping as the brandy burned its way down my throat. It tasted like a cross between turpentine and cold medicine. I'm sure I wasn't drinking it correctly. It was probably insanely good brandy and a connoisseur would be shocked at my guzzling it. However, I wasn't going for refined, I was going for maximum effect.

It occurred to me, belatedly, that the decanter was probably leaded too. Oh well. I took another swig. I could feel the burn of the brandy seeping out from my stomach and invading my limbs. A nice, pleasant sort of warmth. My brain hadn't dulled enough yet for a nap to seem like a good plan.

"To Georgiana," I muttered as I raised the decanter up. The afternoon light coming in through the window sparkled through the crystal and made the liquor inside look like living, burning amber. I took another healthy swig. The taste was growing on me.

I settled back on the settee, propping a pillow behind my head. It was embroidered in the same style as the sampler, and I began to wonder how many of the dratted things poor Georgiana had been forced to make in her time here.

I studied the brandy decanter seriously. Such pretty shifting colors when held up to the light like this...and contemplated who to toast next.

"Hmm, definitely not Wickham...or the odious Mrs. Younge...how about Darcy!" I'm not entirely sure who I was talking to, but I somehow felt less weird drinking alone if I kept up a running commentary. "That's who I really want to see. How tragic to be stuck in *Pride and Prejudice* with no Darcy making an appearance. To Darcy!" I took another gulp. I was beginning to feel more than just comfortably warm. I put my feet back up on the other arm of the settee and crossed my ankles.

"Oh Darcy, Mr. Darcy where are you? Although I guess I'm your sister, so that's, um, awkward." Another gulp, it seemed an appropriate punctuation to the realization that even if Mr. Darcy came sweeping through the door right now, my throwing myself at him would be out of the question—or get me confined to Bedlam. Incest. Not really the kind of topic one finds in a Jane Austen novel.

"You know. I thought Jordan was going to be a Mr. Darcy. He kind of looks the part: tall, dark, handsome, all that nonsense." *Gulp.* "But nooooo, Jordan, you were not quite Darcy were you?" *Swig.* "More along the lines of a Wickham." *Guzzle.* "Damn Wickham! Stuck with you in real life and in—" *Gulp.* "Whatever the hell this is."

Drat. The brandy was gone. How did I not notice that I'd had so much? I let the decanter slip out of my hand and fall to the floor. Luckily, there was a soft ornately woven rug directly under me so it didn't break. My arm felt oddly heavy as it dangled over the side of the settee. Actually, I felt heavy all over. And warm. And lethargic. But for the first time since I'd first opened my eyes in the sitting room yesterday, actually for the first time in as long as I can remember, I felt completely relaxed. Relaxed was good, I thought as I let my eyes drift shut. Relaxed is...

The rushing sound filled my ears and then I felt the push and pull on my body. I blinked against the bright, afternoon sunlight, and clenched my teeth at the sound of Mrs. Younge's grating voice.

"...and I must say, he was paying you particular attention yesterday during our stroll. Did you not notice it? Such charming manners, and so handsome."

Damn.

"Oh, yes. You are right, he is quite handsome," I replied absentmindedly.

I didn't even have a headache from all of the brandy I'd consumed. In fact, I bet if I walked back down the hall to the study I'd find that same decanter refilled and sitting just where I'd found it yesterday (was it yesterday?), as if it had never, ever happened.

Maybe it hadn't, I thought to myself as I mindlessly let Georgiana's hands work away on the sampler and stared blankly at a spot directly above Mrs. Younge's head. I mean, I know I lived through it, but if Kelsey gets drunk in a fictional sitting room by herself and there is no one around to see it does it make a sound? This analogy sucks.

I glanced down at my sewing. The same dratted row of roses. This was now the second time I'd filled them in. And guess what? Tomorrow they'll be unsewn again and I'll sit here and stitch them right back. Ad infinitum. Running screaming out into the street and throwing myself under the first available carriage was beginning to seem less and less like bad idea.

All right, so falling asleep in the same position and same inebriated (okay, fine, slightly more inebriated) state as I had in the real world didn't seem to have caused me to jettison out of the book. Neither had telling Mrs. Younge and Wickham that I was onto their little scheme.

New theory: What if I did something really dastardly and completely out of character for Georgiana, could that pop me out of the book? Or at least out of this same scene? Telling Mrs. Younge off had been out of character for Georgiana, but maybe I had to do something even more dramatic. I didn't want to kill myself but I could kill someone else. Wickham seemed like a good victim.

Hmm, same problem as killing myself—jerk though he was, he was necessary for the storyline. In a way, we have Wickham to thank, odd though it seems, for finally bringing Darcy and Elizabeth together.

Fine, so I wouldn't kill the bastard. I'd just have to come up with something else jarring enough to shake me right out of the book. As I waited for Wickham to arrive, it occurred to me that *Pride and Prejudice* is a romance, maybe my infraction needed to be romantic in nature.

When Wickham came into the sitting room, after the whole bowing and curtsying charade was over and he had walked over to the settee to sit with me, I launched myself at him. I could hear Mrs. Younge's shocked gasp as I flung myself at Wickham, pressing Georgiana's lithe body up against his, wrapping her arms around his neck and kissing him for all I was worth.

It was surprisingly not unpleasant. I mean, I hate the guy so I would have thought kissing him would make me want to throw up, but no. My traitorous body or mind, I wasn't sure which, refused to be completely repulsed by him. I have no defense other than he was really, really attractive. And I am apparently, really, really shallow. And I was kissing for my life. Sure, yeah, that was it. Kissing for my life.

After a brief moment of surprise Wickham started kissing me back. Somehow I'd known he would—he was too much of a rake not to respond. And I hate to sound conceited or anything, but I'm a pretty good kisser. Well, better than Georgiana would have, or should have, been anyway. His arms came up and around my midsection, pulling me even closer, fitting Georgiana's body rather intimately against his. I heard Mrs. Younge say something—I have no idea what, I was really beyond paying attention to her—and then I heard her footsteps leaving the room. The thought that I'd thoroughly compromised Georgiana filtered through my hazy mind as Wickham ran his tongue over mine. Younge was likely headed off to find the butler or another reliable servant to witness my ruining.

Well, I'd shaken things up pretty significantly. This was definitely un-Georgiana-like behavior, and yet I hadn't magically morphed back into Kelsey. I gave in to the urge to bite softly on Wickham's lower lip. He really did have an amazingly kissable mouth. And kissing him was strangely exhilarating. I must have a thing for rakes. On that lowering realization, I drew back with a resigned sigh.

"Georgiana—" he started in a raspy voice. *Oh interesting,* I thought. Wickham wasn't entirely immune to Georgiana. He was definitely attracted to her, but then it was possible he would react that way to anything in a skirt.

"Well, crap," I cut him off. "That was certainly interesting, but unfortunately for me not earth shattering." The look on Wickham's face was priceless. If I hadn't been so frustrated and teetering on the edge of depression I might have enjoyed it. "I suppose I'll see you tomorrow, same Bat time, same Bat channel." I turned and marched out of the open sitting room door, just as Mrs. Younge was skidding up with the butler in tow.

"Hodges," I nodded to the butler as I swept imperiously by. "Don't listen to a thing that crazy woman says."

Hodges's face remained impassive but I could tell by his eyes that it was costing him. "Yes, Miss," he responded gravely.

I marched back up the stairs to Georgiana's room. This was getting old. Sew roses. Cause a scene. Spend the rest of the day up in my room (or like yesterday passed out drunk in the sitting room) waiting for it to start over.

Time for a newer theory: Falling asleep wasn't a good idea. Maybe the scene jumping happened *because* I was asleep. If I could stay up all night could I somehow make it to the next day? It might not even happen right when I fell asleep, what if it happened at midnight—like Cinderella's carriage changing back into a pumpkin? There I was sleeping peacefully, innocently away and then *bam*—right back into the scene.

If I could stay awake and could get past whenever the literary clock was resetting itself I could at least continue on with the book instead of repeating this over and over. I mean, if I couldn't get *out*, getting *through* would be the next best option.

I glanced at the clock on Georgiana's mantel. It was only a few minutes past two in the afternoon. I always "woke up" in the sitting room a little before 1:30. I was looking at possibly staying up for twenty-four hours. I suddenly wished that I'd snagged a book out of the study. I'd seen a few volumes in there, but the thought of reading hadn't appealed to me at the time, I'd only been after the booze. If I was going to stay up for an entire twenty-four hours I needed something to occupy my time.

I spent the first hour or so searching Georgiana's room, hoping she had a novel, or at least a diary, stuffed somewhere that I could waste some time reading. Nope.

I spent an hour sitting in front of the mirror practicing French braiding. I'd always wanted to learn how to French braid my own hair, but had never found the time. It seemed like an opportune time and after about forty-five minutes I'd managed a really spectacular looking braid. I did wonder if I would forget how to do it once I was back to being me again (assuming I ever got back to being me), because I'd mastered the art using Georgiana's hands.

I ran in place for awhile, then did a few pushups. Georgiana was not in very great shape. Honestly, neither was I, as evidenced by the hiking debacle, but I was feeling ungenerous enough to be hypercritical of her skinny little arms.

I sat cross-legged on the bed and sang ninety-nine bottles of beer on the wall at the top of my lungs. Who was going to stop me? Mrs. Younge never seemed inclined to bother me after one of my little outbursts and none of the servants were going to question my insane behavior, at least not to my face. God knows what they were saying amongst themselves though.

I began to feel a little bit like I was in prison. I'm not sure why I'd confined myself to the room. I could have at least brought the brandy with me.

By eleven I had been reduced to obsessively staring at the clock. I was getting tired. Georgiana's body didn't like staying up late. She was going to have to toughen up before she came out and had to spend the season dancing until the wee hours of the morning. I wondered if they started training young ladies the year or so before, having them stay up and exercise late at night so they wouldn't drop dead of exhaustion at their first ball.

I watched the minutes tick down to the next day. 11:57, 11:58, 11:59.

There was the familiar push and pull. It felt stronger now that I was awake for it. The light was so bright it temporarily blinded me.

"...and I must say, he was paying you particular attention yesterday during our stroll. Did you not notice it? Such charming manners, and so handsome." Mrs. Younge's hateful voice filled my ears as I blinked the bright early afternoon light out of my eyes.

I stared down at the row of roses on the sampler in disgust. I *was* Cinderella's pumpkin. Midnight hit and I'd been popped right back into the little scene in the sitting room. Forced to play it again and again.

I felt like crying. Why? If I was going to be stuck in some extracurricular scene from *Pride and Prejudice* why couldn't it have been something fun? Like Lizzy and Darcy's wedding night or something? Why wouldn't time just move on? My hands busily started restitching the row of roses as my brain whirled.

Maybe if I could get through the book, *all* the way through—live the next year and a half or so as Georgiana, I'd get out of it. The book would end and then I'd pop back out to Kelsey. But I'd have to get through it first.

And then it hit me. I'd never actually gotten through it. I might not know exactly how or why Georgiana agrees to elope with Wickham because Austen never spells it out for us. The whole story is only told from Darcy's perspective. In fact, I have been stuck in a paragraph—*a paragraph*—of the novel for the last four plus days. But whether I understand it or approve of it doesn't matter. Georgiana *does* agree to run off with him. I had never agreed to the elopement. The closest had been that first day when I said yes to his proposal but then blew up at him and Mrs. Younge when he pressed me on eloping.

I had to say yes. I had to get to the point of eloping so that Darcy would come and rescue me and then maybe I could move forward. It would be an incredibly boring year and half. Not much really happens to Georgiana beyond being taken back to London and given a new companion. At some point, like in more than a year from now, she goes back to Pemberley and meets Elizabeth who is traveling in Derbyshire, and that is pretty much it. It sounded horribly long and dull but infinitely superior to the nightmare I was currently experiencing on replay.

So I sat and stitched, and gave mindless assents to Mrs. Younge's prattling. I smiled demurely at Wickham when he came. I didn't try to have any fun challenging him. I didn't bat my eyelashes once. When we walked down to the shore and he asked me to marry him I said yes. When he pressed me to elope, I only hesitated long enough to seem realistic.

I completely ignored the triumphant look he and Mrs. Younge shared over my head.

I even managed a shy blush when he kissed my hand as he was leaving. It was a pity no one except Wickham and Younge witnessed my awesome performance. It was Oscar worthy. I briefly considered giving up on my masters program so I could move to Hollywood (all of thirty-two and a half miles from Anaheim) and become an actress. I, apparently, had hidden depths of acting talent that had not yet been tapped.

Mrs. Younge was all sweetness and light to me after Wickham left. We put our heads together and started planning the practical details of the elopement. My things would have to be packed. Wickham had suggested we leave two days hence, and as my new tack was complete complacence, I didn't offer any argument. Mrs. Younge called one of the maids and instructed her to bring Georgiana's trunk to her room to begin the packing.

I meekly followed her up to my room and sat on the bed nodding my assent to her suggestions about which dresses I should take with me. It wasn't like I had any idea what to pack for an elopement. If I'd ever undertaken such a stupid plan in the real world I would have been heading for Vegas, which was only a five or six hour trip from Orange County. I could have just hopped into the car and gone and bought whatever I needed there. Although who I would have been eloping with I've no idea. It's not like Jordan had ever asked, and I would hope that if he had I would have had the presence of mind to say an emphatic no.

After about an hour or so Mrs. Younge finally left me so that I could change for dinner. The maid came in and helped me change to a more formal gown and I went downstairs. It seemed silly to me that I should have to change, as it was just Mrs. Younge and me. Over dinner she was full of excitement and plans for my elopement. And why not? Her cut of my thirty thousand pounds was within sight.

I could only hope now that I'd bitten the bullet and made the mistake of Georgiana's life for her that the storyline would now proceed as normal.

I stayed up again, waiting until the clock clicked down to midnight. When it actually hit twelve I was so relieved I almost passed out. I stared at it as it ticked off the minutes for another quarter of an hour or so, just to reassure myself I was finally moving forward. I collapsed, exhausted, in Georgiana's bed.

CHAPTER
Seven

...a fine figure of a man...

WHEN I WOKE up, sunlight streaming in through the large windows and the sounds of a fire crackling merrily in the grate, I almost wept with happiness. I'd been in *Pride and Prejudice* for days, but this was my first real morning and I was excited to explore the offerings in the breakfast room.

I had to wait for a maid to help me get dressed. This was a new experience for me. As I'd been popping into the dratted sitting room in the middle of the day I'd never had to actually get dressed. It was weird and awkward to have someone hanging around and touching me while I was in various states of undress. But I found that my trick of letting my mind wander and Georgiana's muscle memory take over worked just as well here as it did with the sewing. In no time I was all buttoned up and ready to go.

I could barely contain my excitement as I bounded

down the stairs. I had finally moved past the dreaded *Groundhog Day* replay and felt like I didn't have any other responsibilities to perform as Georgiana. I was free! I'd done what had to be done to further the plot of the story, and now I could just hang around until Darcy got here. And I had serious hope that he would be arriving today. After all, I was eloping tomorrow, so if he wanted to catch us by surprise before the happy day he would need to get here today, or by the latest, tomorrow morning.

The thought that I was going to meet the most desirable man in all of literature made me giddy. I skipped my way to the breakfast room.

Regency breakfast was not exactly the same as The International House of Pancakes. There were quite a few dishes that I wouldn't touch with a ten-foot pole, but I was hungry enough that I managed to pile a plate respectably high.

Mrs. Younge joined me after a few minutes. She was still acting all sweet and motherly. I wondered if when she looked at Georgiana all she saw were dollar, or in her case pound, signs. Of course her world was all unicorns and rainbows this morning, she and Wickham were just slightly over twenty-four hours away from achieving their goal of separating Georgiana from her family and her considerable fortune. I wonder if it bothered her at all that for the deal to be done her lover was going to have to sleep with me. Not that I thought Wickham was at all loyal to her, for him she was likely just convenient.

"Is there much packing left to be done?" I asked.

"No, I had Sarah pack your valise last night. You do not need much else."

"Oh. Then why do we wait until tomorrow to leave?" I hoped my question just appeared naïve and innocent. What I really wanted to know is why Wickham, once he had gotten Georgiana to consent to the elopement, had waited at all. Was it so she wouldn't be alarmed by the pace of events and cry off? If I were him I would have thrown in her in a carriage and set off post haste for Gretna Green. But then he could have had no idea that Darcy was going to just happen to visit his sister and foil the whole scheme. I was thinking like an outside observer. One that had access to the whole plot.

Mrs. Younge smiled, a rather sickly, condescending smile. I wonder if she thought I couldn't wait to be alone with Wickham. "I am sure Mr. Wickham has affairs here he needs to set in order, and of course he needs to see about hiring a coach."

"Oh, I see. So what shall we do today then if all of my things have already been packed?"

"Well, we could perhaps take a stroll, or read? Are there—" Mrs. Younge paused, and seemed to be searching for the right words. "Do you have any questions for me?"

I stared at her blankly. "Questions about what?"

She colored uncomfortably. "Questions about what occurs between a husband and wife."

My eyes widened in shock. Was Mrs. Younge, the woman who I ranked as little higher than a sex trafficker, the woman selling a fifteen-year-old girl down the matrimonial river for cold hard cash and an occasional place in Wickham's bed, asking Georgiana if she had questions about losing her virginity? Was she actually concerned? Or just worried that I would run, screaming in terror, from my bridal chamber and never consummate the marriage. Would Wickham still get the money if Georgiana never slept with him? Probably. Who was going to believe that a young girl like Georgiana refused to sleep with a stud like George Wickham? Nobody, that's who.

"Um, no. I do not think—" I broke off and tried for a blush. "I do not think I wish to talk about it."

Mrs. Younge nodded quickly and returned to her breakfast plate. I stabbed a sausage on my plate viciously and hoped that Darcy would get here soon.

After breakfast we managed to end up back in the sitting room. Seriously, Regency teenage girls must have had the most boring and unvaried lives ever. I was suddenly sorry for all of the times I'd claimed I was bored when I was fifteen. I'd had at least a hundred more options every day then it seemed Georgiana did. I was pleased to see, however, that the row of roses that I had embroidered yesterday had stayed filled in.

Mrs. Younge kept up a steady stream of chatter, mostly vaguely encouraging things about how fortunate Georgiana was to have secured the admiration of such a handsome man as George Wickham. I had to fight against a sudden urge to laugh hysterically. My shoulders shook with barely suppressed giggles. It had just occurred to me that the happy couple would have been *George and Georgiana Wickham* if the elopement had been allowed to go off. Too funny! I'd only read this book a hundred times and hadn't ever caught it. Probably because I'd never been quite this close to the situation before.

Luckily, Mrs. Younge didn't seem to notice my gasping for air as I silently laughed myself silly over these stupidest of things. I'm pretty sure she would have thought I was losing it. I'm not entirely sure that I wasn't losing it. Why, out of all the bad things represented by a union between Georgiana and Wickham, did the fact that they basically shared a first name seem the worst of the lot? 'Cause I'm obviously crazy. I took a moment to revisit the "Kelsey is insane and in an asylum" theory. It wasn't without merit.

My self-examination was cut short by the sound of a carriage pulling up outside. I sat up straighter in excitement, looking expectantly toward the door of the sitting room.

A perplexed look, followed quickly by a look of concern, skated across Mrs. Younge's face. I had a swift feeling of satisfaction that she was about to get it —and get it bad—before I returned to my excited anticipation. This was it! I was going to see *Fitzwilliam Darcy*! In the flesh! I could barely stand it.

The front door opened. The sound of an authoritative male voice came from the front entryway—a question, and the sound of the butler answering. Footsteps coming toward the sitting room...

And then I was face to face with Mr. Darcy.

I'm not sure exactly what I was expecting. I, of course, had a favorite on-screen Mr. Darcy. As I'd blurted to Mark a few days ago, Colin Firth from the 1995 BBC mini-series was my Mr. Darcy of choice. There are those who prefer Matthew Macfadyen, and he was admittedly hot, but his forehead always distracted me a bit. I totally respect the Macfadyen camp, but there was something about the brooding smolder that Firth had perfected that made him the Darcy of my dreams. So, I guess I had kind of expected Mr. Darcy to really look like that.

And he didn't look *unlike* Colin Firth...or really unlike Matthew Macfadyen. They all shared enough characteristics that if I was a police detective putting together a lineup of tall, hot, dark-haired Regency dudes I would have included all of them.

If it was possible, the real Mr. Darcy was even hotter than Colin Firth's portrayal of him. He wasn't shooting smoldering glances about the room at the moment—why would he? As far as he knew he was just visiting his little sister, the world had yet to come down about his ears—but I bet if he did he'd leave Firth and Macfadyen in the dust.

Darcy was tall and broad shouldered and fit-looking. He filled out a pair of breeches rather decently. His hair was very dark, almost black, and a bit mussed as he had just recently taken off his hat. He had incredible cheekbones, deep set hazel eyes, a straight nose, and full, wide mouth and the most amazing dimple in his chin. It was the cleft chin that did me in. If this Mr. Darcy had walked into a room full of women in the twenty-first century, there would have been a blood bath. Cat fight *extraordinaire*. No survivors.

Mrs. Younge and I both stood up in surprise as he came into the room. I'm guessing that Mrs. Younge's surprise was a little bit less of the pleasant variety than Georgiana's would have been. Darcy bowed to us both and then turned a broad smile toward me. I almost died right there on the spot.

I'm his sister. His sister. His sister. I feel nothing but sisterly affection, I lectured myself sternly as he walked toward me, hands outstretched and warmly took my hands in his. *Sister! Sister!* My brain screamed as I tried not to melt into a puddle of goo.

"Georgiana," Darcy said, still smiling warmly down at me. His eyes were insane. They were hazel, but really they were almost a deep, olive green with a ring of velvety brown around the iris. "I hope you are well."

I peeled my tongue off the roof of my mouth and opened my mouth to respond. What did Georgiana call him? You'd think I would have been more prepared, after all I knew he was on his way. I guess I was so excited at the prospect of seeing Mr. Darcy that I hadn't thought through the fact that I was going to have to actually interact with him.

"Yes, I am well, Fitzwilliam. What a surprise to see you here! I did not know you were coming."

His smile faltered, just for a second, as he looked down into my eyes. *Oh my god, he knows!*

"Here, Sweet, sit down," Darcy guided me down to

the settee and then released my hands so he could sit down as well. Out of the corner of my eye I could see Mrs. Younge resume her seat, except that she sat poised on the very edge of the chair, almost visibly shaking with nerves.

"Is something wrong, Georgie?" Darcy asked in a lowered voice, his amazing eyes still searching my face.

Yes, I thought a bit desperately, *something is very wrong. I'm not Georgiana, but a girl from hundreds of years in the future trapped in her body. Oh, and you're fictional. You don't really exist. But I'm horribly, horribly attracted to you and cursing the crappy luck that landed me here as your sister instead of the girl you love.*

Out loud I managed, "Nothing is wrong, brother, but I have some very exciting news." I could still see Mrs. Younge out of the corner of my eye, but pretended to miss the violent shake of her head. Oh well for her...the truth was about to come out.

Darcy's expression became even more concerned. "What news?"

"I am to be married!" I injected as much excitement as I could into my tone and pasted a bright smile on my face. This was a scene that had to be played well: Georgiana, thrilled to be engaged then heartbroken to find that Wickham was a cad. "Are you not happy for me?"

Darcy stiffened, and his expression changed from concerned to cautious, and then almost blank. It was like watching a mask come down over his face. I wondered if this is how he presented himself to

Elizabeth and everyone else: slightly removed from it all, as if he didn't care. Having watched the transformation, I could tell that he *did* care. He cared too much, but was desperately attempting to project an air of neutrality. It was defensive mechanism. He wasn't expecting good things from Georgiana's announcement, but he must think it was better for her to see him blank than angry.

He seemed to be choosing his words with care. "I want for you to be happy, of course."

"I am happy, brother, even more so now that you are here. Now, of course, I see that it would be foolish to go off to Gretna Green. We should be married at home. That would be ever so much better, even if it means having to wait."

I felt horrible. It was like sticking a knife in someone and then turning it this way and that, trying to cause the most damage. I could see the flare of shock and anger in his eyes when I mentioned Gretna Green, but his face remained impassive. And I wasn't even done hurting him yet. This part sucked.

"I am glad I have come when I have. By all means you should be married at Pemberley. You are mistress of it after all. The chapel will be lovely for a wedding —Mother and Father were married there. But tell me, who is your betrothed?" What that even tone of voice was costing him I would probably never know. Darcy was likely seething inside, wanting to tear the head off whatever man had convinced his sister, who was really not much more than a child, to run off with him. And I was about to deliver the death blow.

Mrs. Younge was looking paler by the moment, but I couldn't tear my eyes off of Darcy's long enough to fully look at her. There was something mesmerizing about them. I felt really, really sorry for what I was about to do. If I was to do a character analysis on Darcy I would cite this incident as having changed him, and not for the better. My next few words were going to take a proud and shy man and close him up behind a wall of suspicion and hurt for the next several months. This incident would enhance his tendency to distrust, to find fault with those he met, resulting in him at first alienating the love of his life.

I truly think this was a defining moment for Fitzwiliiam Darcy. A hurtful and defining moment.

Well, crap. This really did suck. All I did was fall asleep with a book on my face and now I got to be the one to damage Mr. Darcy.

"You will never guess! I confess I was surprised to meet with him here as I had not seen him since I was a child—" There it was, the involuntary movement of his hand, the narrowing of his eyes. He had made the connection before I'd even gotten to the name. "George Wickham. Are you not surprised, Fitzwilliam?" I don't know why I added that last bit. Perverseness?

Darcy clenched his teeth together. Have I mentioned his jaw? It was very strong and very...well, everything about him was just "very."

"I am surprised," he admitted. "And I am very glad that I know your plans. And, Mrs. Younge," he turned his head finally to look at my soon-to-be-former companion. "I expect this is the first time you are hearing about Georgiana's engagement?" The sarcasm was fairly dripping off of his voice. I had a moment of absolute admiration for his ability to conjure up such a dry tone when he was so upset.

I figured if I was turning knives, I might as well help turn the one in Mrs. Younge's career as a companion. So I laughed gaily, as if I hadn't noticed the tension in the room. "Oh, no, Mrs. Younge has been helping me pack. She is quite friendly with Mr. Wickham."

"Is she?" Darcy's voice was suddenly very soft. Soft, and lethal sounding. It sent shivers down my spine. From the look on Mrs. Younge's face it was sending shivers down hers too, but of an entirely different variety. "Georgiana, I think it would be best if I spoke to Mrs. Younge alone. Why don't you go up to your room for a bit."

I allowed a confused and worried expression to flit over Georgiana's features. "Is something wrong? Have I done something I should not have?"

Darcy turned back to me and sent me what was probably supposed to be a reassuring smile. "No. You have not done anything wrong, but I do need to speak with Mrs. Younge."

I stood up, actually relieved to be done with the awkward situation for now. Darcy stood up as well and escorted me to the door of the sitting room. As soon as I was out of sight of Darcy and Mrs. Younge I dropped the lady-like gait I had started out with and ran as fast as I could up the stairs and to Georgiana's room.

As I waited in the room, I could hear the maids scrambling up and down the hall, and a raised voice that I knew was Mrs. Younge's. They were helping her pack her things. Darcy had tossed her out on her ear and had made quick work of it. Not even forty-five minutes after he'd first set foot across the threshold I heard a carriage pull up in front of the townhouse to take Mrs. Younge away.

About thirty minutes later, the maid named Sarah came to my room to let me know that my brother wanted to see me in the study. I honestly wasn't sure how to proceed from here, but luckily Darcy was everything that was kind and solicitous. I could tell he really cared for Georgiana's feelings as he explained to me that he was taking me back to London with him until a new companion could be found for me.

I nodded demurely when he told me we would leave Ramsgate in a few days. I knew that from London that Darcy would eventually go to visit Bingley at Netherfield and the actual timeline of *Pride and Prejudice* would commence. I was stuck living as Georgiana for the time being, but I'd always wanted to visit London. And now I got to visit London in the 1800s. I was about to live every geeky literature major's dream.

CHAPTER
Eight

*She did not shut it properly
because she knew that it is very
silly to shut oneself into a
wardrobe, even if it is not a
magic one.*

THREE WEEKS LATER I'd finally had enough.

I had to get out. I couldn't do it anymore. I thought if I could just wait through the year and the half left in the story, it might just pop me out of the novel and back into my life once I reached "The End." But being stuck as a literary character who spends almost the entire time "off-screen" ended up being dreadfully boring. I suppose that if I was a character that had more freedom—like someone who had already been introduced to society—I would have more to do. But Georgiana's options were really limited.

If I could have been Lizzy I'm sure I would have found something to employ my time. Well, first of all, she has a lot more "on-screen" time, being the main character of the novel, but even one of her sisters—okay, honestly, Jane was the only one who seemed palatable as a character—had more freedom at Longbourn than Georgiana had. They were all "out" and therefore could go to parties and dances. Not only that, but they weren't rich heiresses, so they had freedoms I didn't. Georgiana couldn't set foot outside without her companion, but the Bennet girls frequently walked by themselves into the village of Meryton, or went shopping, or visited with their aunt.

I felt like I could kill someone just for a walk outside by myself. I'd off them and stuff them in a closet just for twenty-minutes of productive, breathable, alone time. But it wasn't going to happen.

I spent almost all of my time in the London townhouse practicing piano or painting. Luckily for me, these were activities that Georgiana's body remembered how to do and if I could make my mind blank enough as I had done with the sewing I could accomplish a lot. Painting, playing piano, dancing with the instructor. Repeat. Unfortunately for me this meant I was spending a lot of time with my mind blank. It was starting to scare me. I had never been so purposefully unproductive in my life. I also began to freak out about the amount of time I'd been in the book. Where was I in the real world? Was I still lying there on the couch in some kind of weird comatose state? Was time passing there like it was here?

And I couldn't handle living in the same house as Darcy anymore. He'd come to the sitting room where Mrs. Annesley, my new companion, and I spent most of our afternoons. I'd pour tea and we'd chit-chat about nothing. I think it was probably training for Georgiana to become a hostess, and her brother was nice enough to act as the guinea pig. I usually saw him at dinner too, though often he dined with the Bingleys and I knew soon he would be headed to Netherfield with them and the novel would actually begin.

It kind of felt like being back stage before a production was going to start. Sort of that heightened waiting for the action to begin. But I was the only one who knew we were actors and that there were scenes to be played.

And so after three weeks in the London townhouse I finally snapped. Like a twig. I had to try to get out of the novel. All of my previous attempts had been spectacularly unsuccessful. They'd resulted only in me having to repeat the odious day of Wickham's proposal over and over. What if I tried something again and I got bumped back to that scene? The previous three weeks would have been a total waste of my time.

And what, exactly, was I going to do? The only thing I could think of that I hadn't tried was announcing to another character that I was not, in fact, Georgiana, but Kelsey Edmundson, real person, from the twenty-first century.

Which is how I found myself sitting in Darcy's study—it was much nicer and more homey feeling than the one in Ramsgate—preparing to inform him that he was a fictional character. If I didn't get out of the novel, I expected one of two other things to happen. Either I would be bounced back to the sitting room in Ramsgate and forced to play everything over again, or the timeline would continue as normal, but Darcy would be convinced that Georgiana was completely around the bend. I didn't think he'd be the type to stuff her away in an asylum. More likely that he'd bring in the best private physicians to examine my poor noggin and try to fix me. It would definitely mean even more restrictions on what I was able to do during the day.

I was actually leaning toward the first option. I was pretty sure the rest of the day would be highly uncomfortable, and then at midnight I'd find myself back setting that same dratted row of stitches. The thought was making me physically ill. But I was desperate.

I was smart enough to not tell Darcy I wanted to talk to him privately until the very end of dinner. I figured the closer to midnight it was the better.

"What did you want to see me about, Georgie?" Darcy asked as he sat in the leather chair opposite me.

"I have something to tell you that is not going to make a lot of sense to you, but I need you to keep an open mind."

Darcy looked a little startled at my direct tone but nodded. He leaned forward in his chair, his forehead furrowed in concern.

I took a deep breath. When push came to shove, this was harder to say than I'd thought. "There is a novelist—a woman—her name is Jane Austen. She is writing a book that will be published in a few years. It's called *Pride and Prejudice* and it's going to become a huge sensation. In two hundred years it will be considered a classic and studied in universities all over the world."

Darcy raised his eyebrows in surprise. I suppose he had been expecting me to confess I was secretly corresponding with Wickham or something.

"In fact, two hundred years from now, *I* will be studying it in a university. I know this is going to sound completely insane, but my name is Kelsey Edmundson. I'm trapped in Georgiana's body, but I am a twenty-three year old university student from America. From the future. Well, not even the future, because you see, we are actually *in* that novel. In *Pride and Prejudice*. You're the hero of the novel. You're going to meet and fall in love with the heroine, Elizabeth Bennet, and the two of you will become one the most beloved couples in all of literature."

There was a pregnant pause after this announcement. Darcy was looking at me in shock and concern. I was holding my breath waiting for something—*anything*—to happen. I don't know what I'd been hoping for. Maybe for the walls of the study to be ripped apart and the entire novel to disintegrate around me. Or for me to be whooshed and pushed and pulled and open my eyes on my own couch, none the worse for wear. Anything would have been preferable to the absolute nothing that was happening.

"Georgiana," Darcy said in a carefully neutral

voice. I looked back at him. At least he didn't look like he was going to immediately consign me to Bedlam. "I think you have let your imagination run away with you, and perhaps the wine at dinner did not help."

I sighed. It didn't really matter if he believed me or not. My theory had been that telling another character that we were all fictional would jar me out of the book. That hadn't happened.

"I know you don't believe me. But it's true. I'm just tired of being stuck here. I want to go home. I want to see my friends. I'm running out of theories, and I don't think I can make it through to the end of this book." I stood up and curtsied. "Goodnight, Darcy. I hope you sleep well."

He didn't try to stop me. I walked slowly to Georgiana's room. A small part of me hoping that the effects of my breaking the fourth wall and saying out loud that we were all just characters in a book were just somehow delayed. But I made it safely to Georgiana's room.

I sat, on the edge of Georgiana's bed still wearing the dress I'd worn to dinner, once again watching the clock tick down to midnight. I swear to God, if I ended up in the sitting room with that cursed sampler in my hands once again I was going to meltdown right then and there.

The clock hit 11:59 and I realized that my fingers were hurting from how tightly I was twisting them together in my lap. I tried to tell myself to relax, but I couldn't. I was too freaked out. I thought the ticking of the clock might actually drive me insane. Maybe I would end up in Bedlam after all.

The hands of the clock moved to twelve and I let out a huge sigh of relief. Although this probably meant that I'd spend the foreseeable future being poked and prodded to figure out why I was convinced that all the people around me were fictional characters and I was a novel-jumping, time-traveling girl from the future. Honestly, it was preferable to being back with Mrs. Younge and Wickham.

I wondered if it meant I could try other ways to get out of the story without facing the repercussion of being bumped back to the sitting room.

I finally fell asleep, fully clothed, and utterly exhausted.

I woke up late, but late was normal here. Breakfast wasn't usually available until at least ten. I'd found that I could wander in any time between ten and noon and expect food in the breakfast room. I'd gotten into the habit of eating right at ten. Mrs. Annesley and I usually met in the breakfast room about that time so when I didn't manage to get dressed and down before eleven I felt bad for keeping her waiting. However, I was sure that she'd heard about my little conversation with Darcy last night and probably was more concerned with my mental state than my tardiness for breakfast.

Mrs. Annesley had obviously been in the breakfast room for some time as her plate was almost empty. She looked up as I entered.

"Good morning, Georgiana, how are you feeling this morning?" She smiled at me warmly and if there was a hidden meaning behind her words I couldn't detect one. I smiled back, rather unsure of the footing I was on. She wasn't looking at me like she thought I was nuts, she was looking at me just like she had every morning for the last three weeks.

"I am sorry I am late. I overslept a bit," I finally answered.

"That is quite all right."

I stood there awkwardly for a few moments, waiting for the other shoe to fall, for her to mention something about what I'd told Darcy last night. Honestly, there was no way he wouldn't have told her, right? The woman would have to be warned that her charge was patently insane.

Mrs. Annesley quirked one eyebrow, obviously not sure why I was still hovering just a few steps into the room. "The eggs are especially good this morning," she finally offered tilting her head toward the sideboard.

"Yes. I am sorry. I find myself still a bit tired," I said apologetically and headed toward the sideboard. If Mrs. Annesley wasn't concerned about my mental state, I surely wasn't going to let it interfere with my breakfast.

Mrs. Annesley chatted comfortably while I ate.

After a few moments of idle chitchat I finally got up the nerve to ask about Darcy.

"I have not seen your brother since dinner last night," was the answer.

"You did not see him after I, um, spoke with him in his study, then?"

Mrs. Annesley looked at me curiously. "Did you speak with him in his study? When was that?"

"Last night." She looked so surprised that I added weakly. "Did not I? Perhaps I am confusing my days?"

"You must be muddled, Miss Darcy, for directly after dinner last night your brother went out with Mr. Bingley and you and I stayed up and read that new novel, the horrific one."

I stared at her blankly for a moment. She wasn't describing what had happened last night but what we had done the night *before* last. Could it be possible that I'd been bumped back in the timeline but not all the way to the sitting room in Ramsgate but only one day?

I wasn't quite sure what to think about that.

"Oh, yes, I do remember now. I had trouble sleeping last night and was thinking of something I wanted to discuss with my brother, I must have dreamed that I actually did speak with him."

Mrs. Annesley nodded as if my explanation made sense. It didn't really, but she was too polite to actually say anything.

"I expect we shall see him this afternoon, perhaps you can speak with him then" was all she offered before tactfully changing the subject to some dress patterns we had seen in a magazine.

I didn't ask to speak with Darcy that evening at dinner. I'd tried that and it had obviously not worked. I was grateful that I hadn't been forced back to when I first entered the novel, but I would have been even happier to have awakened as myself. Something *had* happened, though. When I was talking to Darcy about being Kelsey—when I had said my full name—I'd felt more like myself than I had in weeks. As if the real world was somehow just a little bit closer and more reachable than it had been before. I just didn't know how to get to it.

Mrs. Annesley and I continued our reading again after dinner. It was kind of weird to be reading a novel when I knew myself to be in a novel. I wondered briefly if I could jump from *Pride and Prejudice* into *The Mysteries of Udolpho*. Like an infinite regression of novel jumping. Somehow I doubted I'd be able to jump into *The Mysteries of Udolpho* from Georgiana. I'm not sure why, but I just felt like the story wouldn't be strong enough to pull me out.

Why would Austen's story be stronger than Mrs. Radcliffe's? My first answer was "well, because it's a better story, of course." And because I know it better. Perhaps that is why I fell into it, because it's a story that I know.

And for some reason, that is when the idea hit me.

Of all of my theories, and there had been plenty, this one made the most sense to me. I was surprised I hadn't thought of it before.

I had to write myself out.

I was so excited to try it that I could hardly contain myself. As soon as Mrs. Annesley got to the end of a chapter I pleaded tiredness and managed to escape up to my room.

As far as I could tell Georgiana had never kept a diary or anything, but there was a desk in her room stocked with pen and paper. She was a very good student, that much I could discern from her neat little stacks of paper full of French verbs conjugated every which way to Sunday. I'd attempted to be as good a student. I figured since I was stuck here I should take advantage of the situation and at least try to learn something. But French consistently evaded my grasp.

I pulled out a piece of paper, quill and ink and wrote as neatly as I could:

My name is Kelsey Edmundson.

Kelsey Edmundson woke up on the couch in her apartment in Anaheim, California, where she had fallen asleep reading a book.

She was Kelsey Edmundson and only Kelsey Edmundson.

As a work of prose it wasn't very elegant. My brain was scattered and I wasn't sure exactly what I was saying. I just knew, somehow, that it was important to say who I was; to write a piece of my story on that paper.

I folded it neatly in two, creasing it down the middle like a book. I'd fallen asleep basically with *Pride and Prejudice* on my face, so I laid the paper down, face up and open on Georgiana's pillow. I lay down on my stomach with my cheek pressed against the paper.

I don't know how long it took me to fall asleep, but it was a long time. I'd allowed myself to hope that this might work, and the excitement was making it hard for me to relax. Finally my eyes drifted shut.

I woke up, on my own couch, wearing my ratty sweats, with *Pride and Prejudice* still smashed against my face.

CHAPTER
Nine

"...the silliest girls in the country."

THE RELIEF SWEPT over me like a paralyzing wave. I couldn't move. I couldn't breathe. And then I dissolved into tears. I'd started to be convinced that I'd never make it out. That I'd be stuck as Georgiana forever. I'd never seen anything as beautiful as the Southern California sunshine streaming in from our large living room window. Just the feel of it was so totally different from the feel of the sun in England, or the fictionalized England, I'd been living in for the last month.

Crap, how long had I been gone? I grabbed my phone from the coffee table and checked the date. It was the morning after I'd fallen asleep reading *Pride and Prejudice*. I had been stuck as Georgiana for almost a full month, but no significant time had passed here in the real world.

It was barely seven a.m., but I was starving.

Luckily, my local Chinese delivery is open twenty four hours. I called and ordered enough food to feed a family of four for a week and then jumped in the shower. I dissolved into tears again as the warm water pounded down on my head. The amazingness of indoor plumbing cannot be overstated.

Tori wandered out into the kitchen at around 8:15 and looked at me in blurry eyed confusion. "Why are you eating Chinese food at this god-awful hour?"

"'Cause I'm hungry and I haven't had it in ages. It's so good! Want an egg roll?"

"What are you talking about? We ordered from the Emerald Dragon like three days ago."

I stared at her blankly for a minute. "Oh, yeah. Um, the thing is, something weird happened to me last night—"

Tori sat down in a chair on the other side of the kitchen table and looked at me earnestly over an open cardboard box of fried rice. "I know, the whole thing with Ashley. What that little bi—"

"Actually," I cleared my throat. "This doesn't really have anything to do with that whole thing. Well, maybe in a way. I mean, it could have been the inciting incident, but that's beside the point." A crease had appeared between Tori's eyebrows. I knew that crease, it was the "I am becoming increasingly concerned for your emotional stability" crease.

"I need you to keep a really open mind," I added.

"Always." Tori nodded her head sincerely, but the crease got more pronounced.

"So, you know how I've always wanted to meet

Mr. Darcy?"

Tori nodded, looking confused.

"Well, I did."

Blank stare.

"I, um, well the thing is, I got into *Pride and Prejudice*," I continued. "Somehow I jumped into the book and into a character. And I kind of lived there for a few weeks until I figured out how to get out."

"Lived there? As in you lived inside a book?" The crease was reaching new levels of deepness. She needed to stop doing that to her forehead or not even Botox would help her by the time she hit her forties.

"Yes. Like in Regency England, as Georgiana Darcy —that's the character I somehow randomly jumped into—except really, when you think about it, not *actual* Regency England. Frankly everyone was just too pretty for real life."

"Is this some kind of joke?" she demanded.

"No. It's not a joke. I said you have to have a *really* open mind."

"There's open and then there's crazy. How exactly did you manage to get into a book? Magic?"

"I'm not entirely sure about that part, actually. You know," I said slowly, "It's almost like I'm Dr. Samuel Beckett, but for fictional characters."

"What does Samuel Beckett have to do with it?"

"You know, Dr. Sam Beckett from *Quantum Leap*? How he jumps into people?"

Tori's mouth gaped open as she glared at me. "Are you seriously talking to me about a television show from the 1980s right now? That sort of thing doesn't really happen. I mean, it *can't* happen."

"But I think it can. I don't know exactly how it works, just that I fell asleep reading the book and kind of woke up in it. As Georgiana."

Tori's face relaxed. "See, you fell asleep. You must have just been having a really vivid dream." She laughed, but it sounded a bit forced. "How much wine did you have last night?"

"Not enough to make this up. I'm sure this actually happened."

The crease snapped back into existence with surprising speed. "You can't have been inside a book for weeks, Kels. I saw you last night and now here you are this morning. Obviously a dream."

"Yeah," I speared a wonton with a fork and popped it in my mouth. "I think it's like Lucy and the wardrobe. No matter how much time you spend there, not a lot of time will have passed here."

"Honey, you know Narnia isn't real, don't you?" Tori had leaned forward and her voice was gentle, as if she was talking to a child. Or a pet. Or a crazy person.

"Yes, I know Narnia isn't real." I paused for a minute. Did I really know that? I mean, I got into *Pride and Prejudice*, could I get into *The Chronicles of Narnia* too? Or maybe into *Anne of Green Gables*? Or— total nerd meltdown alert—any *Star Wars* book? I felt a cold sweat break out my forehead at the thought. Holy magical book jumper, Batman! Could I *be* Princess Leia?

"Was it only wine?"

I tore myself away from my frantic mental list-making of every book I could possibly try to get into to look over at Tori. "What?"

"Last night, you only had the wine? Nothing... else?"

"Are you asking me if I'm *on* something?"

"Yeah, kind of."

I guess I didn't really blame her, but it still kind of stung. I'd known her fifteen years, in which time I'd never even smoked a cigarette. But I guess if she was telling me something so spectacularly bizarre, I might ask the question too. "Just a glass of wine, not even enough to get tipsy."

"You were really upset. Maybe it's kind of like, well, you know..." she trailed off looking uncomfortable. "Didn't you have that one uncle who..."

"Uncle Greg? He had post traumatic stress disorder. He was in a *war* for goodness' sake! It's not a genetic thing."

"Sorry, I'm just worried." The forehead crease was completely out of control now. Her mention of my uncle had spooked me. Not because I thought she might be right and that I was experiencing a severe mental break (I'd already discarded that theory relatively early on during my stay as Georgiana), but because if she was thinking about my family it might occur to her to call my mother. That could only turn out badly.

I chewed slowly on another wanton. "You're probably right. It was probably just a vivid dream."

Tori looked at me suspiciously. My change of heart was a little bit too quick to be believed.

"Seeing Ashley must have made me overly emotional...and then the wine. And you know how I am about *Pride and Prejudice.*"

"Obsessed?"

"That's one way to put it," I agreed. "I tend to obsess about things, don't I? I guess I just got caught up in a silly dream." The sincerity was fairly dripping off me at this point. I felt bad straight up lying to my best friend, but it was either that or the loony bin. If Tori got ahold of my mother with this kind of story, I could kiss any peace of mind—and any chance at trying to jump into other books—goodbye for God knows how long.

I'm not sure Tori entirely believed me. She shouldn't have, she knew me well enough to know I was lying. But she wanted to believe me, and that went a long way.

"Can you believe Ashley? Do you think she was all over Mark because he was with us, or what?" I figured a change of topic would help. And food. I nudged the package of egg rolls closer to her.

"Probably. Charlie said she attached herself to Mark right after we went to the bathroom." Tori finally accepted my offer of an egg roll. "She's got issues."

"Totally," I agreed. With any luck Tori would launch into a tirade on Ashley's issues and forget all about mine. I could care less about Ashley, but if Tori believed that was the root of my temporary lapse of sanity, she'd let me slide easier.

Luck was with me. Tori spent the next ten minutes going through an entire order of green pepper beef and listing every single one of Ashley's faults and assuring me I was much better off without Jerkface Jordan.

I was relieved that her focus was off me, but the loss of my green pepper beef seemed a high price to pay.

Tragically, I could not be Princess Leia. No matter how hard I smashed the novelization of *A New Hope* to my face before falling asleep, I couldn't get in. This was a blow, but not entirely unexpected. *Star Wars*, no matter what I tell myself, isn't exactly great literature. Maybe whatever this weird novel-jumping ability was, it was limited to classics.

But it turned out I couldn't be Anne Shirley either, or Viola in *Twelfth Night*, or Carroll's Alice. I didn't bother to try any of the Brontë sister's books. They might be interesting to read, but who in their right minds would want to live *Wuthering Heights*? I even tried two other Austen novels, *Emma* and *Persuasion* (Anne might not be the spunkiest heroine of all time, but I could suffer through for Wentworth).

Nothing.

That last bit confused me. If I could get into an

Austen book, shouldn't I be able to get into *any* Austen book? Or what if the whole novel-jumping thing was a one off. What if I couldn't even get back into *Pride and Prejudice*.

I didn't want to end up as Georgiana again. However, I would trade use of a limb to be Elizabeth Bennet. She's not self-conscious and lame around hot guys like I am. She's spunky and witty and charming. She also doesn't allow herself to fall for losers, or at least not fall hard enough that it does her any permanent damage.

If Lizzy was the goal, then picking the right scene was of the utmost importance. There was still a part of me that shied away from Darcy's first disastrous proposal. I'm not sure I could handle that much awkward. I'd probably throw myself at him and agree to marry him, which would just keep popping me back to the start of the scene anyway.

So I found a scene with Elizabeth at Longbourn after she returned from her visit to Charlotte. I figured it might be easier to slip into Lizzy when she was home, in her own surroundings.

I fell asleep on my stomach, my cheek pressed tightly to the page.

Mid-morning sunlight was streaming in through the windows of the small sitting room. I blinked a few times to adjust my eyes. The sitting room seemed packed with women, all with similar curls in varying shades of brown. I looked down quickly at my dress. It was a perfectly serviceable morning muslin, but nothing near as nice as what I'd worn as Georgiana. I could tell that it wasn't new. The top was even a bit tight across my chest like it had perhaps been handed down instead of made for me. Speaking of my chest, Darcy must really have been a saint if what he'd noticed were Lizzy's fine eyes...

I almost squealed in excitement. I'd done it! I'd made it into Elizabeth Bennet! I was Lizzy!

"I am sure I cried for two days together when Colonel Millar's regiment went away. I thought I should have broke my heart."

I looked up from the examination of my chest to gaze across the room at Mrs. Bennet. She was surprisingly pretty. Though why I found that surprising, I'm not sure. Maybe because she's always played older in the movies, but she couldn't have been more than forty. She had, after all, produced five relatively good looking daughters and Mr. Bennet had basically admitted he fell for her looks when they were young.

There was a long pause. I glanced around the room, waiting for Lydia to respond to her mother— I'd re-read the scene a bunch of times before trying to jump and knew they'd be commiserating together over the soldiers leaving town. Mary was the most easily distinguishable as she sat flipping through sheet music in a corner and looking dour. Right next to me was a girl about fifteen or sixteen, so either Kitty or Lydia. Sitting together on the settee each with needlework in hand were two more sisters.

That must be Jane, I thought of the one with the light brown hair. *Wow, she is really pretty.*

The sister next to Jane looked up at me, quirking a dark brow. Her eyes were wide and almost almond shaped. They were a rich chocolate brown framed with nearly black lashes. Fine eyes.

Oh, crap.

"Lydia?" Elizabeth promoted. There was a spark of laughter behind those amazing eyes. "Are you feeling quite well? You look a bit far off."

No, I wasn't feeling well. I'd just managed to pop into possibly the most vacuous, annoying little sister in all of literature. What exactly was Lydia's line? "I'm sure my heart shall break," I sniffed. That wasn't quite right, but close enough.

"If only we could but go to Brighton," Mrs. Bennet sighed dramatically.

Lizzy and Jane shared a small smile. *Yes,* I thought derisively, *if only we could. Oh, but wait, I do! And I hook up with Wickham, the sleaziest of sleazes, while I'm at it.*

"Oh, yes!" I said through gritted teeth. "If one could but go to Brighton! But papa is so disagreeable."

"A little sea-bathing would set me up forever." Mrs. Bennet sighed mournfully at the end of this pronouncement. I resisted the urge to roll my eyes.

"And my Aunt Phillips is sure it would do me a great deal of good," said the girl next to me. Kitty. So that was all the Bennet sisters' identities solved. All the Bennet girls together in one room and I pop into Lydia. The universe obviously hates me.

I made it through an afternoon and evening with the Bennet family. Seriously, Lizzy and Jane must be saints. I was ready to murder both Mrs. Bennet and Kitty at least four times over before sunset. I'm sure the real Lydia had never been so eager to go to bed, but at the first mention of turning in for the night I was upstairs like a rocket.

After everyone was asleep, I snuck downstairs to the small desk I'd spotted in a little nook off the sitting room and pilfered some paper and pen and ink.

My name is Kelsey Edmundson.

I will wake up in my own apartment, in Anaheim, CA.
No time will have passed.

If I hung around for a few days I could probably set myself up for months of partying it up Regency England style at a beach resort. But the thought of spending any more time than necessary as Lydia literally made me sick to my stomach.

I crept back up the steps to the second floor lighting my way with a candle I'd purloined, stopping long enough to look into a mirror. Lydia was very pretty, though her features weren't as fine as Jane's. Her eyes were wide and dark. In fact, they were a lot like Lizzy's. For the first time it occurred to me that Wickham had ruined Lydia because she looked enough like the sister he was really interested in to make it exciting. I felt the bile rise in my throat and turned from the mirror.

Kitty and Mary were both sleeping soundly as I tiptoed back into the bedroom. I felt bad for Mary who was forced to spend so much of her time with such an annoying pair of sisters. It probably made poor Mary even more...well, Mary. I crawled into Lydia's bed, placing the neatly folded paper bearing my real name under my pillow.

"Charlie and his poker group are going to come over tonight and watch a movie," Tori announced.

"The whole group? What's that like six guys?" I didn't bother to look up from my book. After waking up from my little field trip as Lydia Bennet, of all characters, I'd gone on a postmodern library binge and checked out every book that even mentioned blurring the lines between fiction and reality. So far I hadn't found anything that sounded like my own experience. I'd hit kind of a dead end with my internet research too. There were books and short stories written about people who jump into novels, more of them than I'd expected, actually, but nothing with anyone claiming to have actually *done* it.

Though, based on Tori's reaction when I'd tried to explain it to her after I had popped back into the real world the first time, I could see why people would keep mum. Unless they *wanted* to end up in the crazy bin. But maybe people had experienced it, and instead of talking about it, had written stories about it. You know, like how some people thought that H.G. Wells really had time travelled.

I was grasping at straws. But it was better than grasping at nothing.

"Yeah, six or seven, I'm not sure," she answered. I could feel her eyeing the cover of the book I was reading. She was probably still concerned I was delusional.

"Oh." I glanced up at her finally registering the concerned note in her voice. "Are you here warning me because that Mark guy will be coming?"

"Yeah," she crossed her arms and leaned against my doorjamb. "I just wanted to let you know, 'cause you haven't seen him since the Ashley incident. You seemed a little...shaken up...after that."

"Hmm, yeah, no, I'm fine," I said absent-mindedly. My eyes had drifted back to the book. The heroine had finally made it into her novel within a novel. It was a classic too, though not *Pride and Prejudice*. In her case it seemed like a thing some people were just able to do in her alternate universe society.

"Kelsey!" I realized that Tori had called my name more than once and I glanced up guiltily.

"Sorry."

She narrowed her eyes at me. I attempted to look innocent. And as not-crazy as possible.

"He's not dating Ashley."

"Huh?"

"Mark. He didn't go out or anything with her. I just thought you should know." She was still squinting at me like a specimen under a microscope. Waiting for me to show signs of emotional or mental distress.

"That's smart of him. He seemed like he had a decent head on his shoulders," I answered noncommittally. Really, if Mark wanted to date Ashley it was no business of mine. Yeah, it might make it kind of awkward to have him around but I had bigger fish to fry at the moment. Like the fact that I seemed to be able to jump into characters in my favorite novel.

I realized my attitude was a complete reversal from my earlier position on the whole Mark/Ashley situation. But that was two novel jumps and a month in Regency England ago. Although I realized to Tori it had just been a week ago.

"I'm fine. I'm not saying I want to hang out with Ashley or something, but she's not the reason Jordan and I broke up. Well, she may have been the catalyst, but she was a symptom, not a cause. I'm not going to get all uptight around a guy just 'cause Ashley's come on to him. I'd never be able to go to any alumni events if that were the case."

"All very true." Tori gave me another once over and then smiled. "Well, there's going to be pizza and stuff so feel free to come out of your Kelsey cave and mingle. Or at least eat."

"Yeah, sure," I answered, but my eyes had already drifted back to my book.

CHAPTER
Ten

"Come out to the coast, we'll
get together, have a few
laughs..."

I DIDN'T WANT to admit it, but I could tell the minute
Mark arrived. His deep, rumbly voice carried through
the whole house. Not that he was loud or obnoxious
sounding. He was probably more laid back and quiet
than all of the other boisterous guys I could hear in
the front room. But something about his voice just cut
through the rest of them.

Not that I was listening for it or anything. I wasn't
interested in him. It wasn't my fault his voice
sounded like warm honey. It also sounded annoying
cheerful. All the time. Nobody was really that
consistently happy.

I ignored the small voice of reason that whispered
I'd only met him twice, so condemning him as being
too fake-happy was probably unfair, and glared at the
wall that separated my bedroom from the living room

full of men. I heard Mark's voice again, followed by a burst of male laughter and I ground my teeth in frustration. There was no way I was going to get any reading done. Not that I'd admit to myself that it was because I was straining to make out what Mark was saying.

I closed my book with a sigh. It wasn't really helping with my "research" anyway. There weren't really any similarities between me and the main character other than the ability to get into a novel.

I stopped to check my reflection in the mirror over my dresser. Yikes. I smoothed my blonde hair back into a ponytail which helped a little bit. I reached for the makeup bag sitting on the dresser and then stopped myself. I wasn't trying to impress anyone. I was just hanging out in my own apartment on a weekend. There was no reason for me to primp and preen.

Our small living room was crammed with male bodies. I tried not to seem like I was specifically looking for Mark. He wasn't hard to find, he was sitting on the couch, holding a paper plate with pizza on it and chatting with Rick. Argh. Rick I would rather avoid. I veered off into the kitchen were Tori was doling out the pizza.

"Here." She handed me a slice.

"Thanks," I stood there uncertainly for a moment and she gave me a wink and a small shove back out into the living room.

I wandered casually in the direction of the couch, though that required stepping over several pairs of guy legs.

"Kelsey!" Rick had spotted me. "Here, have my seat."

"Thanks." I sat in Rick's recently vacated spot of the couch. He sat on the arm of the couch, really too uncomfortably close for my liking. But the trade off was I got to sit next to Mark.

"Hi." I was going for casual acquaintance and not "last time I saw you I ran off 'cause I saw a slutty girl I know draped all over you."

"Hey." Mark smiled at me, his dark eyes warm. Was it possible I'd forgotten, in just a week, how ridiculously hot he was? Apparently, yes. I could actually feel my brain turning to jelly. "We seem to be making a habit of invading your apartment."

"At least this time I'm actually dressed for the occasion, and not in my pajamas." I pulled a funny face.

Mark chuckled. He really did have the most amazing laugh. It made me want to be witty and clever just so I could keep hearing it.

"I thought you looked great," Rick said eagerly.

I grimaced. "Thanks for the compliment, untrue as it may be."

"No, really, you have great legs." Rick blurted out, then a dull red infused his cheeks. I sincerely hope that he'd meant to only think that and not say it out loud. I resisted the urge to look down at my shorts-clad legs, or to turn to see if Mark was looking at them. "Um, you don't have a drink, do you want a Coke? I can go get you one," Rick added hastily.

"That'd be great," I said sincerely.

"Be right back." Rick bounded across the room in the direction of the kitchen and after a moment, I breathed an audible sigh of relief.

"He's not a bad bloke." Mark broke the silence.

"Rick's a nice guy. But then, he isn't making awkward comments about your legs."

Mark laughed again. "True. I could see how that would change one's perspective."

I smiled back and looked up to where Charlie and another guy I didn't know were engrossed in debate in front of the DVD player. "What movie are you guys watching?"

"Last I heard it was the latest *Die Hard*, though I think Derek was lobbying for *Tron: Legacy*."

I rolled my eyes. "I hope Charlie wins. I love *Die Hard*."

"Really? Not a lot of girls do."

I gave him a mock glare. "I am not a lot of girls. I adore McClane. You know, 'on a good day he's a great cop, on a bad day—'"

"'He's the best there is.'" Mark finished for me.

"Damn straight." I grinned. I was doing it! I was having a normal, almost flirty conversation with Mark Barnes.

"Here's your Coke, Kelsey."

I resisted the urge to yell at Rick to go away. "Thanks," I said instead as I accepted the cold can.

A silence settled over the three of us.

"Do you have a movie preference?" Mark asked Rick over my head. "Kelsey was just telling me she prefers *Die Hard*."

"Oh, that's awesome. I love the *Die Hard* movies."
Rick leaned closer to me. I surreptitiously scooted
closer to Mark and answered Rick with a nod. I didn't
want to encourage him.

The great movie debate was finally decided and
Tori flicked off the overhead lights. I kept hoping that
Rick would move away from. Like, sit on the floor or
something, but he somehow kept getting closer and
closer to me. I'd scooted so far across the couch that I
was nearly touching Mark by the time the opening
credits scrolled on. I'm not sure what was making me
more edgy, Rick, or my proximity to Mark. Okay,
that's a lie. It was totally Mark. He smelled amazing.
His profile was ridiculous: strong jaw and nose.
Though now that I was this close, I could see a small
bump near the bridge of his nose, like maybe it had
been broken at one point. Somehow it made him seem
even sexier. I turned back to the screen and tried not
think about draping myself all over him *à la* Ashley.

I shouldn't have thought about Ashley. The image
of her with her red claws digging into Mark's arm
popped into my mind and refused to leave. Tori had
said that he wasn't seeing her, but what did Tori
know?

Rick moved even closer to me. He was pretty much
off the couch arm now and completely onto the
couch. He was also basically pressed up against my
right side. But I was frozen.

"You've still got a few inches," Mark said in a low
voice. I swallowed and glanced over at him. He
nodded to the small space between us and then

looked significantly past me at Rick.

If I moved I'd be pressed up against him. The thought had appeal, but I couldn't get the image of Ashley caressing his arm out of my head. "Sorry, I'm not like Ashley." The snide comment was out before I could call it back. I saw his eyes widen in surprise. I should have just apologized. I should have tried to make it into a joke. Okay, that probably wouldn't have worked. But I should have done something. Instead I just sat silently as he shrugged and turned back to the movie.

I sat through another fifteen minutes of the movie, Rick breathing down my neck on one side, and Mark completely ignoring me on the other. Then I quietly got up, dumped my pizza in the kitchen trash and snuck off to my room and back to my books.

I stood uncertainly outside the large double-doored entrance to McKinney's pub. I was still not sure how I'd let myself be talked into going on a blind date. But Tori had been persistent. Really, when wasn't she persistent? I'd given in this time because I had been hoping it would stop her from worrying about me. She could obviously tell I wasn't over my "little *Pride and Prejudice* fixation" in spite of my best efforts to act normal around her.

So here I was, about to go on my first date since

Jerkface Jordan. I closed my eyes for a moment in a silent prayer that the evening would not be a complete disaster and reached for the handle of the door.

"Here, let me," a deep voice said from beside me. A deep, sexily accented voice that I probably would have known anywhere. I snapped my eyes open. There was a large hand on the door handle, pulling it open. A large hand that was attached to a very muscular, and familiar, arm. *Oh no, no, no, no.* I glanced up in shock.

Mark.

He looked amazing. Really, really amazing. Like slacks and a button up shirt that fit way too well to be from a department store, amazing. He could not possibly be getting those clothes on a teacher's salary could he? He must be so much better with money management than I was.

"Kelsey?" Mark looked down at me in surprise. He was holding the door open, but neither of us was moving. I was frozen with shock and a dawning feeling of dread. "I'm sorry, I didn't recognize you."

That was lowering. I briefly rallied, thinking it was probably because I usually looked like something the cat dragged in around Mark, but I'd made an effort tonight. He just didn't recognize me 'cause I was looking totally hot. Then I remembered he'd seen me in my mini skirt/boots combo. Tonight's jeans and slightly off one shoulder sweater did not begin to measure up.

"Oh," I managed. *What witty repartee, Kelsey. You're*

going to earn a conversational award with that comeback. "I...uh..." And that's when it hit me. I was here for a blind date. Set up by Tori. My friend. My soon-to-be-former friend.

Mark took in my face—eyes wide, mouth hanging slightly open. I'm sure I looked like a fish gasping for air. I could tell the moment it hit him too. His eyes narrowed and something...odd... flashed in their dark brown depths. To his credit he didn't turn around and run, screaming, back to the parking lot. "I take it you're my date for the evening?" He even managed a smile.

"I'm guessing so." I was proud of how casual my reply sounded. Until I realized we were both still standing in the doorway of McKinney's, Mark still holding the door open for me. "Sorry," I muttered and walked into the pub. He followed, letting the door close behind us. The sound of it shutting seemed somehow final to me and I turned quickly toward him.

"Look," I said, "you don't have to have dinner with me. You were obviously brought here under false pretenses." I actually shudder to think what Charlie had told him about the girl he was setting him up with. I could only hope that the terms "desperate" and "recently cheated on" had not been used. Whatever it was Charlie had said, it obviously hadn't been "Oh, and by the way, it's Tori's roommate, Kelsey."

"If you want to just call it a night, I'm totally okay with that, I mean, don't feel like it'd be hurting my feelings or anything." I was rambling. *Stop talking,*

Kelsey.

Mark was still looking at me with that sort of half smile. "Kelsey, it's just dinner. I don't have a problem with it if you don't." He raised an eyebrow at me. I took it as a challenge. I'm not sure why. Maybe he was just trying to get me to bow out so he didn't have to be the one to do it. More likely, I was reading way too much into everything and he was just being a nice guy. I'm not sure why the idea of Mark having dinner with me just because he was a nice guy bothered me so much. But it did.

"Sure, let's have dinner," I heard myself saying.

As I slid into the booth across from Mark I was already regretting my decision. I don't know what it was about him, but I just had this sense that whenever I was near him I would end making myself look like a total idiot. I folded my hands on my lap under the table. I was committed to not knocking any drinks on myself tonight.

After we gave our orders to the waitress, silence descended on our table.

"So, uh, how do you like teaching?" I finally asked.

Mark's eyes crinkled at the corners as he smiled. "Love it."

"Did you always want to be a teacher? You don't really seem the type." I hoped that didn't come out as condescending as I thought it did.

"More the dumb jock type?"

Oh man, it *had* come out that condescending.

"I'm sorry, it was more a commentary on my high school teachers than on you." There was a bit of an awkward pause, after which I added "And I suppose my high school teachers are now your colleagues, so I should probably just stop talking."

Mark shrugged, letting me off the hook. "I did sort of fall into it in school. I just ended up loving history. A professor of mine suggested I pursue a teaching degree. I was just as surprised as anyone that I ended up enjoying it so much."

"I think it's awesome. I wish more teachers really loved what they do."

"Yeah, I agree. If someone decides to teach just because they can't figure out what to do with their degree, then they're probably the last people that should be in front of a classroom."

I fought the blush that was trying to make its way onto my face. I wasn't going to admit to him that I'd thought about teaching for that very reason. But the ever practical Kelsey had gone for earning more useless degrees instead. Not that I had any plans for what I was going to do with my MA.

"So have you always wanted to get your Masters in Literature?" he asked.

Why did he have to ask that? Could he hear my thoughts somehow? Was I usually this paranoid?

"I've always loved literature," I hedged. "The written word is powerful. *Stories* are powerful. They tell us about ourselves, our society, but they also have the ability to take us away from ourselves...to immerse us in other worlds." I realized I was leaning forward earnestly. Way, way too earnestly. And gesturing with my hands like someone proselytizing on a street corner. I sat back and folded my hands back into my lap.

That odd light was back in Mark's eye. "That's one of the things I love about history." he said. The waitress appeared again and slid our plates of food onto the table. "Thanks." He smiled up at her. A predatory look crossed her face. I could tell she'd weighed and measured me and decided I wasn't a real threat.

"No problem," she purred. I raised my eyebrows. Threat or not, I was sitting right in front of her. Did women just always throw themselves at him this way? I'd seen it that night at the party and again with Ashley. Mark didn't seem to be in any need of help in the dating department. I had no idea what Charlie had told him to get him to go on this blind date.

"History really is just a series of stories," Mark continued turning back to me. He hadn't been rude at all to the waitress: in fact, I doubted he'd even noticed her come on. I resisted the urge to shoot a triumphant glance up at her as she stood, slack-jawed, at our table for a brief moment before sidling away. "Stories of heroes and cowards, winners and losers, great men and women. What makes it interesting, what makes it powerful, isn't the recitation of names and dates, but their stories."

I blinked at him. I'd never once thought of history that way. I mean, the whole real people and their lives thing, yeah, but never with the kind of passion that was currently pouring out of Mark. I have to admit that amount of intensity coming out of that attractive of a guy was...extremely hot.

"Your students are lucky," I said as I picked up my fork and dug into my shepherd's pie. "I wish I could be that passionate about history, but real people don't interest me as much as fictional characters do." As soon as I said it I felt like kicking myself. Even though it was true, it sounded creepy. And rude.

"But I bet you know a lot about each of your favorite authors. How their stories fit into the pieces of history around them."

"Yes," I admitted. "I guess so. Although the characters in stories are almost stronger than their authors a lot of the time."

Mark grinned at me. The single dimple on the right side of that grin slayed me. "Yeah? So who's your favorite fictional character then? Han Solo? John McClane? Or maybe your Mr. Darcy?"

"Darcy." I blurted out without thinking and then blushed bright red. There'd been my chance to pretend to be normal. *Swing and a miss.* "Well, actually Elizabeth Bennet," I amended. "If I could be anyone from a book, it would be her." Why was I still talking?

"Huh, I've never given much thought to what fictional character I'd like to be." He looked thoughtful for a moment. "Can't think of anyone. I mean, it might be fun for a day to be someone else. But that's what your Halloween is for, right?"

I took a huge bite of shepherd's pie in a last ditch effort to stop myself from blurting out that I actually *had* managed to be someone else and for much longer than a day.

"You don't have Halloween in Australia?" I asked once the shepherd's pie had burned its way down my throat.

"Not really, no. There are always a few kids that dress up, but nothing like here. Did you know there's a year round Halloween Warehouse off the 5?"

"The one in Buena Park? Yeah, it's awesome, I went there last year to get my Leia costume for the convention—" I broke off in embarrassment. That was way too much information for a blind date. What was with me and my big mouth around Mark? He could ask me for my social security and pin numbers and I'd probably hand them right on over.

Mark laughed. "Well, there you go. Not just for Halloween. There are plenty of days that you get to be someone else."

"Not enough," I thought. Mark looked surprised and I realized I hadn't just thought it, I had actually said it. I winced. I could see whatever glimmer of interest Mark might have had in me fade right before my eyes.

I should have laughed it off, made a joke of it like "see this is why I need to take turns being other people, 'cause I say crazy stuff without thinking about it." But I didn't. I just retreated into myself. Apparently this was my go-to response around Mark. I could never get a firm grip on myself or the situation when I was around him. Which is why if Tori had told me who I was meeting for this blind date I would have just said thanks, but no thanks.

Our conversation got more stilted. I wasn't doing

much to help it along, honestly. He asked me how my food was, and I said it was good. I think I asked him if his burger was good—they have really great burgers at McKinney's—but I don't remember. Around Mark I felt like I was Alice falling down the rabbit hole, but instead of ending up in Wonderland I kept finding myself in the Land of Uncomfortable Social Situations. Awkwarder and awkwarder.

He paid for dinner. I felt bad because I'd been a horrible date. I felt bad because I'd really been starting to like Mark. And then I'd totally blown it and instead of trying to salvage it, I'd blown it more.

I was starting to think that I really was destined to just always appear at my worst in front of him.

"Thanks for dinner." I finally managed to break our silent walk out toward the parking lot. "I'm sorry I wasn't a better blind date."

"You don't need to apologize."

The guy really was too nice. What was wrong with me? Here was this really amazingly smart, interesting, handsome, and genuinely nice guy that I was totally interested in. Was I going to let my own insecurities screw it up for me?

I took a deep breath. "Look, Mark. I like you. I know I come off as a total ditz sometimes, but I'm not really…well, I don't think I really am, lately it's been kind of hard to tell. Every time I'm around you I do and say really stupid things and I have no idea why."

He opened his mouth like he was going to say something in response, but for some reason words kept pouring out of me. "I don't know what Tori and

Charlie were thinking. Someone like you, obviously, wouldn't ever go out with someone like me. It's okay, I get it—"

"Kelsey," Mark finally got a word in edgewise. "You're right, I probably wouldn't have asked you out."

"Oh. Well then, have a nice night." I attempted to gather what was left of my dignity—honestly there wasn't much—and turned toward my car.

"Not because I'm not interested in you," he said quickly, "You're smart and obviously attractive."

I stopped and turned back around. Obviously might be overstating it, but that didn't sound totally unpromising.

"But I wouldn't have asked you out because you are obviously still a bit unbalanced—"

"You think I'm unbalanced?" I interrupted him. "I'm not unbalanced! I mean, I might be a little kooky sometimes...is this about the *Star Wars* stuff?"

"No," Mark ran his hand through his hair in frustration. "I'm not saying you're actually unbalanced, I'm saying you're still off-kilter from your breakup. Even if Charlie hadn't told me you'd recently broken up with someone after you pissed off after the hike, I would have guessed it."

"Pissed? Yeah, I was pissed!" I bit out.

"What? You were pissed after one drink?" he asked. "You don't have to make excuses—"

"I'm not making excuses! What are you talking about? Sorry if I didn't react well to seeing Ashley for the first time since she attempted to stick her tongue all the way down my ex's throat."

Mark stared at me for a moment before letting out a bark of laughter.

"What?" I demanded defensively.

"I think we are speaking at cross purposes," he said. "I meant pissed off as in left quickly. I was forgetting to translate into Yank. You can react however you want to seeing anybody. I'm more talking about how you seem to run hot and cold, one minute you're funny and clever and the next minute you're silent and withdrawn. I'm honestly just not sure how to read you."

He wasn't wrong, but for some reason that made me feel even angrier. "Thanks for dinner," I said again, just because I couldn't think of anything else to say.

Mark stuffed his hands into his pants pockets, looking even more frustrated than he had a few minutes before. We stared at each other for a long minute. Finally he nodded. I turned back toward my car, fishing for my keys in my purse, and cursing myself, Tori and Charlie, and the universe in general for how the evening had gone.

"Which one are you?"

"I'm sorry?" I looked over my shoulder as I unlocked my car.

"Which Kelsey are you?" He shrugged, hands still in his pockets. I refused to notice how the movement caused his shirt to tighten across his shoulders. "Do you even know?"

I gaped at him. What the hell kind of question was

that? To suggest I didn't even know who I was?

"I—I—" I stuttered. Why couldn't I just tell him off? Why couldn't I just say "I'm beyond funny and clever, and you've officially missed out, Buddy?" I hadn't been at a loss for words when my heart had actually been broken by finding Jordan and Ashley together. I'd been able to rip Jerkface to shreds with nothing but words. And yet here was this guy basically questioning my sanity and I had nothing. Maybe it was because he actually looked sincerely confused. Maybe it was because I was starting to realize that I had been more interested in him than I'd admitted to myself.

"Night, Mark," I finally managed before I slipped into the car and slammed the door behind me. He was still standing in the parking lot as I drove away.

Chapter
Eleven

...in every respect entitled to
think well of themselves, and
meanly of others.

"YOU," I SAID accusingly, as I slammed the front door. "Are both in a crap load of trouble."

Tori and Charlie looked up from the couch with twin expressions of guilt.

"It, um, didn't go well, then?" Tori asked in a small voice.

"Yeah, 'well' wouldn't not be how I'd describe the epic fail of that 'blind date.'" I made quote marks in the air around the phrase because I knew how much it annoyed her when people did that.

"I'm sorry." She jumped off the couch and walked toward me, a contrite expression on her face. "I really thought you guys had some chemistry, but I didn't think you'd go if you knew it was Mark." I continued to glare at her and she came to a faltering stop a few feet from me. "I'm really sorry; I shouldn't have done it."

"No, you shouldn't have. I can safely say that if Mark was ever even slightly interested me, he isn't anymore."

"I'm—"

"I'm going to bed," I cut her off before she could try to apologize again. I knew that if she did that I would probably forgive her and I wasn't in a forgiving mood. I wanted to bask in my self-righteous anger for a bit longer.

I slammed my bedroom door behind me and huffed out an angry breath. The more I thought about it, the more annoyed I became. Which Kelsey was I? I was just me. So sometimes I was quiet and awkward and sometimes I was outgoing, and let's admit it, still awkward. The problem was probably that I had no real internal filter. Around Mark I wanted to seem less like a goof so in lieu of a filter I just shut down.

Still, how dare he suggest I not know who I was? Argh. I could only imagine what he'd say if he knew I was literally jumping into other people's bodies. Other people who don't even really exist. That'd send him running for the hills.

I hadn't even considered jumping back into *Pride and Prejudice* since last weekend's little Lydia mishap. I picked the book up from night table and stared at it.

I was jealous of Elizabeth Bennet. She made Darcy fall in love with her without even trying. She didn't withdraw and get all tongue-tied. She was funny and witty and vibrant. I could manage funny, but as soon as that small voice inside my head whispered that is was more likely that people were laughing *at* me than with me I veered off course, crashed, and burned.

Who was I? I was a girl who could jump into her favorite novel. How many people could claim that? And I was going to end up as Lizzy Bennet.

I flipped through the novel looking for a good scene. No more Longbourn family gatherings. If ended up as Mary I might leap off a cliff.

It took me a long time to fall asleep. I kept replaying my fight with Mark. I couldn't stop his words from repeating in my mind.

I was in a well-lit drawing room, sitting on a chair near a beautiful piano, my fingers idly flipping the pages in a book I held on my lap. I could feel the soft silk of my pale lavender gown pressed against my legs. It occurred to me that it was a much nicer dress than Elizabeth Bennet should have. The thought made me start. I looked up quickly. There was Mr. Darcy a few feet away from me, writing at a desk. Just the sight of him caused an almost painful contraction in my chest. I heard a laugh and turned my head to see a man who must be Mr. Bingley standing in front of a settee, conversing with a seated woman whose face I couldn't see.

This was my first time seeing Bingley. He had sandy blond hair and a ridiculously good chin. He and Jane would make gorgeous babies together. I leaned forward a bit so I could see who he was talking to—I still couldn't manage to see her face but I recognized her dark curls. I had, after all, just played the part of her sister for half a day.

Once again I had managed to perform my miraculous, literary quantum leap into entirely the wrong character.

The disappointment was almost overwhelming. I took a steadying breath and looked around me further. I recognized Mr. Hurst snoring in his chair across the room, and Mrs. Hurst sitting, bored, on the piano bench looking at some sheet music.

Wait a minute.

Wait just a *damn* minute!

The drawing room at Netherfield, with Darcy, Lizzy, Bingley, and the Hursts accounted for. Which left...

"Oh, hell no!" I burst out.

Every head in the room, with the exception of Mr. Hurst, who continued to snore away, swiveled toward me in shock.

"Caroline?" Bingley's voice was filled with concern. "Are you quite well?"

I took a moment to compose myself, searching through the frustration and panic clouding my brain for some more Austenesque phrasing. I was quite certain, judging from Darcy's raised eyebrows and Mrs. Hurst's slack jaw, that Caroline Bingley had never before had such an outburst. At least not in front of other people.

I managed a small smile.

"Oh yes, Charles. I do apologize; I was just reading aloud from my book. I didn't realize I was so loud. Quite a scandalous novel."

I glanced down at the book in my lap and grimaced. *The Sonnets of Shakespeare*. Fabulous. Well, hopefully no one had noticed what I'd been reading.

I saw Elizabeth's eyes dart from my face to the book and back, and I realized she must know I was lying. I don't suppose it mattered. I pretty much detest Caroline as a character, so would it really be horrible if every other character temporarily thinks that she's gone off her rocker? I planned to spend as little time as possible in her skin anyway.

"Actually, Charles," I said, standing up and holding the volume down at my side to conceal it with my skirts, "I confess I am feeling a bit fatigued from our earlier..." I trailed off, trying to remember what we would have been doing earlier. I distinctly remember there being walks in the shrubbery, but I couldn't be sure which evening of the whole Jane-and-Lizzy-stuck-at-Netherfield scenario we were on. "From earlier." I finished, lamely. "I think I shall retire early."

Charles looked even more surprised. "I say, Caroline, are you feeling that unwell? I do hope you are not becoming ill. Here, let me take your arm and help you up the stairs."

I tried not to pull a face. Caroline's feet could find the way on their own very well, but Bingley looked so sincere I felt bad refusing him.

Once in Caroline's room, after several assurances

to Bingley that I would be fine, in response to his repeated expressions of concern and promises to make sure Caroline's maid came up directly, I pilfered her desk for a paper, pen, and ink. I managed to find a few loose pieces, folded them in half to create a makeshift book, and started writing.

Kelsey Edmundson woke up in her own bed in her apartment in Anaheim, California.

Everything was as before.

Nothing had changed, and no time had passed.

I wrote it over and over until I filled up every single page of my makeshift book. I was just shoving it under one of the pillows on the bed when Caroline's maid knocked quietly on the door. As soon as I was out of my evening dress and into nightclothes, I jumped into bed. I double-checked that my head was on the right pillow and wished for sleep to come as soon as possible. Even a few hours as Caroline Bingley had been too long.

The loud whooshing sound filled my ears. I could feel the pushing and pulling as I was sucked back into the scene.

I was sitting on a chair near the piano. There was Mr. Darcy at the desk and Bingley speaking to Lizzy just as he had been before I went to sleep.

I was still Caroline Bingley.

The bolt of pure panic was like nothing I'd ever felt

before. It started with a squeezing feeling in my chest and shot through the rest of my body like an electric current before settling, heavy and nausea inducing, in the pit of my stomach.

This was very, very bad.

It was worse than when I'd first been stuck as Georgiana. Then, at least, there had been the novelty of experiencing my first literary quantum leap and the steadfast hope that I had simply not hit on the right method for jumping back out of the book—that the next thing I tried might work. This time I *knew* what should work to get out, and it *hadn't*. For some reason, I hadn't been able to write myself out of *Pride and Prejudice* and back into my real self. I'd been popped right back into the scene as punishment for not playing it right.

Elizabeth was laughing at something Mr. Bingley said and Darcy was looking at them in a disgruntled fashion from his seat at the desk. I forced myself to concentrate.

"I see your design, Bingley," said Mr. Darcy. "You dislike an argument and want to silence this."

"Perhaps I do," laughed Bingley. "Arguments are too much like disputes. If you and Miss Bennet will defer yours till I am out of the room, I shall be very thankful, and then you may say whatever you like of me."

I breathed a small sigh of relief. It was Lizzy's first night at Netherfield. Jane was sick upstairs, Darcy had been writing a letter to his sister, I'd—well *Caroline*—had just been insisting that Darcy include her raptures about Georgiana's design for a table or some such nonsense. Then there was the whole discussion about how Bingley writes letters which was basically an excuse for Lizzy and Darcy to match verbal swords and for Darcy to start his tumble into love with Lizzy.

Caroline had probably been sitting here stewing during that conversation, possibly planning several horrific deaths for Elizabeth, when I'd popped right into her. And then popped right back in after messing up the scene the first time around.

"What you ask," Elizabeth returned to Bingley, "is no sacrifice on my side; and Mr. Darcy had much better finish his letter."

I forced myself to sit quietly. At some point Darcy would finish his letter and suggest that Lizzy and I play piano. Then I'd get to clamber all over myself trying to impress Darcy with Caroline's awesome piano playing skills, during which time he'd just be making eyes at Lizzy and basically asking her to dance of all things. Though she'd be too clueless to get it, thinking he was making fun of her. I wondered if Caroline figured it out. Probably.

It promised to be an absolutely fan-freaking-tastic evening.

Twenty minutes later I was absent-mindedly watching Caroline's hands fly over the keys in front of me, straining my ears to hear what I knew Darcy was saying to Elizabeth. If I could get past this part I could go straight up to bed and get on with trying to write myself out again.

And there it was: Darcy asked Lizzy about being seizing the opportunity to dance a reel (is that what I was playing?), she ignored him, he repeated the question. She was replying, *"Blah blah blah,* despise me if you dare..." I never thought I'd be irritated with Elizabeth Bennet, but really, did she need three whole sentences to get to the point? I was dying to get out of here.

"Indeed I do not dare," Darcy said with a mixture of stiffness and surprise.

I screamed "End scene" in my mind, but I waited a good thirty seconds before stopping my fingers from their busy work and jumping up from the piano bench.

"I fear I am a bit tired. I shall see you all in the morning at breakfast. Goodnight!" And before anyone could respond I was out the door like a shot and up the stairs to Caroline's room.

I wasn't sure why I hadn't been able to write myself out the first time. Just a few quick sentences had been enough to get me out of Georgiana and Lydia. But Caroline was a stronger character, maybe I needed more specifics.

Kelsey Edmundson, age twenty-three, youngest daughter of Richard and Marianne Edmundson, a grad student with way too much school debt, woke up in her own apartment in Anaheim, California.

She was not Caroline Bingley, she was Kelsey Edmundson, no time had passed.

I kissed the page for luck and then placed it between my head and Caroline's pillow. *Please work*, I prayed as I finally slipped off to sleep.

It didn't work.

I woke up in Caroline's bed, staring in shocked disbelief at the molded ceiling above me. I tried not to panic. Really tried. Then I got up, located the chamber pot, and tossed whatever was left of Caroline's dinner from the night before.

The page with my brief biography was still crumpled against the pillow. I grabbed it, smoothing it out, staring at the words as if they might hold the answers I needed.

"Think, Kelsey. Think." Obviously I'd played the scene the night before well enough to move forward in the timeline of the novel, the same way I had eventually as Georgiana. But writing myself out still hadn't worked. Why?

I stood up and paced the length of the room then squeezed the paper into a ball and tossed it into the fire crackling merrily in the grate. Some poor servant had already been up and in Caroline's room before I'd woken up. That had always creeped me out as Georgiana, knowing people were walking around in my room while I was asleep. Now I was too frustrated to be creeped out.

I'd been feeling really annoyed the whole time I'd been Caroline, actually. I wondered if it was just because I so desperately didn't want to be here as her, or if just inhabiting her body meant that her permanent bad temper was rubbing off on me.

I stopped mid-pace. Was that possible? Could Caroline be a strong enough character that her irritation would affect me? Now I really *was* creeped out. I didn't really have an answer. But I did know that what I'd written earlier wasn't as strong as Caroline Bingley. I mean, honestly, just reading her lines in the novel makes me want to smack her. How could I think a simple paragraph about who I was and who my parents were could overcome that

So I sat back down at Caroline's small desk and pulled out two clean sheets of paper. This time instead of filling up the pages with the same paragraph over and over I wrote out the story of my life. I included everything, from my birthday, to my first crush, to my novel-jumping adventures, to my fight with Mark. I wrote in tiny, cramped, sentences, filling both sides of each piece with as much information as I could.

Once I was done I ran back to the bed, eager to fall asleep and try out my new escape hatch. Unfortunately neither Caroline's body or my mind seemed in the least bit inclined to sleep.

After thirty minutes of staring up at the ceiling listening to Caroline's stomach rumble, I finally jumped back up off the bed and rang for her maid. Might as well at least go down to breakfast.

As Caroline's maid helped me into yet another one of her lovely gowns, I stared vacantly at the mirror in front of me. I wondered why more movies didn't cast her as a blonde. She had lovely, almost too pale hair. Coupled with her snotty attitude and her penchant for pale silk gowns, it gave her the appearance of an ice queen. How unfortunate for her that Darcy preferred the dark, liveliness of Elizabeth.

"It'd help your cause if you smiled once in awhile, Caro," I muttered under my breath.

"I'm sorry, Miss?"

"Nothing, Mary, I'm just talking to myself."

As I walked down the stairs, I wondered if smiling would be breaking some kind of Caroline code that would pop me back into the earlier scene. Or if I could manage a somewhat pleasant demeanor as long as I didn't do anything that directly altered the storyline. What was on the agenda for today? Walking in the shrubbery with Darcy and then after dinner the big, dramatic pride discussion between Lizzy and Darcy. I was torn. Part of me wanted to stick around for that, because, well, that's an awesome scene, and the other part of me realized that participating in that scene as Caroline Bingley was going to be borderline torture.

"Good morning," I said as I swept into the breakfast room. I must have sounded even cheerier than I thought because both Darcy and Bingley looked surprised as they stood up and bowed.

"Good morning, Caroline, did you rest well?"

"Yes, Charles, I did. Thank you for asking. Oh,

Miss Bennet," I turned with a gracious smile as Lizzy walked into the room. "How are you this morning?"

I almost giggled at how startled she looked. Her eyes darted between me and the bowing gentlemen as if waiting for some unseen ambush. Not that I blamed her.

"I am well. Thank you, Miss Bingley."

"And your sister?" I asked, following her over to the sideboard and filling up my plate. "I do hope that our dear Jane is feeling better."

"Oh yes. I believe she is. I am hoping she might be able to join us tonight after dinner."

"That is wonderful news!" Bingley positively beamed with excitement. "I am so glad to hear it."

"Thank you, Mr. Bingley," Lizzy replied as she sidled away from me and toward the table. I let her escape to the relatively comfortable company of Bingley's enthusiasm and sat a few seats down the table from Darcy and applied myself to my eggs and toast. I felt, more than saw, Darcy glance my direction in confusion a few times. My guess is Caroline probably spent most of her time throwing herself at him (I mean, who wouldn't?). Under normal circumstances I probably would have been drooling over him too, but I was starving. And knowing as Kelsey that Caroline had absolutely no chance made my breakfast infinitely more interesting than drooling over Mr. Darcy.

The only one who had a chance was Lizzy. Though now that I wasn't his sister throwing myself at him during our upcoming stroll held some appeal. The worst that could happen would be that I'd pop back into the scene where I'd become Caroline. I'd have to wait for midnight. I could end up being a very awkward pumpkin as I sat around the rest of the day waiting for midnight to chime after having just mauled my brother's houseguest. This was Mr. Darcy, after all, so he most likely wouldn't respond with the, say we shall...*enthusiasm*...that Wickham had responded with when I'd tried a similar tactic on him.

The fact was, Darcy wasn't going to fall in love with Caroline. If I wanted to get a chance at kissing the actual hero of the novel I was going to have to get out and find a way to get back in as Lizzy.

CHAPTER
Twelve

*"I can't go back to yesterday
because I was a different
person then. "*

KNOWING CAROLINE HAD no chance didn't stop me
from clinging just a little too tightly to Darcy's arm as
we strolled in the shrubbery later that morning. Who
are we kidding? The clinging was entirely in character
for Miss Bingley, so I was well on my way to making
it through another set of scenes with flying Caroline
colors.

Mr. Darcy had really, really nice arms. He was tall
and I was shorter than my usual Kelsey self. I was
truly enjoying the petite girl next to the tall,
handsome, breech-clad gentleman phenomenon I was
currently experiencing. I batted Caroline's pale
eyelashes up at Darcy and contemplated the fact that
Mark, handsome and ridiculously buff as he may be,
does not quite match Darcy for height. Or, you know,
the wearing breeches thing.

I almost tripped over the hem of my gown. Why was I thinking about stupid Mark Barnes when I was on the arm of Mr. Darcy? There was no good answer. If I could explain the workings of my brain, I wouldn't need the years of therapy that were obviously waiting for me outside of *Pride and Prejudice*.

Mr. Darcy looked at down at me, his dark brow knitting in concern. I allowed myself a moment of positively drowning in his amazing hazel eyes before I pulled myself together and turned on the Miss Bingley Annoys Darcy by Teasing Him About Elizabeth act. Clueless Darcy had been dumb enough to mention that he thought Lizzy had "fine eyes," and Caroline had decided the best response was to constantly tease Darcy as if he were planning to propose to Elizabeth. Caroline meant to point out all of Lizzy's flaws, but honestly, all she succeeded in doing was to keep bringing Darcy's attention back to her rival.

"I was just thinking, Mr. Darcy, of what dress I shall wear to your wedding." I honestly had no idea how Caroline brought the subject up. Jane Austen was a huge fan of dropping into a scene mid-conversation. As, apparently, am I. I always managed to pop into a character when a line is expected of me. "I hope you will give your mother-in-law a few hints, when this desirable event takes place, as to the advantage of holding her tongue; and if you can compass it, do cure the younger girls of running after the officers—"

I nearly lost my train of thought when I Darcy's

jaw clench as I recited, with as much enthusiasm and slyness that I could muster, Caroline's little lecture. 'Cause. Um. Darcy's jaw. Yummy. *Get it together Kelsey.*

"—And, if I may mention so delicate a subject, endeavor to check that little something, bordering on conceit and impertinence, which your lady possesses."

God Almighty. Caroline Bingley said some really craptastic stuff. I didn't realize just how bitchy that whole speech was until it had to come out of my own mouth. I'm surprised Darcy didn't just turn around and walk back down the path to the manor. I would have. Well, after I smacked her across her stupid face.

Mr. Darcy, obviously, had more class than me. Or he was a glutton for punishment. Or something. He merely raised an eyebrow and quirked up a corner of his mouth in a slightly mocking smile. I almost shivered. Kelsey could see, even if Caroline obviously hadn't, that his smile was a warning. "Have you anything else to propose for my domestic felicity?"

I tilted my head and smiled coquettishly up at him. *This, Caroline dear, is where you should shut up and pretend to play nicely with others.* But that wasn't in Caroline's make-up. She'd find a stab at Lizzy's extended family too fun to pass up. "Oh! Yes. Do let the portraits of your Uncle and Aunt Philips be placed in the gallery at Pemberley. Put them next to your great uncle, the judge. They are in the same profession, you know; only in different lines. As for your Elizabeth's picture, you must not attempt to have it taken, for what painter could do justice to those beautiful eyes?"

I felt momentarily sorry for Caroline, she just didn't know when to stop talking. Maybe things just came out of her mouth without her meaning to say them and she was as horrified as everyone else that she'd said it but just passed it off as no big deal.

"It would not be easy, indeed, to catch their expression, but their color and shape, and the eyelashes, so remarkably fine, might be copied," Mr. Darcy said.

I smiled weakly, really it was more of a grimace, in response. I was too preoccupied with my assessment of Caroline to take any great delight in his zinging her with the "Lizzy is hot" commentary.

Could Caroline and I be more alike than I wanted to admit? I almost always said the wrong thing. Look at my last few encounters with Mark. I opened my mouth and stupid, stupid, stupid things came out. And then I didn't know how to react to my own stupidity so I freaked out and shut down. Caroline just hadn't gotten to the stop-talking-altogether part of the complete social lameness equation. She would keep digging until someone else bailed her out by stopping the conversation.

Poor Caroline Bingley.

And poor me.

More like poor everyone else around us.

And on cue, Jane Austen bailed Caroline out of her own conversational idiocy by bringing Elizabeth and Mrs. Hurst around the corner to interrupt her tête-à-tête with Darcy.

"I did not know you intended to walk," I said in my best surprised voice to Caroline's sister and Lizzy.

"You used us abominably ill," answered Mrs. Hurst, "in running away without telling us that you were coming out." She darted forward and snagged Mr. Darcy's other arm so that Lizzy would be forced to walk alone as the path was only wide enough for three.

Mr. Darcy attempted to drop both of our arms, but we both clung on for dear life. "This walk is not wide enough for our party. We had better go into the avenue."

But Lizzy, who never seemed to have a problem expressing herself, laughed gaily and answered. "No, no; stay where you are. You are charmingly grouped, and appear to uncommon advantage. The picturesque would be spoilt by admitting a fourth. Goodbye." She turned off and nearly ran down the pathway, eager to be away from us. I could see the shock and disappointment flash across Darcy's face. Poor sucker, he already had it really bad for her and she could literally not wait to be rid of him.

I'd feel more badly for him if I wasn't wrestling with finding commonality with Caroline Bingley of all people. I sighed. I'd played the scene well enough, it was time to be done. "All this walking has quite done me in. If you don't mind, I would like to return to the house now."

Mr. Darcy nodded, looking ridiculously relieved. Mrs. Hurst quirked her eyebrow at me in surprise, but I didn't offer any other explanation as we made our way back to the manor.

I took myself up to Caroline's room and fished my biography out of the desk. I read over it, looking for flaws. It was fine, even if I wasn't. Then I flung myself on the bed and cried myself to sleep.

I woke up as myself.

Traumatized. There was no other term for it. My experience as Caroline had freaked me out. I was less upset now over the not being able to write myself out on the first two tries—Caroline was a stronger character, so it made sense that I'd have to flesh out my own character more to get out of her. What was really causing me some serious panic was my complete inability to jump into Elizabeth Bennet. So far I'd managed to get into Georgiana who barely qualified as a character—I don't think she even has a line of actual dialogue in the novel. Lydia, quite possibly the stupidest character in the book. And now —Caroline. If *Pride and Prejudice* has a villain, it's her. Okay, that might be harsh—Wickham is a scoundrel, Darcy's Aunt Catherine de Bourgh is a witchy old harpy, so they could qualify as villains. But nope, if I had to pick one, I'd totally go with Caroline. So why in the heck would I have ended up as her?

I was really afraid the answer was that I was too much like her: socially lame and rather self-obsessed.

And like her and the other two characters (and unlike Lizzy) I was the kind of girl who would never end up with the good guy. Georgiana and Lydia both were taken in by Wickham, so I shared the propensity of dating jerks with them. Caroline had better taste, she was in love with Darcy after all, but that love was as unrequited as the day is long.

Maybe even in a fictional reality I was destined to never find happiness.

Or maybe I needed to stop trying to be someone else—it obviously wasn't working out well for me—and fix my own problems.

I put the book back up on my bookshelf and resolved to put the whole novel-jumping thing out of my mind. It was easier said than done. There was a part of me that was just dying to try jumping one more time to see if I could manage Lizzy. There was another part of me that was scared of what character I could end up as next.

But I was done being the girl who never got the good guy.

"Hey."

Mark looked surprised to see me. In all honestly, I was kind of surprised to be there myself, casually leaning against his car in the parking lot of my *alma mater*. I hadn't even been back here since I graduated.

"Hey, Kelsey."

"I just wanted to apologize for dinner the other night," I said. "Not dinner, really, but my behavior."

Mark raised an eyebrow. "You don't need to apologize. I probably should, though. I shouldn't have said what I did in the parking lot. I let my frustration get the best of me."

"No, you were right. I have been acting weird. I can see how that would be confusing. And now here I am at your place of employment, which probably comes off as a bit stalkery, but I didn't have your number and I didn't want to ask Charlie for it. But I felt like I should apologize."

Mark grinned. "Well, we can stand here and argue over who should apologize or we could go get a coffee."

I gaped at him. "Yeah, I'd love to get coffee," I said sincerely as soon as I recovered.

Ten minutes later we were ensconced in one of the back booths at the Caffeination Station, its proximity to Whittier Prep, and the amount of coffee you could get for a relatively small amount made it a favorite student hang out. Probably about half the kids in here, judging by the number that had said hi to Mark —or Mr. Barnes—as we ordered, must have been students at Whit Prep. I hadn't been back to the Station since I'd graduated, but it hadn't changed much.

The caramel white mocha sitting in front of me was roughly the size of my head and was giving me major flashbacks of hanging out here during high school.

There had never been quite this hot of a guy sitting across the table from me when I was a teen, though.

"That's some drink." Mark glanced at my oversized cup piled high with whipped cream and white chocolate shavings as he took a sip of his black coffee.

"You've no idea. It's amazing. I'd forgotten how good."

"Did you used to come here when you were in school then?"

"Yup, in the grand Whit Prep tradition, I hung out here way too many afternoons pretending to be cool."

Mark raised an eyebrow at me in consideration.

"What? Do I have whipped cream on my face?" I wiped at my mouth.

He laughed. "No, I was just trying to imagine what you were like in high school."

I shrugged. "I was a floater. I got along with everyone, but I didn't really have my own group, not at school at least."

"Ah, see I thought you'd be part of the popular group."

"Me? Um, no. I mean, they didn't bother me or anything, I got along with the popular kids, and with the geeks and chess club."

"But you dated a football player, isn't that what Charlie said?"

I looked up, surprised that he'd remembered.

"Briefly. Extremely briefly." That high school heartbreak had led me to the determination that had Darcy been a modern American high-schooler he would not have been a football player. Wickham on the other hand—I'd lay good money on him being a quarterback. "But what about you? Did you go to high school here or in Australia?"

"Oz. Uni here."

"Is your family still there?" I asked.

"Yeah."

"It's got to be hard living that far away from them," I said sympathetically. "No matter where I go in Southern California I'm never more than ten minutes away from some member of my extended family. They're probably a little too close, actually."

He laughed at the face I pulled. "It's a bit lonely at the hols, but I survive. I think I miss my sister most. She's younger than me. Kind of a brat, but I love her."

"Little sisters are supposed to be brats, it's in the job description. I know because I am one. Have you been back much since college?"

"A few times. She visited me once. I love home, but I fell in love with America when I was in school."

"And you were a jock in school, I bet. I mean that in the best possible way."

"Yeah, I can tell." He grinned, dimple winking at me. It was suddenly really hot inside the coffee shop, as if they'd turned the heater on full blast even though it was at least eighty degrees outside. I tried not to fan myself.

"I meant, you obviously enjoy an...active lifestyle. I mean you seemed to enjoy climbing up that damn mountain, so I bet you played sports in school."

"Kelsey, that wasn't exactly mountain climbing."

I tried to look affronted. "Hush. I like to think it was. It makes me feel better about almost passing out twice."

"Well, if it makes you feel better—"

"It does," I assured him.

"Everest has nothing on it." He nodded solemnly. "But yes, I played baseball growing up. Got a scholarship for uni because of it."

"Seriously? I didn't know they play baseball in Australia."

"Not that many people do. I got into it when I was young because of my grandfather. He was American. Everyone else I know played cricket. I play a bit, but baseball was a passion. If you want to get anywhere with it, you have to leave Oz. So I did."

"Wow. And you decided to teach instead of pursue baseball?"

He shrugged again. "I wasn't good enough to make the pros, and teaching became a new passion. I still love the sport, but it's not like I'm up nights mourning some baseball career that didn't happen. There's an opening for a coaching position at Whit Prep though: they've asked me to fill it."

"You'd be a great coach," I said sincerely. "Keeping in mind I have no idea what constitutes a great coach seeing as I avoided participating in all organized sports like the plague, so my basis for comparison is basically bad sports movies. But I'd cast you as a coach…Wait, baseball or girls softball?"

"Girls."

"Oh god, no. Bad idea. You're going to break all

their poor young hearts. The crushes—seriously at that age—they could be emotionally crippled for life."

He crossed his arms and leaned back in the booth. "You might be exaggerating just a bit."

"Nope." I took another sip of my drink. "Not at all."

"So then you think I'm crush-worthy do you?"

"That is the worst kind of fishing, Mark Barnes. Like you don't know you're totally, ridiculously attractive. You have to go and make me actually say it."

"But I have no way of knowing what you find attractive." He was still sitting casually but that light I'd seen in his eyes the other night was back. The intensity of that look made me swallow against the butterflies that had suddenly burst into life in my stomach.

"Back atcha," I said as flippantly as I could manage.

Mark leaned forward, crossing his arms on the table. I swallowed again. For some reason it was getting harder to swallow. And hotter. Definitely hotter. Maybe someone really had turned on the heater. Or I was coming down with the flu.

Or I was totally overwhelmed by Mark's dark chocolate colored eyes.

"You. I find you very attractive."

My first reaction was to tell him that he couldn't possibly. That my hair was too straight and my chin too square and that he was basically one step away from a GQ model. Not even a big step, like a teeny tiny baby step. But luckily, something, my brain, or my mouth, or my heart, overrode that first instinct.

"Back atcha." Except it wasn't flippant this time. At all.

He smiled at me then. The force of it almost knocked me over. It was a good thing I was sitting already. "You have whipped cream on your nose."

"Of course I do," I replied with a mock grimace. "I find wearing dairy products is a great way to break the tension during these types of really intense conversations."

His laugh, oh my gosh, if I could bottle that laugh I'd be a billionaire. Lonely women everywhere would hand over their life savings. But I'd be too stingy to ever sell it. I'd be a Mark laugh hoarder.

I laughed with him. 'Cause there wasn't anything else to do. I obviously had it bad. This level of bad couldn't even be quantified.

"Are you going to let me take you to dinner?" he asked as he reached out with a napkin and wiped the whipped cream off my nose.

"Yes, I think I am."

CHAPTER
Thirteen

"My life is a perfect graveyard
of buried hopes."

THE NEXT MORNING I floated out of my bedroom and down the hall to the kitchen. I'm pretty sure my feet didn't actually touch the ground once.

Tori looked up at my from the table where she sat eating a bowl of cereal. "You seem unusually happy this morning."

"Hmm? Oh do I?" I grabbed a bowl from the dishwasher and pirouetted over to the cupboard where I knew she'd hidden the Coco Puffs. "You know I'm gonna find these, why do you keep hiding them from me?"

"'I want them to last more than a day?"

"Hurtful." I spun my way back over to the fridge for milk.

"Are you humming?" she demanded.

"Maaaaaaybe."

"Oh my good lord, singing *and* dancing. Tell me what is going on. Did you win the lottery?"

I giggled. "Kinda." I sat across from her and dug into my cereal. "Mmm, chocolate for breakfast is such a good idea."

"Would your current state of Disney princess level happiness have anything to do with not being home for dinner last night? What time did you get home anyway?"

I crunched through two bites before I answered. Messing with her was so much fun. "Late."

"Oh really? This gets more and more interesting. Did you have a date last night?"

"Yup." I paused for effect. Really I just wanted to see how far up on her forehead her eyebrows could get as she waited for me to elaborate. Surprisingly high. "With Mark."

"Mark Barnes? As in the guy I tried to set you up with and you freaked out and said I was dead meat?"

"You set us up on a double blind date. It was trickery and I wasn't prepared."

"Ha! But I was right! You guys have chemistry." Tori looked way too smug for her own good.

"Mmmhmm. Yes, *chemistry*."

"Are you going to tell me how much chemistry? Inquiring minds want to know."

She wished. "No, I am not."

"That is so unfair." She huffed in mock frustration. "And I assume from the singing and dancing that you're seeing him again."

"Yup, he's taking me to a baseball game tonight."

Tori dropped her spoon. "A baseball game? As in a professional sporting event? You?"

"Don't look so shocked. I've been to them before."

"In the last decade?"

"Well, no. But it should be fun."

"I'm sure you'll find something to do at least, even if it's not watching the game." Tori waggled her eyebrows at me suggestively.

"I'm shocked at you, Tori Mansfield. Shocked." I shook my head as I took my now empty bowl over to the sink to rinse it out. "So, are you going to help me pick something to wear or what?"

Her eyes lit up. "Oh babe, we should just go get something. I've already seen your closet. Pathetic."

"Hey." I wasn't really offended, because she was right. "I can't believe I am saying this, but I will wear whatever you tell me to wear."

"The power is mine!" Tori cackled evilly as she dumped her bowl in the sink next to mine. "I promise not to abuse it. At least not too horribly."

The baseball stadium was packed with people. I drove by it all the time and saw the full parking lots, but I never realized how many people could fit inside. The atmosphere was electric, and we had really great seats. Or at least that's what Tori told me when I texted her and Charlie a picture of our view of the field while Mark was off getting us drinks and nachos.

Also, thanks to Tori's shopping efforts I didn't look entirely out of place. She'd made me buy a red v-neck t-shirt, assuring me I'd blend in. She was right, the stands were overflowing with red, broken up by the occasional white jersey. The jeans she'd picked out were a little bit tighter than I normally would have bought, but they emphasized my long legs. I was already aware of the hotness differential between me and Mark and losing the ability to breathe normally seemed a small price to pay to help close the gap.

"So what position did you play?" I asked once Mark had returned with our snacks.

"Outfield. Usually right field."

I looked up at the player currently standing in right field—luckily I knew where to look because I'd asked Tori while we were shopping for a quick update on the general rules of baseball.

"No, it's not like stage left and right." She'd doubled over laughing.

"Shut up." I'd smacked her on the arm.

"You poor thing. If you date him for more than a week I'll buy you a book. You'll be an expert in no time."

"Your confidence in this possible relationship is underwhelming," I'd replied acidly.

"Hey, I'll invest the fifteen bucks in *Baseball for Dummies*, all I'm asking for is a commitment of a week. I'm a good friend and you know it."

I squinted out at the player in right field. He was not unattractive. Seriously, who knew there were so many hot guys in baseball? I've obviously been missing out. I attempted, unsuccessfully, not to imagine Mark wearing baseball pants. It's probably a good thing I didn't know him in his baseball playing days. My heart wouldn't have been able to handle all the excitement.

Not that he wasn't looking ridiculously attractive in his jeans and t-shirt. The man did things for t-shirts. I averted my eyes from his arm as he offered me the nachos, choosing to stare at the gooey chips instead. Hopefully if I accidentally drooled he'd just think I really liked nachos.

"Do you miss it?" I asked as I selected a chip and concentrated on maneuvering into my mouth without getting any cheese on my new shirt.

"Sometimes. It's fun being part of a team."

"Is it? I always hate group projects at school, but I guess that's not really the same thing?"

Mark laughed. "Poor Kels, do you work for everyone else's A?"

"Yes, yes I do." I grinned up at him, probably looking like a total fool. The fact that he had just used my nickname had sent me soaring into the stratosphere. "You know I know nothing about baseball, right? I'm counting on you to tell me when to cheer."

"I know, but I'll bet you'll pick it up pretty fast. Fans and sportswriters can get really into the stats—there's a statistic for everything in baseball—but it's a pretty straightforward game."

"That's comforting."

"Here's a fun fact for you. Did you know your Jane

Austen was the first author to ever mention baseball?"

I looked up in surprise. "I did not. Oh! Catherine Moreland in *Northanger Abbey*? She plays baseball—is that really the first reference to it? I'm kind of impressed that you know that."

"Yeah, might be the only Austen fact you'll ever get out of me, so enjoy it while you can."

I looked up at him through my lashes. "Oh, I am enjoying it. Trust me."

And I enjoyed the game. Mark was right that it was easy to follow. Being part of a huge crowd cheering for the home team gave me a weird sense of euphoria. As did Mark holding my hand through the entire ninth inning.

I enjoyed it even more when Mark walked me up to my apartment door when he dropped me off.

Then he kissed me.

I'd always dated guys who were taller than me. Not that Mark wasn't, he had a good two inches on me, but I didn't have to tilt my head all that far back to kiss him. When I leaned into him I could feel the entire length of his body against mine. We fit together in a surprisingly easy and comfortable way. Like puzzle pieces. Really, hot, steamy, knee-wobbling, insides-melting puzzle pieces.

I tried not to cry when he ended the kiss. Or beg him to keep kissing me. Or throw myself bodily at him.

"Goodnight, Kelsey." Mark tucked a strand of hair behind my ear and then leaned back in to kiss me on the nose. "Sweet dreams."

"Night," I whispered back, somehow managing to get my key into the lock as he walked down the apartment steps then turned back again to wave. I waved back and then floated inside.

I was three dates into my fledgling relationship with Mark and I had yet to say anything totally stupid or slip into weird, awkward Kelsey mode. Maybe I was starting to overcome my own natural tendencies. Of course, even thinking such a heretical thought set me up for total disaster.

I sat across the table from Mark at the Italian restaurant by the theater discussing the book that the movie we'd just seen was based off of. I can't remember the last time I went to a movie adaptation with a guy who'd actually read the book. Probably never.

"The book was better. They did a decent job with it, but it was missing that underlying tension the book has," Mark said as he looked at the menu. I was supposed to be looking at my menu too, but I was too busy staring his mouth as he talked about the novel.

"The book is always better. Always," I agreed absently. "It's amazing how much better *Pride and Prejudice* is than any of its adaptations. Like, I thought they'd done an okay job with casting, but when you're actually *there* you realize they didn't even get close."

"Huh?"

"Hmm, what?" I realized I was still staring at his mouth and refocused with a start. "Sorry, what?"

"What do you mean, 'when you're there?'"

There was a long silence. I could almost hear my brain whirring as I searched frantically for a way to explain what I'd just said. I wonder if Mark could hear it too.

"Um..." That's when I made the stupidest decision. Ever. In the history of Kelsey. And that's saying a lot. "Well, I had an interesting experience recently."

"Yeah?"

"Yeah. You know how *Pride and Prejudice* is basically my favorite book of all time?"

Mark nodded. So far, so good.

"Well, and this is going to sound a bit out there," way to understate, Kels, "but um, I've kind of managed to get into *Pride and Prejudice*."

Mark's forehead creased in confusion. "What do you mean into? Aren't you already into it?"

"No, well yes, but I mean—and again, I know this sounds unbelievable, but it's the honest truth—I have jumped into *Pride and Prejudice*, like into the characters—and, like, *lived* in it."

There was a long pause.

"Is this a joke?"

"Um, no. I'm being completely serious. This has happened to me. Three times actually, three different characters. It was an accident the first time, but the last two times I jumped in on purpose."

"You're saying you've lived inside a novel? A piece of fiction?"

"Yeah, I know it sounds crazy—"

"Fair dinkum."

I blinked. "I don't even know what that means."

"I'm agreeing with you. You're crazy."

"I'm not saying I'm crazy! I'm saying that I know it *sounds* crazy. That doesn't make it any less true!"

There was another long pause. I stared miserably at the tablecloth, not even able to look up at him. I didn't want to see the look on his face.

"I'm sorry, I shouldn't have told you," I muttered.

I heard him puff out a breath. "I don't know what to say, Kelsey. You've had some hard times recently, with your break up—"

"That was months ago. I'm not emotionally fragile and I'm not retreating into some imaginary world if that's what you're getting at. I shouldn't have said anything, it's just that I like you and it feels weird to keep that big of a secret." I finally glanced back up. Mark didn't look upset or angry, he looked concerned. The kind of concerned that you look when someone is standing on the edge of a bridge and threatening to jump. He really did think I was insane. I felt tears prick behind my eyes. This was a spectacularly bad idea.

"So you really think you're able to be other people? Fictional people?"

"I don't think it, I *know* it. I've been three different characters."

"Kelsey," he leaned forward and put his hand over mine where it rested on the table. "That is just not physically possible. Have you thought about...talking to someone...about this?"

I laughed, bitterly. "Like a psychiatrist or something? I'm not crazy. I hoped you'd understand...I don't even know why I thought you might."

The frustration finally broke through Mark's calm demeanor. "I'm trying to understand, but you've obviously got a serious problem. I didn't realize how close to the truth I was when I asked if you even knew who you were."

I looked back down at the tablecloth, trying to compose myself. His bringing up the conversation outside McKinney's pub had caused a little crack in my already tender heart.

"I'm sorry. I have to go." I said numbly, pushing my chair away from the table.

"Kelsey, don't...wait a second." He started to stand up, but I'd already turned and fled the restaurant.

By the time I got home I'd managed to work myself from heartbroken into a rage. Yes, I realize the whole thing made me sound Cuckoo for Coco Puffs, but what was I supposed to do? Go through my life lying by omission to the people that mattered to me? And how dare he go back to the not knowing who I am crap? I know who I am. Just because I occasionally spend a bit of time as characters in my favorite novel didn't mean I was a weaker person. In fact, I'd just proven that by finally writing myself out of Caroline. I *did* know who I was.

I sat fuming in my room, working myself further into a state of righteous indignation. A completely undeserved indignation—if I'd been Mark and he'd told me something similar I'd probably have snuck into the bathroom and texted Tori to come rescue me —but somewhere between the restaurant and home I'd lost all perspective.

Was I supposed to just never tell Mark? Or should I have waited longer? What's the appropriate number of dates before you tell someone that you can jump into a novel? I'm sure there's an appropriate number before you discuss past relationships, future plans for kids and marriage. But novel-jumping is not something that most relationship advice columns ever cover.

We'd had two great dates, not counting our disastrous blind date—2.5 if you included the Caffeination Station—and we were well on our way to a decent third date with the movie and then dinner. That's like regular couple type stuff. I should've just kept my mouth shut, pretended to be totally normal, and kept *Pride and Prejudice* up on my top shelf where it belongs. But it's kind of a big thing not to share. I mean, right? Could Lois Lane and Clark Kent ever really have a relationship if Lois has no idea that Clark is Superman? Not that I'm comparing myself to Superman. Well, maybe a little bit.

And if I never tell, does this mean I can never read *Pride and Prejudice* again? What if Mark and I date for years, get married, have gorgeous, red-headed, baseball-playing, history-fact-spouting babies, and one night I forget myself and fall asleep reading and *poof!*—mommy's gone.

Obviously, I am borrowing trouble here. First of all, I'm perfectly able, the Caroline debacle notwithstanding, to write myself back out of the book. Secondly, it was only our third date. However, I've never been accused of being the most calm, rational person. Or of being able to stop the stupid confessions that somehow pour out of my mouth.

My phone kept buzzing. I didn't respond to any of Mark's texts. There were three, and one call that I hit decline on. The last text was:

— Please call me. I'm worried about you. —

For some reason that made me even more frustrated. Like if he really did care he would have believed me, not just texted.

I tossed my phone on my nightstand and yanked *Pride and Prejudice* off the shelf. Jumping while angry wasn't really the best idea, I'd demonstrated that by ending up as Caroline-*freaking*-Bingley of all people, but I had something to prove. I'm not sure who I was trying to prove it to. I already knew I could jump. It's not like I could record it or take anyone with me. I was destined to be the only one who knew I was telling the truth.

It made me angry.

I slammed the book open, verified that Elizabeth's name occurred on the page and lay down on the bed, covering my face with the book and closed my eyes.

I could feel my tears getting the pages wet.
I woke up as Elizabeth Bennet.

CHAPTER
Fourteen

"Headstrong, obstinate girl!'

I WAS IN a small but neatly furnished bedroom. I was standing by a window that looked out over an extremely tidy garden. If the hedges hadn't been green, I would have assumed they were some kind of wall instead of plants. They were trimmed within an inch of their lives. Only one gardener that I could think of would have such obsessive-compulsive habits.

Mr. Collins.

I ran to the vanity table on the other side of the room and stared excitedly into the mirror.

Elizabeth Bennet's almond shaped, dark eyes gazed back at me.

"Oh my god, I did it!" I breathed as I ran my hands over Lizzy's face and dark curls. "I am Elizabeth Bennet."

I could barely contain myself. Luckily, I seemed to be alone in Lizzy's room at the Collins's, so I gave into my excitement and danced around the room singing "Lizzy, Lizzy, Lizzy Bennet, yeah!" in a manner entirely inappropriate for a Regency lady.

After my little victory dance, I plopped down on the bed and thought through my situation. I was Elizabeth, and I was obviously on my visit to Hunsford parsonage during which I would encounter Lady Catherine (argh), and Darcy and his cousin Colonel Fitzwilliam (yes!), and suffer through the disastrous first proposal. Unless I already had. Maybe it was the day after and I was reading Darcy's letter.

I stood up and searched the room for Darcy's letter, silently berating myself for not paying more attention to the scene I was jumping into. I should make a list of jumping rules, put them on sticky notes, and plaster them to the front of the book.

Rule One: Never Jump Angry

Rule Two: Pay Attention to What Scene You Are Jumping Into

Rule Three: Avoid Scenes With Caroline Bingley in Them as if Your Life Depends On It.

I had completely ignored rules one and two when I jumped after my confession to Mark. Thankfully, I had managed to at least pick a scene without Caroline.

There was no letter from Darcy to be found in Lizzy's room so I had to assume we were pre-proposal. But when?

The answer came in the form of a huge commotion downstairs, the sound of feet running up the stairs, and someone calling "Eliza! Eliza!" in a high-pitched squeal. The words I had glanced at before I cried myself to sleep fell into my mind just as I opened my door so I wasn't surprised to find a panting Maria Lucas standing in front of me looking as frazzled as if someone had just announced that the world was ending in five minutes.

"Oh, my dear Eliza! Pray make haste and come into the dining room, for there is such a sight to be seen! I will not tell you what it is. Make haste, and come down this moment."

"What is happening, Maria?" I asked, though I knew she wouldn't tell me, as I allowed myself to be dragged downstairs. Maria lead the way to the dining room, and we peered out the window to see Mr. Collins and Charlotte talking to two women in a phaeton that was stopped outside the garden gate. I knew it was Mrs. Jenkinson, the companion of Lady Catherine's daughter Anne, and Anne herself, but of course Lizzy didn't know that. I was mentally searching for Lizzy's lines and trying to calculate the timeline. This was Elizabeth's second day at Hunsford, how many weeks did that leave me until I saw Darcy?

"Is this all? I expected at least that the pigs were got into the garden. This is nothing but Lady Catherine and her daughter!"

Honestly, the pigs probably would have been more interesting. I was still trying to figure out the ETA of Darcy as I stared out at poor Charlotte getting blown about by the wind as she chatted with the ladies from Rosings. It was early March and it looked ridiculously cold out if the steel grey skies and brisk wind were any indication.

"La! My dear, it is not Lady Catherine. The old lady is Mrs. Jenkinson, who lives with them." Maria could not have sounded more shocked if Lizzy had confused Mrs. Jenkinson with the Prince Regent himself. Mr. Collins had obviously instilled The Awe of Lady Catherine in his young sister-in-law. "The other is Miss De Bourgh. Only look at her. She is quite a little creature. Who would have thought she could be so thin and small!"

A huge gust of wind blew through the front yard, causing the front gate to bang open and closed with a huge sound. I swear Charlotte tipped over sideways before recovering herself. "She is abominably rude to keep Charlotte out of doors in all this wind. Why does she not come in?"

Maria turned her saucer-like blue eyes to me, her blonde curls swishing around her face. She looked a bit as if I suggested inviting the Christ child in for tea. I mentally snickered. "Oh! Charlotte says she hardly ever does. It is the greatest of favors when Miss De Bourgh comes in."

We both turned to stare out the window again. Mr. Wickham had told Elizabeth that Mr. Darcy was to be betrothed to his cousin. Of course it wasn't true no matter how much his aunt, Lady Catherine, might wished it. Lizzy didn't know that though, as far as she knew she was looking at the future Mrs. Darcy.

"I like her appearance," I repeated one of my favorite Lizzy lines. "She looks sickly and cross. Yes, she will do for him very well. She will make him a very proper wife."

Maria looked at me with her too-wide eyes again, but I didn't explain what I was talking about. I've always enjoyed Lizzy's little snarky asides, I know that they were indications that she was too quick to judge people, but it's not like she was alone in those judgments. Everyone in Hertfordshire had thought Darcy was a proud, stuck up prig. Anne de Bourgh looked like a cross between a wraith and an unhappy bumblebee. The weird yellow and brown striped spencer she was wearing did not help her sickly, sallow complexion one bit. Nor did the perpetual frown.

I frowned in response. I'd just finished the math in my head. I had about three weeks until Darcy showed up at Rosings. Could I handle three weeks of living with Mr. Collins? That seemed an extreme price. But then, here I was, finally, as Lizzy. What if I jumped back out of the novel to try to get closer to a Darcy scene and ended up not being able to get back as Lizzy? That would suck.

So would sitting through the first proposal and breaking Darcy's heart, because unlike Lizzy, I knew Darcy wasn't a complete and total jerk. But he needed that first rejection to become the great romantic hero we all know and love. I'd already broken his heart once as Georgiana. His sister's almost elopement had really shaken him, and playing that scene had not been a walk in the park. Breaking his heart as Lizzy, saying the truly hurtful things she said to him, that wasn't going to be fun.

You should have thought this through before you decided to just jump, willy nilly, into to the book, Kels.

However, there was plenty of Darcy goodness before the proposal. There's no reason I couldn't enjoy that while it lasted. If I could just get through the next three Collins-tastic weeks, I'd be rewarded by several Darcy-centric days.

Decisions.

I hadn't been trying this long and hard to be Elizabeth Bennet to back out now. I squared my shoulders as the phaeton drove away and Mr. Collins and Charlotte returned to the parsonage. I even managed to greet them and Charlotte's father, Sir William Lucas, as they all tumbled through the front door, breathless with stories of the graciousness of Miss de Bourgh and her invitation to dine at Rosings the next day.

Living in the same house as Mr. Collins was slightly less torturous than I'd assumed it would be. This was mostly because Charlotte had him so well managed that during the day we rarely saw him. We had to sit through his soliloquies at dinner and our occasional trips to Rosings Park were excruciating tests of my ability to respond politely to absurdity. Mr. Collins at Rosings was quite possibly the most socially uncomfortable thing I had ever witnessed. Which is saying a lot because I'd sat through the last half of my blind date with Mark.

Then there was Lady Catherine de Bourgh to contend with. She really was an imposing figure. I could see similarities in her coloring and features with Darcy, and she certainly shared his propensity for thinking he knew what was right. However, Darcy had nothing on this harpy. Seriously, the things that came out of her mouth should probably get her smacked, or at least cast on The Real Housewives of Regency England.

As it turned out, my obsession with Elizabeth Bennet had born the fruit of me being more familiar with her lines than anyone else's so I was more than up to playing her part against Lady C during what I termed "The Quiz." On her first visit to Rosings, Lady Catherine asks Lizzy all about herself and her family, and basically disapproves of everything. Seeing her reaction to Lizzy's answers was almost worth the price of having jumped into Lizzy a little too early.

"Upon my word, you give your opinion very decidedly for so young a person." I once pulled the exact same face that Lady C was staring at Lizzy with. I'd eaten an entire bag of Sour Patch Kids and was having a mini-meltdown. "Pray, what is your age?"

I smiled Lizzy's not-quite-saucy smile. I was really in love with that look, I'd entertained myself the night before by practicing it repeatedly in front of the mirror. "With three younger sisters grown up your Ladyship can hardly expect me to own it."

The Sour Patch Kids overdose face got even more

pronounced. I almost expected her to start twitching. Lizzy's description of Lady C as "dignified impertinence" was spot on.

"You cannot be more than twenty, I am sure. Therefore you need not conceal your age."

Talk about an obsession with youth. Hollywood has nothing on the Regency era. Though I suppose if your life expectancy was closer to forty than eighty the focus on marrying at a young age was to be expected. I suppose that at twenty-three I would be nearing old maid status. Except that I wasn't Kelsey, I was Lizzy Bennet and a full three years younger.

"I am not one and twenty."

And Darcy was twenty-eight, I knew this because by the end of the book—next year—he'd be twenty-nine, the same age as Mark. The gap between Lizzy and Darcy was a full eight years, whereas between me and Mark it was six. Actually, it was really only five and half. Wait a minute, why was I comparing myself and Mark to Lizzy and Darcy of all people? I mean, comparing me to Lizzy I get because I'd been doing that for roughly half my life, but Mark to Darcy?

I was jarred out of my musings by Sir William and Mr. Collins rejoining the group. In a way this saved Lizzy from further questioning because Lady Catherine turned the full force of her meddling personality on Mr. Collins and the hapless parishioners that he represented.

Thankfully our visits to Rosings happened only once or twice a week. They were all "off-screen" in the novel, so I didn't have a script, but I figured if I acted as Lizzy-like as possible the novel would just keep chugging forward. I managed to not do anything, either at Rosings or Hunsford, that bumped me backward in the timeline.

I found myself, surprisingly, becoming good friends with Charlotte. I guess it shouldn't have been that surprising to me that she had a dry, sly wit and was always good for a laugh, but somehow it did. There must have been a reason that Elizabeth and Charlotte had been friends: it wasn't just that they were of a similar age and lived near each other. Charlotte was seven years older than Lizzy. Jane was the eldest Bennet, yet it was Lizzy and Charlotte who were good friends.

Other than the spectacularly lame decision to set her cap at Mr. Collins (and could I really blame her? It was live with stupid, simpering Mr. Collins in her own home, or live with her stupid, simpering parents in theirs), she turned out to be sensible and easy going. I actually started enjoying our daily chats in the sitting room and walks along country lanes. Charlotte had managed to make a comfortable life for herself and had an uncanny ability to minimize her husband's influence on her day. After her father returned to Hertfordshire, Charlotte, Maria, and I had even more time to ourselves.

"Are there any new gentleman come to Meryton since I have been gone?" Charlotte asked one day while we were in her sitting room.

"No. Though the militia are still there which means my sisters have plenty of handsome men in red coats to pine after."

"And are you pining after a certain man in a red coat?" Charlotte quirked an eyebrow at me. Her face was very expressive. It wasn't typically beautiful, but she was pretty enough that I wondered why she hadn't married before twenty-seven. The answer, of course, was that Austen needed her character to save Lizzy from Collins and also provide a way for Lizzy to visit Darcy's aunt's home so she could run into him. Poor Charlotte was just a plot device.

"I suppose you are referring to Mr. Wickham. I must admit that I am not pining for him or for any other gentleman." I answered. Although, as I said it a certain gentleman's face flashed into mind.

It wasn't Darcy's.

That night I dreamed of Mark. The dream was unsettling. It was a distorted version of my telling him I could jump into *Pride and Prejudice*, but instead of me running away at the end of the conversation it was Mark running away from me. I ran after him but I couldn't reach him.

I woke up in a cold sweat and vowed to myself that I wasn't going to think or dream about Mark again.

The Darcy countdown had begun. In fact, everyone at Hunsford knew that he was expected soon at Rosings. Mr. Collins spent the better part of two dinners waxing poetic about how gentlemanly he was when they had met at Netherfield. I smiled into my wine glass, knowing that Darcy had been horrified when Collins had approached him without an introduction. But I nodded and kept my own counsel.

Lizzy would not have been looking forward to Darcy's impending arrival, but I sure as heck was. Finally the day was upon us. Charlotte had seen Mr. Collins approaching the parsonage with Mr. Darcy and Colonel Fitzwilliam in tow and had dashed into the sitting room to tell Maria and me.

"I may thank you, Eliza, for this piece of civility. Mr. Darcy would never have come so soon to wait upon me."

I started to protest. She was right of course, but Lizzy was still absolutely clueless that Darcy had designs on her. My protest was cut short by the gentlemen coming into the room. They bowed. We curtsied. I attempted not to throw myself at Darcy. Okay, that may have been overstating it, but after weeks of Mr. Collins being the only male in the general vicinity, the introduction of the hotness that is Darcy was almost too much to take.

His cousin, Colonel Fitzwilliam, wasn't anywhere near as attractive as he was. In fact, Austen clearly states that he is plain. I thought that was a bit of harsh of Austen, to deliberately make him a plain character. But even though he wasn't handsome, he was very charismatic and dashing. And very male.

Next to Darcy and Colonel Fitzwilliam poor Mr. Collins looked like a mouse.

Mr. Darcy paid his compliments to Charlotte, but didn't say anything to Lizzy at first. Colonel Fitzwilliam was more than charming, however, asking me how I liked Hunsford and the surrounding area. I began to wonder if he knew that Darcy liked

Elizabeth and was trying to get a rise out of his cousin. He was almost just a little too flirty.

"I trust that your family is well, Miss Bennet," Darcy finally broke into my conversation with Colonel Fitzwilliam. Oh, the poor sucker. He truly was jealous of his cousin. Having played the part of his sister, I had seen Darcy with his guard down and so I could recognize the jealousy even behind the mask of indifference he wore so well.

"Yes, thank you. They are well." I paused deliberately. "My eldest sister has been in town these three months. Have you never happened to see her there?"

"I have not been so fortunate as to meet with Miss Bennet," Darcy answered as confusion chased across his face. Poor man, he had no idea what kind of a grudge Lizzy was nursing about the treatment of Jane.

Stop worrying about Darcy! I needed to be less in tune with Darcy's feelings and more in tune with Lizzy's. If I wanted to play these scenes right I needed her sassy indifference to him at my immediate command.

Soon after this uncomfortable exchange Mr. Darcy and Colonel Fitzwilliam rose to leave. This was disappointing because I knew that we wouldn't be dining at Rosings for a week. This whole waiting for the best scenes was a serious time commitment.

But I was excited to get to play one of my favorite scenes with Darcy the next time we were at Rosings.

CHAPTER
Fifteen

*A dream is a wish your
heart makes.*

I FOUND MYSELF, annoyingly, dreaming more and
more of Mark at night. The dreams had slight
variations but were mostly along the same theme. I
was always running after him. Sometimes I'd try to
reach him and fail. Sometimes I'd catch up with him
and he'd turn around and look at me with a blank
expression as if I was a total stranger and he wasn't
quite sure why I was accosting him.

It was frustrating to have finally made it into the
book as Elizabeth and to be spending my nights
pining for someone in the real world. I'm not sure
pining was the right word. I wasn't even sure what
our status was in the real world. We'd only had three
official dates. Does that count as dating? And if it
does, then what would our current status post I-can-
jump-into-novels reveal be? I hadn't stuck around to
find out if he was "breaking up" with me. Do people

break up after three dates? Or is just like, "hmmm, maybe I don't want a fourth date."

'Cause you're a crazy person who doesn't know who she is.

That's what he thinks of me at least.

Honestly, all of this self-examination was kind of pointless. For right now I was Elizabeth Bennet. Insecure, un-self-realized, crazy person that might make me but I was going to take as much advantage of it as possible.

A week passed before we were invited to Rosings again. I'm sure it was killing Mr. Collins slowly and painfully, but he managed to keep a relatively stiff upper lip. He only mentioned Lady de Bourgh, Rosings, Anne, Mr. Darcy and his cousin, or some grand feature of the manor and park twenty or so times a day. For Mr. Collins this was quite a feat and I'm sure that all of the ladies at the parsonage, myself included, appreciated it. Some of his anxiety was relieved by the fact that Colonel Fitzwilliam had visited us twice, but the Colonel seemed much more interested in socializing with Charlotte, Maria, and me, than spending any quality time with Mr. Collins. Really who could blame him?

The extended break from all things de Bourgh and Rosings was easier for me than it was for poor Mr. Collins whose entire world revolved around Lady Catherine. I knew exactly how long it would be before we were invited back to Rosings. Our next big scene there was to be on Easter when would see the Rosings Park gang at church and be invited over for the evening.

It was to be a rather momentous week in my life as Lizzy. The Easter evening visit to Rosings would be followed by a visit from Darcy the next day, and shortly thereafter with the first proposal. So, I had flat-out rejecting a proposal of marriage from literature's most eligible bachelor to look forward to. It was going to require my best acting skills, because really I just wanted to say "Yes, marry me, sweep me off to Pemberley, and make all the world's problems disappear." My previous experiences had taught me that if I did say yes, instead of Lizzy's rather more than emphatic no, the scene would just reset itself. I was seriously considering it. I probably would just play the scene through, but it would be so much fun to see what would happen the rest of that day if Lizzy professed herself to be in love with Mr. Darcy.

My dreams stubbornly remained full of a certain red-headed Aussie. There was really no reason I should be thinking about Mark at all. I should be thinking about Darcy 'cause Darcy was hot. And one of the best romantic heroes of all time. I shrugged off the little voice reminding me that since jumping as Lizzy Darcy's hotness had been registering more as a fact and less as something that personally affected me. I had an entire week of exciting Darcy events to look forward to. Spending time thinking about Mark was pointless and counterproductive.

If only my subconscious would get the message.

Easter morning came and we all filed off to church to hear Mr. Collins's sermon which was horribly dry, rather pointless, and not quite doctrinally sound.

Lady Catherine issued her invitation to Mr. and Mrs. Collins with an expression that let us all plainly know she hadn't really wanted to invite us, but her invitation couldn't be refused—and wouldn't have been by Mr. Collins in this lifetime...or the next either. The most immediate effect the invitation had was basically ruining our own Easter meal plans, as Mr. Collins spent the entire mid-day meal gushing over our Rosings invite. These exclamations of delight followed us into the sitting room, where we would usually have respite from him, and I was only able to escape his soliloquy by proclaiming Maria and myself in need of extra time to dress for the evenings festivities.

"Of course, my dear cousin," Mr. Collins said beatifically as I rose from the settee and pulled Maria up with me. "I am sure you feel the honor of such an invitation greatly. Though you cannot have finery enough to truly grace the halls of Rosings Park as it deserves, I understand you desire to prepare as much as possible. Lady Catherine, after all—"

"Yes," I cut him off with a quick smile. "Lady Catherine is goodness itself to invite Maria and me and I am sure she will understand our lack of finery. However, we must be as presentable as possible, so off we go. Maria, come along." I tugged her firmly by the arm, propelling her out of the room forcefully. Charlotte shot us a longing look as we exited, but I could only rescue so many people at one time. It was like war. You only saved the ones you thought had a chance of survival or had the least likely chance of fending for themselves. Poor Maria was already so awestruck over everything having to do with Lady Catherine that another thirty minutes of Mr. Collins waxing poetic might actually do her in for good.

As much as I found Mr. Collins silly and annoying I had to admit I was kind of nervous about the evening as well. In the book it's a pretty important scene between Lizzy and Darcy, with Colonel Fitzwilliam playing a helpful third. The conversation over the piano is likely what propels Darcy into finally deciding to pay his addresses to Lizzy. I'm pretty sure that after so many rereads I had it memorized word for word, but I was a little freaked out about getting it all right. As Caroline there had been plenty of scenes that I had fudged my way through, adding in as much as I could remember of Austen's actual dialogue, and filling in the rest with how I thought Caro would act. It had seemed to work out okay, I had been able to get enough right to not keep getting bumped back to the place I first entered the scene as Caroline. But those scenes weren't quite as important as this one. At least in my estimation. The nerves were getting to me and warring with a sort of weird, giddy excitement. The whole thing kind of made me want to throw up.

And Mark wouldn't get out of my damn head.

Every time I closed my eyes I could see his easy, lazy smile. Or the sad look in his eyes when he talked to me about knowing myself. I didn't want to think about knowing who I was as Kelsey, or about Mark at all. Why should I be wasting any thought process on him when I had the delightful Mr. Darcy to look forward to tonight? Well, okay, not quite delightful. He doesn't get totally delightful until after I shred his heart next week.

Oh my god. I might really be sick.

I knew Mr. Darcy was well on his way to being in love with Lizzy, but I took extra special care getting ready, picking out her best dress to wear. I figured it wouldn't hurt.

During the walk to Rosings later that night I gave myself a lecture on appearing just as carefree and content as Lizzy always did. She would have no expectations for the evening and no idea that Mr. Darcy was interested in her. When we finally entered the sitting room at Rosings I had managed to get most of my nerves under control enough to present a complacent, smiling, and disinterested front.

Mr. Darcy and Colonel Fitzwilliam both rose and bowed, and we all curtsied in return while Mr. Collins bowed so low I was afraid he might tip right over and land on his face. As soon as Mr. Darcy looked up and met my eye my heart skipped a beat. He really was extraordinarily handsome. I'm not saying there weren't attractive guys during the Regency era, but the portraits that have survived don't necessarily lead one to believe that Calvin Klein models were walking the streets in waistcoats. But Mr. Darcy could give any modern day hottie a run for his money. I suppose, because he was a made up character, he could be just as attractive as the author wanted to make him in her head.

Apparently, Jane Austen had really, really good taste.

The first hour or so was full of the mindless trivialities I'd come to expect from this kind of social event mixed in with a good measure of pedantic advice and pronouncements from Lady Catherine on every possible subject. It really was almost impossible to keep from rolling my eyes at the woman.

It was kind of entertaining to watch Darcy's reaction to his aunt. That he found her pronouncements and interferences annoying was evident in his face and demeanor. A few of her more absurd and ill-bred comments even brought a dull flush to his high cheekbones. I watched the blushes spread with interest, wondering how, even now as he was embarrassed by his aunt that he could tell Lizzy in just a few days that her relations were what made her so inferior to him. Honestly, I couldn't find much difference between Lady Catherine and Mrs. Bennet other than that Mrs. Bennet had to worry about money while Lady Catherine had the comfort and assurance that no matter how much of a witch she was her money and name would still demand that people treat her with respect. Of the two, I vastly preferred Mrs. Bennet's silliness. She, at least, was harmless.

Colonel Fitzwilliam was sitting next to me. He was just as flirtatious as he had been during his visits to the parsonage and started in on a spirited conversation on music with me now. Darcy kept eyeing us, I'm sure with jealousy. Although, I suppose to Lizzy, who had no idea of his affection for her, it would have seemed as if he wanted to intimidate her. He was obviously not amused by my intimate conversation with Colonel Fitzwilliam. I glanced up through my lashes at the Colonel and wondered again how much of his flirting was just him messing with Darcy's mind.

The Colonel smiled at me before glancing, covertly, at Darcy to gauge his reaction and I knew I'd had it right. He wasn't truly interested in Lizzy, how could he be? Even though his father was an Earl, he was a second son and would need to marry someone with a fortune that Lizzy was sorely lacking. He was trying to provoke Darcy into something. I guess it worked, because Darcy would declare himself just a few short days from now.

Unfortunately, my conversation with Colonel Fitzwilliam had attracted more than just Darcy's interest.

"What is that you are saying, Fitzwilliam? What is it you are talking of? What are you telling Miss Bennet? Let me hear what it is." Lady Catherine's high, nasal voice cut through our conversation like a scythe. All other conversation in the room also ceased, because as soon as Lady Catherine opened her mouth on any topic, Mr. Collins would shush his wife and sister-in-law, Mr. Darcy hadn't been speaking at all, and Anne de Bourgh basically never uttered a word.

Colonel Fitzwilliam grimaced slightly as he looked up at his aunt. "We are speaking of music, Madam," he said. His exaggerated politeness made me want to giggle, but that would really bring the wrath of Lady C down upon me.

"Of music! Then pray speak aloud. It is of all subjects my delight. I must have my share in the conversation, if you are speaking of music. There are few people in England, I suppose, who have more true enjoyment of music than myself, or a better natural taste. If I had ever learnt, I should have been a great proficient. And so would Anne, if her health had allowed her to apply. I am confident that she would have performed delightfully. How does Georgiana get on, Darcy?"

It was actually a blessing that Lady Catherine had ended her bizarre speech with a question about Georgiana so that Darcy at least would have something to reply. The rest of us would have had no idea how to respond to such a ridiculous and self-aggrandizing speech. Mr. Collins, likely, would have found some odious and smarmy way to agree with her ladyship, but the rest of us would have just been left with mouths slightly agape, and no proper response.

"Georgiana does quite well, Aunt. She possesses a rare natural talent for music and it is a delight to hear her play." Mr. Darcy's expression warmed as he talked about his sister. His affection for her was really quite endearing. I happened to know firsthand how gentle and kind he was with her. I also had the best firsthand knowledge of how well Georgiana "got on" with her music lessons. She fell basically somewhere between extremely dedicated brilliance and pure genius, but it wasn't as if I could just go ahead and volunteer that.

Lady Catherine expressed her approval thusly: "I am very glad to hear such a good account of her, and pray tell her from me that she cannot expect to excel, if she does not practice a great deal."

Really, it was almost as if the woman could not allow the conversation to stray from her as its central point for more than thirty seconds.

Darcy answered, with almost the same tone of exaggerated civility that Colonel Fitzwilliam had just used—I wondered if they'd perfected it while dealing with their aunt. "I assure you, Madam, that she does not need such advice. She practices very constantly."

Lady Catherine harrumphed, probably disappointed that Georgiana could not benefit from her instruction. "So much the better. It cannot be done too much; and when I next write to her, I shall charge her not to neglect it on any account. I often tell young ladies that no excellence in music is to be acquired without constant practice. I have told Miss Bennet several times that she will never play really well unless she practices more—"

I felt, rather than heard, Colonel Fitzwilliam's quick intake of breath at what was a pretty spectacular insult of me. I smiled, waiting for the insult to go from spectacular to nuclear in 3...2...1...

Lady Catherine turned her watery, but still piercing blue eyes on me and followed through with "And though Mrs. Collins has no instrument, she is very welcome, as I have often told her, to come to Rosings every day, and play on the piano forte in Mrs. Jenkinson's room. She would be in nobody's way, you know, in that part of the house."

Mr. Darcy didn't deign to answer his aunt. I could see the dull crimson infusing his cheeks again and I knew he was ashamed of her. His cheekbones were really amazing, giving his face a sort of chiseled out of stone appearance. Mark had great cheekbones too. I shook my head. Wait a minute, why I even thinking about Mark again? Dreaming about him at night was one thing, or even ruminating on his words about knowing myself while I was getting dressed, but thinking about him while Mr. Darcy was *in* the room? Unacceptable.

Luckily, we were all saved from having to respond to Lady Catherine's outrageous proclamation by the coffee being served, after which Colonel Fitzwillaim reminded me that I had promised to play for him.

I sat down at the piano and the Colonel seated himself near me. I took a deep breath and willed my mind blank as I let Elizabeth's fingers move over the keys. It worked like it had when I was Georgiana, although Elizabeth was nowhere near that level of skill. I was concerned that once Darcy removed himself from his aunt, who after listening to me play for a few moments had returned to questioning him and dispensing advice about goodness knows what, and came towards us that I would not be able to think and play at the same time as I knew I must for the scene to progress properly.

Making my mind as blank as possible was

beginning to backfire on me. Every time I let my thoughts drift, even just a little, I started thinking about Mark. I actually felt like smacking him at the moment. How dare he keep invading my thoughts, especially at a time when I needed them to be as much my own as possible? I felt my fingers faltering on the keys and willed Mark back out of my head.

Darcy eventually made his way toward us in a very determined fashion. He stood quite near the piano and directly in my view.

Ignore him. Ignore him. I focused on a point slightly above his head, shoving all other thoughts from my mind as my fingers finished out the song. Once it was done, I sighed in relief, paused for a moment to mentally locate my place in Austen's script and then smiled up archly at Mr. Darcy.

"You mean to frighten me, Mr. Darcy, by coming in all this state to hear me? But I will not be alarmed though your sister does play so well. There is a stubbornness about me that never can bear to be frightened at the will of others. My courage always rises with every attempt to intimidate me."

Darcy raised an eyebrow and looked down at me with a half-smile. I'd actually seen Mark look at me in a similar way. *Curse you, Mark, get out of my head!*

"I shall not say that you are mistaken," he replied. "Because you could not really believe me to entertain any design of alarming you; and I have had the pleasure of your acquaintance long enough to know, that you find great enjoyment in occasionally professing opinions which in fact are not your own."

I laughed at Mr. Darcy's description of Lizzy, as I knew I ought, and then turned to Colonel Fitzwilliam. "Your cousin will give you a very pretty notion of me, and teach you not to believe a word I say. I am particularly unlucky in meeting with a person so well able to expose my real character, in a part of the world where I had hoped to pass myself off with some degree of credit. Indeed, Mr. Darcy, it is very ungenerous of you to mention all that you knew to my disadvantage in Hertfordshire—and, give me leave to say, very impolitic too—for it is provoking me to retaliate, and such things may come out, as will shock your relations to hear."

"I am not afraid of you." That damn half smile again. On Mark it looked different, more relaxed and less sardonic. I blinked. My vision blurred for half a second and I could see myself running after Mark like I had in my dreams. Running after him and reaching out for him.

"Pray let me hear what you have to accuse him of." Colonel Fitzwilliam's amused voice brought me back to the present, and I blinked a few times in rapid succession to clear my vision again. "I should like to know how he behaves among strangers."

I leaned in toward Colonel Fitzwilliam, as if I was about to share a secret, but I kept my eyes on Darcy. He kept his warm, hazel eyes trained on me as well. How could Lizzy not have known he was into her? That smoldering look would very likely send me up in flames at any moment.

"You shall hear then—but prepare yourself for

something very dreadful. The first time of my ever seeing him in Hertfordshire, you must know, was at a ball—and at this ball, what do you think he did? He danced only four dances! I am sorry to pain you—but so it was. He danced only four dances, though gentlemen were scarce; and, to my certain knowledge, more than one young lady was sitting down in want of a partner. Mr. Darcy, you cannot deny the fact."

Mr. Darcy shifted slightly, and I could tell that I'd scored a direct hit. "I had not at that time the honor of knowing any lady in the assembly beyond my own party," he replied.

I smiled again and shook my head. "True; and nobody can ever be introduced in a ball room. Well, Colonel Fitzwilliam, what do I play next? My fingers wait your orders."

Before the Colonel could reply, Darcy took a step forward, adding in almost an urgent manner: "Perhaps, I should have judged better, had I sought an introduction, but I am ill qualified to recommend myself to strangers."

He looked so earnest and sincere in that moment that I wanted to stop the entire conversation and assure him that I knew he was rather shy and that this compounded his sort of natural arrogance. That everything would work out and once he attempted to fix the latter the former would be easier to overcome. Of course, I couldn't quite do that so I continued on with the script addressing the Colonel.

"Shall we ask your cousin the reason of this?" I asked still looking up at Darcy, with barely a sideways glance for the poor Colonel. "Shall we ask him why a man of sense and education, and who has lived in the world, is ill qualified to recommend himself to strangers?"

As soon as I said "man of sense and education" I thought of Mark again. It was almost like I could see him, as if he were not quite physically in front of me, but if I reached out for him I would be able to grab him. My fingers twitched against the keys and I had to keep myself from lifting my arms. I was barely heeding Colonel Fitzwilliam's reply, focused as I was on my own bizarre internal meltdown and not letting it ruin the scene.

"I can answer your question, without applying to him. It is because he will not give himself the trouble."

I watched Darcy's face color a bit, but there was now a sort of hollow rushing sound in my ears that I was fighting against. I shook my head slightly to try to dispel it and the annoying image of Mark that was stuck behind my eyes.

"I certainly have not the talent which some people possess," began Darcy after a moment's pause, "of conversing easily with those I have never seen before. I cannot catch their tone of conversation, or appear interested—"

The rushing sound in my ears suddenly stopped. At the same time Darcy broke off. He seemed to almost shimmer in front of me for a moment and I was afraid that I was going to pass out. What was happening? Why did he stop talking? He was supposed to say "appear interested in their concerns, as I often see done," but instead he was glancing about the room in what seemed like confusion. His eyes darted quickly from me to the Colonel then to the group on the other side of the sitting room.

I paused, not sure what to do. Should I just continue on with Lizzy's next line as if he hadn't stopped mid-sentence? I'd never had this happen before. The only time Austen's characters ever strayed from their lines was if I had done something to mess up the storyline. Then once we hit midnight it was back into the same scene again so I had a chance to get it right. The hiccup in the dialogue was always, *always* my fault.

I decided to forge ahead as if nothing had happened.

"My fingers do not move over this instrument in the masterly manner which I see so many women's do." Mr. Darcy stopped glancing about the room and focused on me as soon as I started speaking. The look in his eyes was one of utter confusion and I stumbled over the next phrase. "Th-they have not the same, um...force or rapidity, and do not produce the same expression. But then I have always supposed it to be my own fault—because I would not take the trouble of practicing. It is not that I do not believe my fingers as capable as any other woman's of superior execution."

Mr. Darcy's only response was to shake his head slightly and to reach up and tug on one ear, almost as if he'd been underwater and was dealing with the aftereffects.

"Mr. Darcy?" I asked quietly. My voice was filled with more fear than Lizzy's likely should have been, but as Kelsey I was suddenly afraid that something far beyond verbal sparring over the top of a piano forte was at stake.

"I—I'm sorry, are you speaking to me?" Mr. Darcy asked. A look of surprise flitted across his face and he cleared his throat, twice, rather loudly.

The edges of my vision started to blacken. *Don't freak out! Don't freak out!*

"I say Darcy, are you feeling quite well?" Colonel Fitzwilliam's concerned voice cut through my internal drama. His face reflected the same level of concern as his voice, and as Darcy continued to stare at him for a moment without responding, the Colonel half rose from his chair.

Darcy took an odd half-step backward. "No, I mean, er, yes that is, I am feeling fine. I think I'm dreaming."

Colonel Fitzwilliam laughed heartily at that as he stood up, although to my ears his laughter sounded strained. "No, cousin, you are not dreaming, though I could see how you would think so with such a vision of loveliness as Miss Bennet before you." Darcy blinked at me again and I managed a half-hearted smile.

"Our ride this afternoon must have been too fatiguing," the Colonel continued. "Perhaps you should retire for the evening and I shall make your excuses to our aunt?"

Mr. Darcy nodded slightly, then looked around the

room again, as if not sure which way to exit. Colonel Fitzwilliam, now looking extremely worried, grabbed him securely by the elbow and directed him toward a door that would let him exit the room without passing by Lady Catherine. "This way, Cuz," I overheard Colonel Fitzwilliam say in a low voice.

CHAPTER
Sixteen

*"I'm afraid I can't explain
myself, sir. Because I am not
myself, you see?"*

I SAT AT the piano in a state of absolute shock and
confusion. I bit my lip in indecision. I'd never had to
guess quite like this before. Either scenes played out
according to plan, or I was the one in charge of
plotting the temporary new course.

"Where are my nephews going off to?" Lady
Catherine's shrill voice cut through my panic. "I say,
Miss Bennet, what have you done to make them run
off like this?"

I stood up from the piano and walked back over to
where the others sat on the opposite side of the room.

"I am sorry Ma'am, I believe Mr. Darcy suddenly
felt ill and Colonel Fitzwilliam is assisting him."

It was basically the truth, and the only explanation
I had to give. The problem is that people here didn't
get sick unless it fit the plot. I'd been in pieces of *Pride*

and Prejudice for weeks on end without even seeing a case of the sniffles. The only real illness had been Jane Bennet's cold at Netherfield and that was because Austen had written it in. In a way it was kind of a perfect world. Bad things only happened if they were necessary for the story to develop. Almost everyone (except characters that had been written deliberately unpleasant looking like Collins or specifically said to be plain like Colonel Fitzwilliam) was rather annoyingly attractive. People could eat too much without worrying about getting overly fat—they'd still just look however they'd looked when Jane Austen imagined them in her head and wrote them down with her pen.

Which left with me with absolutely no explanation of why Darcy had wigged out. I had a sinking, sick feeling in my stomach that I'd finally broken the book somehow.

"Ill? My nephew? We must call for a surgeon immediately!" How Lady Catherine's voice managed to get even more shrill I have no idea. I'd really thought that she'd already reached ten on that particular scale, but count on Lady C to find a way to crank it up to eleven.

"Perhaps it may be best to see what Colonel Fitzwilliam advises when he returns. I am sure he will join us any moment." Everyone in the room wore almost identical expressions of shock at my talking back so directly to Lady Catherine, including the lady herself, whose mouth gaped open like a fish. "However, it may be easier if we were to leave you for the evening now. I confess, I am feeling a bit fatigued, and I dare say Ma—" here Maria shook her head, begging me not to pull her into my mutiny against Lady Catherine, "my dear Charlotte," I said instead, "must also be tired from all of our Easter celebrations today."

Charlotte looked confused but readily nodded her assent. "Yes, Lady Catherine, we are so exceedingly obliged to have been invited to your home on this holiest of days, but we would not want to overstay our welcome. Do be so good as to give our respects to the Colonel when he returns."

Lady Catherine and Mr. Collins both protested, but ineffectually. When Charlotte had her mind set on something she managed it quite nicely, and she trusted Lizzy enough to know if I said we should go that we should go. I doubt that Lady Catherine really wanted us to stay (Mr. Collins would have stayed all night if allowed), but she wanted to be the one to suggest our leaving. Heaven forbid anyone *want* to leave Rosings before she dismissed them.

There was much hustle and bustle, but we managed to finally make it out the front door. Colonel Fitzwilliam still hadn't returned to the drawing room. I was becoming more and more frantic in my anxiety for Darcy's wellbeing.

Mr. Collins chastised me, and his wife, the entire way home for daring to leave Rosings before we were dismissed. I felt bad for Charlotte. I could escape to my room when we got back to the parsonage, but she was stuck with Collins.

I lay awake in bed, going over the evenings events in my mind. It had to be something I had done, but what? I was pretty sure that I'd nailed all the dialogue word for word. Was it such an important section that how I spoke the lines, or how I looked at Darcy, could have caused a problem if I hadn't been perfectly like Lizzy?

Well, if it was something I'd done, I had until midnight to worry about it and then I'd be bumped back. To where I wasn't sure, either to the drawing room if I was lucky, or back several weeks to when I'd first made the jump as Lizzy. Crap. More time staying with Mr. Collins. Every girl's dream.

There wasn't a clock in Lizzy's room, but I knew it was already past eleven. I waited quietly until all the sounds in the house had stopped and I was relatively sure that Mr. Collins and Charlotte had gone to bed. I opened the door to my bedroom as quietly as possible. It creaked a bit and I was surprised that Lady Catherine in her grand sweep of the parsonage before Mr. Collins's marriage hadn't ordered it oiled or fixed. I crept down to Charlotte's little sitting room in the back of the house where there was a clock.

It showed 11:43. I curled myself into a chair and watched it tick down the last few minutes until twelve. Midnight passed without incident. I was neither magically transported back to the piano at Rosings, nor to my first day at Lizzy. I sat, confused and upset, in Charlotte's sitting room, until I finally drifted off to sleep.

I woke with a horrible crick in my neck. It was five am, and still dark outside the window with not even a glimmer of dawn. I felt sick to my stomach as I crept back up to my room.

The story had kept going. Time hadn't stopped. And yet, what was supposed to happen last night in the drawing room hadn't happened. Well it had partially, but we hadn't finished our conversation and I had a feeling that the *entire* conversation was vital to the story line of *Pride and Prejudice*.

I slipped back into bed, the sheets cold against my skin as I pulled them up over my head. I didn't know what to expect. I felt like I was flying as blind as I had been the first time I'd made the leap. Even more so, because I'd figured out the pattern pretty quickly and had been able to adjust my reactions. Even when I was stuck as Caroline everything had followed the same predictable patterns.

Now I had no idea.

Today Mr. Darcy was supposed to visit the parsonage. Charlotte and Maria would be out and Lizzy would be there by herself and we'd have one hell of an awkward conversation. As a reader, I knew that just a few days later Darcy proposed for the first time, so today's little piece of awkwardness was his futile attempt at testing the waters—trying to see if Lizzy would be open to his proposal. Lizzy must have just been totally confused by the whole thing.

I had to assume he was still coming. Time had continued on, so therefore, whatever had happened last night in the drawing room hadn't damaged the plot enough for a restart to happen.

With this in mind, I dressed with extra care once I got up, and declined to go walking into the village with Charlotte and Maria. I set up shop, letter-writing and all per Austen's description, in the little back sitting room and waited.

And waited.

He never came.

I tried not to panic. I really did. Gave it the good old college try and everything.

Why didn't he come? It didn't make sense. We made it to the next day so things should have progressed. What would it mean for the plot that he hadn't come? Could I have somehow finally changed *Pride and Prejudice*? And not, apparently, for the better. But what did I do?

I was still in the sitting room when Charlotte and Maria returned from their business in the village. I was calmly employed in writing my letter—I'd rushed back to it when I heard them coming up the walk, the rest of the afternoon having been spent in frantic pacing and self-recriminations. If either of the other ladies thought it odd that Lizzy was still working on the same letter (apparently the wordiest in history), they declined to mention it.

"Did you see anyone from Rosings during your walk?" I finally ventured after the first few minutes of chatty news from the village had been offered by Charlotte.

She looked surprised. "Why no. Although we do not often see either Lady Catherine or Miss Anne in the—Oh, you mean the gentlemen, I suppose. It would make sense that they might be out more than the ladies. No, I cannot say that we saw them."

I settled into a moody silence. If Darcy wasn't here, where he should have been, then where in damnation was he? After today's little visit, Austen states that Darcy and Colonel Fitzwilliam are frequent visitors to the parsonage—the guy comes to propose Thursday (it was now Monday) so that left only a few opportunities for these frequent visits. Should we expect him tomorrow? And if not tomorrow than definitely Wednesday...

The next day brought no visitor to the parsonage and no invitation to Rosings. Something was beyond wrong. I needed to talk to Darcy, but how? It wasn't like I could just walk over and ask to see him: that would be the height of impropriety. On the other hand, maybe if I did something like that, the story would finally reset itself. I debated with myself endlessly. Both Charlotte and Maria commented on my unusually dull mood. I was trying as hard as I could to maintain Lizzy's upbeat demeanor, but it wasn't until Mr. Collins mentioned at dinner that he had seen Mr. Darcy walking in the woods near Rosings that morning that I formed a plan of action.

I rose especially early. Elizabeth was an early morning person. She loved to take walks before most of the rest of the polite world was up out of their beds, and I was lucky enough to have acquired her body clock, so it wasn't too hard to be up and out of the parsonage before almost anyone else was awake.

The air was cool and soft. I tromped toward a stand of trees to one side of the park, I figured there wasn't anyone around to comment on my unlady-like gait so I let myself just enjoy being by myself outdoors. There weren't many opportunities for a Regency Miss to be truly alone.

I walked around the grove a few times without success. I eventually headed down toward the little pond I'd discovered on an earlier walk. It was a bit farther out, but I had nothing to do but walk.

By the time I'd made a circuit of the pond the sun was significantly higher in the sky and had begun to burn off the last remnants of the pearly grey fog. I trudged back toward the stand of trees. Stray hairs were starting to stick to the back of my neck and I'm sure my face was turning an unbecoming shade of bright red.

I saw him half a second before he saw me. He was standing under a tree holding his hat in his hands as he absent-mindedly turned it over and over. I stopped short in confusion, just a few feet from him. He looked different. I couldn't quite put my finger on it, but something was different about the way he was standing. Something different and familiar at the same time.

He turned and looked at me. A quick moment of confusion passed over his face, as if he couldn't quite place me—at which my heart plummeted to my feet.

"Miss Bennet, is it?" He said offering me a half-hearted bow. It was really not much more than a dip of his head.

"Mr. Darcy," I replied, my flush of mortification at being so easily dismissed heating my cheeks. "I did not expect to meet with anyone else this early."

"Is it early? The sun seems high enough." He turned his face up toward the sky and the bright sunlight glinted off his dark hair.

Something was desperately wrong. In fact, *everything* was wrong. The way he was standing, the way he was speaking, the fact that he thought it wasn't early—any decent Regency gentleman would have been surprised to see a woman exerting herself before breakfast.

Wrong. Wrong. Wrong.

"Mr. Darcy, is something the matter? Are you not feeling quite yourself?"

Mr. Darcy laughed. It was a weird sound, somewhere between desperate and resigned. "No, I can most definitely say that I'm not feeling quite myself."

I recognized that tone of voice. I'd used it myself previously.

It wasn't possible. Was it?

"I am sorry to hear that," I said carefully, watching his expression intently. "I have felt like that myself sometimes. As if I have woken up in someone else's body or that I could not quite wake myself from a dream."

Mr. Darcy visibly started, he stared at me, narrowed eyes raking over my face, searching for something.

"Is it a dream, then?" he asked. "This whole thing? Can I still wake up?"

The world was tilting on its axis. The ground under me felt unstable and I'm sure if I looked up at the sky I would see it swinging in drunken circles above me.

"Mr. Darcy," I took a tentative step forward on legs that seemed no longer able to fully support me, stumbling a bit before catching myself. "Are you, in fact, not Mr. Darcy at all?"

He puffed out a frustrated breath, although his hazel eyes held a light. "No, I'm not your Mr. Darcy at all. Not that I can get anyone to believe me."

"Did you get in through the book?" I asked hoarsely. I needed something to hold onto before the earth, or my knees, completely failed me. I made it the next few steps to the nearest tree and leaned gratefully against its trunk. I pressed my gloved hands against the bark, hoping I could somehow ground myself.

He looked confused for a moment. "The book? Oh, you must mean *Pride and Prejudice*, that's where we are, right? God, as if I haven't had enough of that in the last few days."

I nearly passed out at his casual mention of the title of the book. I'd never said it out loud before while actually *in* the novel. I wondered if he would somehow spontaneously combust or something now that there'd been an open acknowledgement of where we were. "I don't know what you mean, but no there wasn't a book."

"How—how did you get in then?"

"I don't know. I was just sleeping. At least I think I was sleeping. I'm not sure, I think I was—then there I was, watching you play piano and stuck in this Darcy character." Darcy crossed his arms over his chest and leaned casually against a tree. I'd never seen Darcy look so naturally relaxed, and here was this guy, his world totally upside down and inside out completely at ease. "I'm not really sure what's going on. I haven't quite figured out yet how to wake up or get out, or whatever." He shrugged one shoulder to punctuate this statement.

He looked like Darcy, he really did, as much as I looked like Lizzy Bennet, but everything about his attitude and posture was screaming another name at me.

"Oh my god..." I whispered.

He looked up at me, cocking his head to one side—questioning.

"Mark." I breathed. "Oh my god, Mark..."

CHAPTER
Seventeen

*"Well, I'm not really supposed
to talk to strangers, but we've
met before."*

HE PUSHED AWAY from the tree in a swift, compact motion that was so unlike anything I'd ever seen Darcy do that I knew I was right. Beyond a shadow of a doubt.

"Are you someone else too?" he demanded. "Are you Kelsey?"

I gaped at him, my mind completely gone—like a nuclear bomb had been set off in my head and all that was left was scorched earth and the charred remains of everything I thought I knew about how this whole jumping thing worked.

"Yes, it's me." I swallowed painfully. "Kelsey." The name felt weird on my lips, somehow foreign.

A strange look skated across his face. I'm not sure, but it looked almost like disappointment.

"So, does that mean this isn't a dream, then?"

I shook my head. I still hadn't been able to let go of

my death grip on the tree. "I'm sorry, it's not a dream. It's real."

"Real? As in we are really in *Pride and Prejudice* as other people?"

"Yes. As in, I'm not crazy. I was telling the truth about being able to jump into the book."

He narrowed his eyes at me as he leaned back against the tree and crossed his arms again. "Yeah, obviously you were telling the truth. But the crazy is still up for debate."

I flushed hotly. "That's a jerky thing to say. It's real, not something I've made up inside my head."

"I get that it's 'real.' I still don't get why you'd keep jumping into different characters."

"Because I want to be Lizzy! Who wouldn't want to be one of literature's greatest heroines if they had the chance?" My voice was getting louder and louder. Someone was going to hear me yelling if I wasn't careful.

Mark—I couldn't think of him as Mr. Darcy now, even though he was looking at me with Darcy's eyes set in Darcy's face—shook his head. "I don't know, I think most people would be weirded out by being someone else. You know, when I asked if you knew who you were—"

"Don't even!" I cut him off. That had angered me. It seemed somehow wrong to bring up our fight in the real world when we were standing there in the bodies of one of the world's most famous romantic couples. Which was probably stupid of me. What was wrong was that Mark and I were representing Darcy and

Lizzy at all. It suddenly seemed like a horrible travesty to me.

"I can't seriously believe you're going to bring that up right now." I finally let go of my grip on the tree and stomped off a few feet toward the parsonage before whirling around. "You're experiencing a totally amazing and mind-blowing event—you're inside one of the greatest novels ever written, literally inhabiting one of the most beloved literary characters of all time and all you can think about is starting in on the 'Kelsey doesn't know who she is' crap again?"

Mark threw back his head and laughed. This had the effect of irritating me even more, but I had run out of things to say and so I fumed in silence.

"Yeah, I'm sure it's all very exciting, getting into an Austen novel and all that. Likely more for you than for me. But after the first few days it gets kind of old, wouldn't you agree?"

I crossed my arms over my chest and avoided his eyes. After a pause he asked, "Kels, how long have you been here? I'm guessing more than a few days." He had that tone of voice again, the one he had used at the restaurant. As if he was a concerned citizen and I was standing on a freeway overpass threatening to swan dive into rush hour traffic.

The tree branch over his head was suddenly very fascinating to me. I kept my eyes fixed on it when I answered.

"A few weeks." A little over four could still be considered "a few," right?

"A few weeks? Dear God, Kelsey, really?" He ran

his hand through his hair. He'd dropped the hat when he'd first leaned back against the tree and crossed his arms. It killed me, it was a gorgeous hat. I glanced over at it: there it was, still lying on the grass, probably getting all wet with dew. Mark noticed my lack of response and eye contact. "A few weeks, total? Or just this time?"

The hat was getting wet, I could see the discoloration from the dampness. It was probably going to be stained beyond repair. Darcy's valet would likely have a fit. And he should, it was a really nice hat. Or it had been before Mark had let it fall to the ground.

"This time," I mumbled.

"So, if you had to take a guess at the grand total of time you've been here in an entirely fictional world, what would that number be?"

I was seriously running out of things to look at. There wasn't much going on in the grove. The bark on the tree Mark was standing by looked like it had the potential to be fascinating.

"Um, maybe, um, a little over two months." The last word was more of a mumble than an actual word.

"Two, what? Weeks?"

"Um, months." I didn't even have to be looking to know what his reaction was.

"Months? You've been here, playing someone else, for *months*?"

I finally snapped my eyes back to him. "Yeah? So what? What do you care? I'm not hurting anybody or anything!"

"Except yourself. It's not exactly healthy, is it?"

"Who are you, my father? My shrink? Go away. I don't want you here." I turned back around and crossed my arms. It may have been a little childish. All right, it was a lot childish, but I'd never had to explain my jumping or my reasons for staying to anyone and I was kind of upset that it was Mark I was having to explain myself to. It made me feel horribly inadequate and like he was disappointed in me. I didn't want to examine why it would matter to me if Mark was disappointed in me. It shouldn't matter to me at all.

"Are you sure about that?"

I tried ignoring him, really I did. I held out for thirty whole seconds. "Sure about what?"

"The whole not wanting me here thing?"

"Of course I'm sure! Why wouldn't I be sure?" I threw over my shoulder. "You're screwing up my favorite novel! You're ruining the most dashing and romantic hero *of all time!*"

Mark snorted. "I only ask because I think you brought me here."

At that I spun back around, Lizzy's skirt swishing around my legs. "I highly doubt that!"

"Yeah, remember how I said I was dreaming and then suddenly I was here? Well, I was dreaming about you—"

"You were?" I tried in vain to keep the hot blush from spreading across my face. Damn Elizabeth and her pale, English skin.

"Last few nights before I 'jumped' as you call it,

actually. It was weird, I could see you, and you'd reach for me, but I was just a bit out of your reach and then I'd wake up. But the other night the dream was different. I could see you reaching and then you finally caught up to me. You grabbed me and pulled and then all of a sudden I was Darcy."

I bit my lip. I had been thinking about Mark a lot recently. Not that I was about to admit that to him. Torture and wild horses couldn't pull that little gem out of me. "So, you're saying I *pulled* you in, instead of you jumping in yourself?"

"Well, I certainly didn't have any thought of entering *Pride and Prejudice*."

"Neither did I. At least not the first time."

"How did you get in the first time?"

"I fell asleep reading it, and I guess I sort of slid into the scene I was reading. Well, sort of, I was reading Darcy's letter to Elizabeth, and I ended up as Georgiana like during what was going on in the letter."

Mark looked at me in utter confusion. "I have no idea what the hell you are talking about, but I trust that you do."

"Haven't you ever read *Pride and Prejudice*?" I asked, horrified.

"Kelsey, I'm a guy."

"What the hell is that supposed to mean? It's classic literature! Didn't you have to read it in school? As a history person shouldn't you have read it for a greater understanding of the Regency era?" I was outraged. My voice was getting higher and higher with every sentence.

"Okay, okay, I've read it. Years ago. Maybe high school? As in, I read it *one* time, as required reading, at least a decade ago. I obviously do not have your level of, uhh, *intimacy*, with this book."

I bristled at his inflection on the word "intimacy." As if, my level of knowledge of the intricate details of the novel was somehow wrong or unhealthy. Okay, he may have a point regarding the whole "being" in the novel as other people thing, but previous to jumping, my level of obsession was normal-ish.

I mean, I had to be somewhat detail orientated about it. Literature was my field of study after all, and I specialized in Regency Literature. There was a certain level of professional pride...

I realized I sounded like a completely insane person and could only be thankful that I wasn't saying any of this out loud. Regardless, Mark could take his sarcastic inflection and stuff it.

"This whole conversation is pointless. It's getting late. Someone is going to start wondering where I am."

He stared at me. "So, what, you're upset with me so you are just going to leave me here? Not even tell me how to get back out to the real world?"

I shrugged. "You write yourself out."

"What?"

"It's a book...a story. The best way to get out is to write yourself out. Like, take a book or some paper and write your story on it. Then I put it under my pillow at night or whatever. But that's how I get in. I fall asleep reading *Pride and Prejudice*. I get out by reading my story."

"Like my life story?"

"Yeah. I've noticed with the stronger—or more main storyline, characters—it's better to be really detailed in your life story, as in names and dates and all that. Darcy is a pretty strong character, so you'd better write a lot about yourself."

"Okay, I can do that. And just sleep with it?"

"Uh—huh. I'm assuming you're trying it tonight?" At his nod I sniffed. "Good, you're messing up the story, somehow. I don't know how. Hopefully it's not screwed up forever."

"Messing up the story, how?"

"Darcy hasn't done what he is supposed to. He was supposed to visit Lizzy on Monday, and really pretty much every day this week. Then tomorrow he is supposed to propose to her for the first time."

Mark laughed. "Oh, poor Kels, are you worried I'll mess up your big romantic proposal?"

"It's neither big, nor romantic, because you—I mean, Mr. Darcy—completely blows it. However, it is vital to the storyline of the book, so I'd rather it actually goes off as written."

"Maybe you should write yourself out too. Wouldn't it be better to just leave? If the proposal is for Elizabeth, wouldn't it be better if it was directed actually to Elizabeth?"

I huffed out a frustrated breath. "I could try to explain it to you, but my guess is there is no way you'd ever understand."

He shrugged, and I'd never been so annoyed by his laid back attitude. Although, to be honest, I would have given my right arm to be as calm and collected. I could put on a pretty decent show. For example, I was about to convince the Collinses that I'd experienced nothing more interesting on my walk than repeated viewings of local flora and fauna, but inside I was a roiling mess of nerves, frustration, and stress. But I suppose that was the difference between me and Mark. My calm facade was just that, a facade, and he really was that chill. Right now I hated him. And I was mad enough to pick a fight.

"You know what your problem is?"

He smirked at me. "I wasn't aware I had one. Other than having been pulled into a piece of fiction by my almost girlfriend."

"Your problem is that you're too damned laid back. Seriously. Like embrace life a little. I know you're mad at me, why not show it?" My brain eventually caught up. "I'm sorry, what was that?"

"You heard me. So I'm too laid back, huh? What is the appropriate reaction, Kelsey? What would you like me to do? Yell at you? What is that going to accomplish? Should I ask you why you can't just be you instead of having this bizarre desire to be fictional characters? Should I punch something? Put my fist through Darcy's hat? Would that make you feel better? What would your precious Mr. Darcy do in this situation?"

I stared at him, eyes wide. "I have to go."

He shook his head and sighed. "So I guess I'll see you in the real world then?" he asked.

"Sure." I started to walk past him on my way back

to the parsonage, but stopped. "Oh, in your life story thing just say that you woke up in your own bed and that no time had passed. That way you won't have missed any time back home."

"I wondered how you were managing that."

"The time thing?"

"Yeah, I just saw you two days ago, but you've been here as Elizabeth for weeks."

I started walking again. "Yup, well, now you know. Just stick that in there and you'll be fine."

"Good to know. Enjoy your proposal."

I muttered something derisive and offensive about his parentage under my breath as I stormed off. He must have heard me 'cause he snorted in laughter again. I didn't turn back to look at him. I'd see the real Darcy tomorrow evening, hopefully, and I didn't want to give Mark the satisfaction of thinking I cared enough to look back.

I maintained my furious pace—I was referring to it in my head as outraged stalking off stage—as long as I could. Eventually the burn in my thighs was too much and I slowed back down to a normal pace. It was probably good in the long run. I didn't want to arrive at the parsonage all sweaty and flushed and obviously having just come from an altercation of some kind (because outraged stalking off stage immediately suggests that the heroine has just had an altercation with person or persons of interest).

I entered the parsonage as if nothing had happened, ran up to my room to dispose of my bonnet and spencer, and then joined Charlotte and

Maria who were still chatting over breakfast. Through the window I could see Mr. Collins puttering around in his garden. I counted my blessings that he hadn't decided on an early morning walk as well. Nothing would have made my little meeting with Mark in the wood more awkward than Mr. Collins happening upon us.

"Good morning, Eliza, how was your walk? You look quite invigorated," commented Charlotte as I sat down across from her.

"Hmm. The weather is quite lovely today. Beautiful day for a walk." I reached for the marmalade and slathered a roll with it.

"Did you meet anyone?" There was something about the light in her eye that made me wonder if there was something more to the question.

"No, it was a quiet, solitary sort of walk. Why do you ask?" I took a bite of my roll and pasted an innocent look onto my face.

"Oh, Mr. Collins was out earlier and noted Mr. Darcy walking in the park, so I had wondered if perhaps you ran into him at all."

I nearly choked on my roll. "Why, no, I did not have the, um, honor, of coming across Mr. Darcy in my walk."

Charlotte smiled at my sarcastic tone. "Pity, I did hope to hear if he was recovered from the other night. However, if he is out walking the grounds we must assume that he is indeed fully recovered."

"Yes, we must. Well, perhaps we shall see him on the morrow with his cousin," I replied sweetly. God, I hoped we'd see him, or more specifically that *I'd* see him, stiff and formal and mucking up his proposal. And none the worse for having been inhabited by Mark Barnes of all people.

I waited up late again to see if anything would happen as Mark was writing himself out of the novel. I wasn't exactly sure what I thought would occur. Perhaps once he was gone the scene would reset back to the evening at Rosings and the real Mr. Darcy would be able to play out the last few days correctly. But time just kept chugging on like normal.

The fact that days were moving ahead when scenes hadn't been played right was stressing me out. I wondered how long that could keep happening before the storyline was so muddled and messed up that it would be visible from the outside. Were readers all around the world suddenly noticing that Mr. Darcy was no longer visiting Hunsford between Easter and the proposal? The "what ifs" were keeping me up, my mind racing with possibilities. I finally resorted to sneaking a glass of Mr. Collins's inferior brandy in hopes that it would help me sleep.

In the clear light of morning I was a little bit more level-headed. I supposed even if the days weren't going to repeat, we could still get the story back on track once Mr. Darcy had full control over his own body. I'm pretty sure he'd already decided to propose to Lizzy by the time Mark had made his jump—or been pulled into the story by me. Not that I wanted to examine any of implications surrounding my newly revealed ability to pull people into works of literature, or the fact that the person whom I chose to exert this bizarre superpower on was Mark Barnes. Mr. Collins most definitely did not have enough brandy to cover that.

The important thing is that Mark was gone. He'd written himself out of the novel and we could now attempt to restore order and proceed as if nothing had occurred.

I knew something was wrong the minute Mr. Darcy and his cousin walked through the doorway of the sitting room. Not only was Mr. Darcy still walking completely wrong—way too relaxed and casual—but his hair was red!

It wasn't quite the red-blond of Mark's unruly locks, but his hair was most definitely not dark brown anymore, it was somewhere between the two colors. And it was curly. And significantly longer than it had been the night before. I gaped at him. Mark—because it had to be Mark and not Mr. Darcy—took the opportunity to wink at me slyly. I glanced around the room wildly, wondering why no one else was reacting to the fact that Darcy's hair was quite obviously the wrong color. The three others in the room—Charlotte, Maria, and Colonel Fitzwilliam—were consumed with the ritual greetings of the Regency era, and apparently not at all concerned that Mr. Darcy's hair had changed overnight.

Colonel Fitzwilliam seemed to be in his usual good mood. After asking after my and Charlotte's health he launched into a light-hearted teasing of Maria Lucas, who blushed under his attentions. Charlotte, laughing, came to her sister's defense, and while they were thus occupied, Mr. Darcy took the opportunity to sit near me.

"Miss Bennet, I hope you are well today," he said as he settled into the seat near mine.

I stared at him. Oh my god, were his hazel eyes starting to turn dark brown? There was now just as much of Mark's deep brown as Darcy's olive green. I swear to heaven above, if I saw Mark's eyes looking out of Fitzwilliam Darcy's face I could not be held liable for my actions.

I tried to smile politely, although it was more of a grimace. "Sit up straight," I hissed at him through my teeth.

Mark straightened. It was nowhere near Darcy's exacting posture, but I suppose if no one was commenting on the red hair, the likelihood of anyone outing him because of a slight slouch was slim to none.

"Yes, thank you, I am well," I answered his original question, my fake smile still in place. "Why are you still here?" I hissed again.

"Not sure, Kels. Your little writing tip didn't seem to do the trick." He lifted one shoulder in a shrug and I resisted the urge to slap his shoulder back down.

"Don't call me that where people can hear you," I shot back quietly. "We need to talk."

He raised an eyebrow. "Aren't we talking now?"

"Yes, all my family is fine. In fact, I recently had a letter from my sister Jane," I answered more loudly. Charlotte had looked at me questioningly. My hissing may have carried further than I'd intended.

"I am glad to hear it," Mark pitched his voice at the same volume as mine. "Er, it's always, uh, good to keep in contact with family."

I rolled my eyes at him, knowing that the back of his head was effectively blocking my expression from Charlotte.

"Hey, I'm new at this, cut me some slack," he said in an undertone.

"Thank you, Mr. Darcy. I am sure that you and your sister keep up a most faithful correspondence. I remember at Netherfield you were always writing the most charmingly long letters to her."

Charlotte had returned her attention to Colonel Fitzwilliam and Maria's conversation, but I didn't want to take any chances. I leaned forward so Mark could hear me better as I lowered my voice to barely above a whisper "Tonight, I'll plead a headache and stay home, which Lizzy is supposed to do anyway. You need to get out of dinner and come meet me here."

Mark chuckled quietly. "Meet you here alone, Miss Bennet? Isn't that scandalous?"

I gritted my teeth. "You are supposed to be coming here to propose anyway," I muttered.

CHAPTER
Eighteen

"In vain have I struggled. It will not do. My feelings will not be repressed."

I SAT WAITING nervously in the sitting room. Unfortunately, the nerves were not because I was waiting for the dashing Mr. Darcy to come propose (badly) to me, but instead because I was waiting to hear Mark's explanation of how he had managed to *not* write himself out of *Pride and Prejudice*.

Mr. Collins, Charlotte, and Maria had set off for Rosings over half an hour ago, so I was expecting Mark any moment. I was trying not to jump to any conclusions until I was able to ask him more specifically about what he'd written in his attempt to get back out of the novel. Hopefully there was something obvious that I'd be able to point out to him. Darcy had to be a pretty strong character: it had been hard enough for me to get out of Caroline. Maybe all Mark needed was a more detailed retelling of his life to get him out of Darcy and back home.

I was avoiding thinking about the fact that Mr. Darcy was starting to look like Mark. I'd never altered the appearance, purposely or accidentally, of any character I'd been in.

There was a slight knock at the sitting room door, and then it opened to reveal Mr. Darcy...or Mark masquerading as Mr. Darcy.

"Hey, Kels," he grinned as he entered the room, closing the door firmly behind him. It was a pretty compromising position, but as no one had burst in on Lizzy and Darcy during that first awful proposal, I could only assume that nobody would now.

"Mark, what the hell is going on with Darcy's hair?" I skipped straight past any pleasantries.

"I'm not sure. It seems to be turning a color closer to mine, doesn't it? And his eyes too. Was like that this morning when I woke up."

"Has anyone noticed? I mean, has anyone said anything?"

"Nope, no one has even looked at me twice. Of course, the first few days they must have thought this Darcy bloke had gone completely 'round the bend, but I've been attempting to act more like you do. Not one word from anyone over at that Rosings joint about the hair or eyes."

"So what exactly happened, then? You just woke up—still here, obviously—and your hair was different? Did you write your story like I told you?"

"Yup. Put it all down on paper. Though let me tell you, getting the hang of the quill took me a good hour or so. It's a bit scratchy, but it's legible. Here, I've brought it for you. I figured you'd have more questions." He tossed it to me. It was several pages folded together almost like a letter. It wasn't in Darcy's neat handwriting, but in what I recognized as Mark's more rangy scrawl.

I sighed as I smoothed the pages out and started reading. It was actually very interesting. I didn't know much about Mark's early life, and he had apparently taken my instructions to heart and included a lot of detail: names, dates, random memories.

"Your sister's name is Kazza?" I asked in surprise. What kind of a name was Kazza?

"Yeah. Oh. It's actually Karen. But everyone calls her Kazza."

"Why?"

"Everyone named Karen gets called Kazza. Aussies will take the opportunity to turn any r into a zed."

"Weird."

"Thanks." He rolled his eyes at me.

I ignored him and kept reading. "There's not a lot about you currently, maybe that could be a problem?" I wondered out loud as I reached the end of the letter.

"There's about three paragraphs," he pointed out. He'd stretched out on the small sofa, propping his feet up on one of the arm rests. If Charlotte could have seen him she likely would have had a coronary.

"Hmm." I looked back over those paragraphs. "Yeah, they're mostly just about where you live and what you do for work and what day of the week it was when you got sucked into the book. I don't know...try adding some more personal stuff. It seems really fleshed out otherwise. This would have gotten me out of Caroline Bingley, and let me tell you, she turned out to be hard to get rid of." I tapped the papers against my forehead as if hoping to divine from them why they hadn't worked to my expectations.

"Personal stuff like what?" Mark asked as he studied the ceiling.

"I included a lot of relationship stuff. Like who broke my heart and who I had a crush on in the third grade. I added the whole Jordan debacle in there too. It's a romantic novel after all, so I thought that love life information might be helpful."

"Do you really think that whatever metaphysical force is holding me here cares about my third grade crush?" Mark asked. He didn't sound like he was making fun of me, more like he was genuinely curious, but it still riled me.

"I don't know. It's just a suggestion. I'm just telling you what worked for me before. I thought it was important to set myself up in opposition to the character, to make my story on par with theirs, and something most of the characters in this novel are concerned with is love and marriage. They're written that way."

I tossed his letter back at him, frustrated. He caught it mid-air without moving from the couch.

"I have never," he announced, half-laughing, "been more glad I was a History Major. Opposition to the character? I mean it makes sense, I suppose, but the fact that we are having this conversation at all is evidence that all you lit people think too much."

"Is there such a thing as 'thinking too much?'"

"Let me rephrase. Over-think things that in the grand scheme of life likely don't matter."

Instead of addressing this little speech I crossed my arms and leaned back in my own chair. "You seem surprisingly unstressed for a man who finds himself trapped in a romance novel."

"Yes, you mentioned yesterday that being laid back is a fault of mine. I could freak out and run around in circles waving Darcy's arms wildly in the air if that would make you feel better."

When I didn't laugh he finally turned his head to fully look at me. "Kels, I'm just joking. Am I a little concerned that I didn't wake up as myself? Yes. But you've been here before. This happened to you and, smart girl that you are, you managed to figure it out. So I'm hoping together we can pinpoint where I went wrong and fix it. I just don't see any point in getting all worked up over something that didn't work the first time. We'll just try again, right?"

I was slightly mollified by this. At least I still had "smart girl" going for me, although how much that would outweigh "emotionally unstable" and "would rather be another person" in the balance of my non-relationship with Mark was up for debate.

"Well, there are a few things that concern me about the whole situation," I finally said. "Speaking objectively as someone who has been here before and done this before."

Mark raised an eyebrow at me and I added, "As objectively speaking as a lover of Austen and literature in general can be."

"All right, and what is concerning you?"

"Two things. First of all, there are scenes that we've skipped. I've never been allowed to skip scenes, or really even to mess them up too much. If I did something that was out of character or would mess up the storyline, I was bumped back to earlier—either where I first entered the novel as a certain character, or kind of to the last place I'd done mostly everything right. Kind of like a video game; if you die you go back to your highest saved level."

"I guess that makes sense. So you weren't able to alter the storyline of the novel then. Whatever it was before you got here, it had to stay that way."

"Yeah, but *you've* altered it. The fact that we're sitting here talking about it at all proves that. You should have been bumped back until you got it right."

"But if I would have been bumped back, what would happen to you? Would you have had to replay the scene too?"

I paused. "I hadn't thought of that. Do you think it might have something to do with two of us being here at the same time? That we can't both simultaneously be moved back earlier in a scene."

"It's a decent theory. Everything at this point is just theory, right? But you're right, I haven't experienced that being put back to the starting point. That must have been disconcerting for you at first."

"It was, but I figured it out pretty fast." That may have been a slight exaggeration, but whatever, I didn't need to go into detail with Mark about all my escapades as Georgiana. I remembered making out with Wickham and felt my face color hotly.

Mark noticed. He had to have, he was staring at my face, but he was nice enough not to ask any questions.

"It's a bit weird for me to be talking to you like this," he said. "You look and sound nothing like yourself, but yet you sound like you. Your speech patterns and phrasing I mean."

"Lizzy's pretty, isn't she?" I agreed absently. I was back to studying his hair. He was right, it was weird to talk to someone, knowing they weren't who they appeared to be. But yet, Darcy's physical characteristics were changing. There had to be a clue there.

"Bloody hell, Kelsey, that isn't what I meant. Yes, Lizzy is very pretty, but she isn't any prettier than you. She's just different looking."

I was surprised out of my musings by the frustration in his voice.

"Oh, well, thanks. Sorry. I was just thinking. Here's the second problem: I still look like Lizzy. No matter if I was Georgiana or Caroline I always looked just like them, nothing about their physical appearance changed at all. Yet here you are with red hair and darker eyes."

"I really don't have an explanation for it. Like I said, I just woke up like this." Mark sat fully up on the couch, swinging his legs back down to the floor. "How long do you think that it's safe for me to be here, before people start noticing that Darcy is gone?"

"Not sure, I'm guessing the proposal and subsequent rejection took no more than ten minutes or so. Then you go back to Rosings and sometime during the evening write Lizzy a really long explanation about all the stuff she accuses you of during the verbal smack down she gives Darcy."

"I remember that part from the movie, something about the other dude, his name starts with a W."

I gave him the evil eye. "Wickham."

"That's the bloke. I'm sorry I messed up your verbal smack down of Mr. Darcy. Do you have the whole thing memorized?"

"Yes," I muttered.

"That's impressive."

"And by impressive do you mean crazy?"

"I don't really think you're crazy. I guess I can see the appeal of living out your favorite story. You do at least always come back."

I didn't bother to point out that I always came back because I was in the wrong character. I mean, I was planning to jump out of Lizzy. Eventually.

"I guess I'll go back to Rosings and try to write myself out again. See you when I see you?"

"Yup. It'll be like no time has passed."

"This must be a simply enormous wardrobe." He winked at me and left. I stared after him. Why did he have to throw a Narnia reference at me? Just to prove he was like two steps past perfect? It was a good thing he'd left, or I might have thrown myself at him right then.

I went to bed early, before the others even got home from Rosings, determined to get a good night of sleep and not stay up watching the clock and wondering if Mark had made it out of the book. My stress and worry were pointless. Either it was going to work or it wasn't.

I got up at the crack of dawn again and headed out for a walk. I tried not think about the fact that this was the early morning walk on which I should be receiving Darcy's explanation letter after the botched proposal. I was just hoping that sometime throughout the day I'd come across the real Mr. Darcy and we could get things back on track.

It was a beautiful morning. The air was cool but the soft morning light warmed me as I walked. I began to feel more upbeat than I had for the last few days. I really think that getting a full night's sleep had been the best choice. I actually started whistling quietly as I walked. It felt like all was right in Austen's little world.

The whistle died on my lips as I strolled into the stand of trees on the far side of the park and almost ran smack dab into Mark.

"Oh no!" I burst out before I could stop myself.

Mark looked up at the sound of my voice and grimaced. "I figured that'd be your reaction."

I stared at him, my mouth agape. Not only was that most definitely Mark's voice and not Darcy's, he looked as if he'd been almost transformed overnight. If yesterday glimpses of Mark were beginning to show in Darcy's appearance, now I had to search for glimpses of Darcy. He was several inches shorter. Darcy was probably about an inch or so above six feet, but Mark was closer to 5'11 or so.

He was also significantly broader across the chest and arms. Mr. Darcy wasn't a slouch, you could always tell he was fit and trim, but it seemed more of a lean strength, while Mark was most definitely muscular. You could see the fabric of his coat straining against his biceps. The weird thing is that the coat didn't look too tight or overly long, as you'd expect if Mark had put on clothes tailored for a taller, slimmer man. It looked like it had been made for him, he just filled it out...differently. Really, a Regency jacket did things for Mark's physique that no t-shirt could have accomplished. And I'd always been a big fan of Mark in a t-shirt.

I tore my eyes off his biceps, coloring slightly. His hair had made the complete transition to Mark's unruly mop of sandy-red curls. Those were most definitely Mark's dark chocolate eyes looking out of a face that was a mix of Mark's and Darcy's features. Not even a true mix, the only thing that still even seemed to remain of Mr. Darcy was his long, straight nose. Mark's had a slight bump in it, like it had been broken when he was young.

Mark smiled at me, almost apologetically. "Kels, I'm sorry, it didn't work. That look of horror you've got on your face is killing me."

I narrowed my eyes. He certainly didn't look as if his feelings were hurt. As he smiled, I noticed that Mark's dimple was missing too. So that's it. A nose and a lack of a dimple were all that remained of the most dashing hero in all of literature.

I seriously considered fainting. I'm not really a fainting kind of girl. But it seemed like an appropriate reaction and a few minutes of unconsciousness sounded like a pleasant little break from the nightmare that *Pride and Prejudice* was quickly becoming for me. I'm not saying I actually fainted. I'm just saying I considered it. Seriously considered.

Mark stepped forward and grabbed my elbow. "You okay? You're looking a little wobbly there."

"I'll live," I sighed as he steadied me. "I'm just, um, surprised to see you here. Like to see *you*."

"Yeah, I seem to have woken up still here and looking even more like myself. I'd ask if you thought it was an improvement to Mr. Darcy's looks, but I already know how you'd answer."

I bit my lip. What was I supposed to say to that? My penchant for Mr. Darcy was widely known. I mean, all one had to do was read the magnets on the fridge in my apartment to realize the man was my ideal. Although, if he'd noticed me drooling over his arms earlier he might realize that I didn't necessarily think all of the changes were bad ones.

"I am partial to his nose, though. What do you think? Too bad I can't keep it when I finally get back home." Mark dropped my elbow and turned to the side as if to model Mr. Darcy's nose. It was kind of unsettling to see it there on his face, as if he'd had some weird plastic surgery procedure. I sniffed. I kind of liked Mark's nose bump, it gave it character and hinted at a wild and rough past. Not that I'd ever, ever admit this to him of course.

"That is if you can get back home," I said. "I'm beginning to get a little bit concerned."

"As am I. Really thought adding more details into your little story writing idea would work, but here I am."

"I wonder what you're doing wrong. Did you bring your story with you again?"

"Uh, no."

"Why not?"

"I don't really need you to grade my life story like a teacher. It didn't work. Maybe it worked for you, but you got into the book a different way than I did. It might just not work for me."

I leaned back against a tree and eyed him thoughtfully. There was a slight red tinge to his skin.

"Mark Barnes, are you blushing?"

"What? No."

"Is there something in your life story you don't want me to read?"

The red spread across his cheeks and I realized I was right. My mind whirred with curiosity. What could he possibly have put in there that he didn't want me to see? Something about himself when he was younger? I really wanted to think it was something that had to do with how he felt about me, but I was too scared to actually think it.

"Well, I suppose I'll just have to take your word for it then," I said folding my arms across my chest.

Mark leaned against an opposite tree and mirrored my pose. "I guess you will."

I tried not to pay attention to the way the fabric of his jacket stretched across his arms, but I found myself holding my breath waiting to see if it would actually rip.

"I—It's not like you *want* to be here. You obviously would have done everything possible to leave."

"Obviously."

I glared at him for a moment. He stared back, but his look was more considering.

"I don't suppose anyone has commented on your appearance changing?"

"Nope. Darcy's valet didn't even bat an eyelash when he came in this morning to help me get dressed. I really thought he might. I mean, at this point I look nothing like the bloke. But no reaction from him or Colonel Fitzwilliam. Saw him this morning on my way out. And the clothes seem to fit right." He pushed away from and held his arms out, inviting closer inspection of his outfit.

I was really trying to not pay attention to the way his clothes were fitting. I wonder if he knew that and was deliberately taunting me. I glared harder at him, but he was wearing an expression of benign innocence that didn't give anything away.

"Yes, how lucky for you that your clothes are fitting correctly," I said drily.

I had been Elizabeth for weeks, and while I'd always thought Mr. Darcy was swoon-worthy handsome I hadn't really felt any actual physical desire for him. Barely a day in Mark's presence and I was already burning up for him. It was distracting.

I stood on tiptoe, looking up at him. My hands came forward to rest on his chest. I told myself it was to steady myself, catch my balance. It wasn't that I wanted to feel his muscled chest through his shirt and vest. My face was inches away from his. Even though he wasn't quite as tall as Darcy, he was still a lot taller than Elizabeth was.

He looked at me with serious eyes. The teasing light had all but gone out of those dark depths. I wanted to drown in them. It would be like drowning in espresso. I loved coffee.

The air between us felt like it was crackling with electricity. My chest was so tight, I wasn't sure I could breathe. I felt like if he didn't kiss me right now I was going to shatter into a million pieces and I wouldn't ever be able to put myself back together.

I licked my lips and his eyes left mine and focused on my lips before flicking back up to my eyes.

"Kelsey," his voice was low, almost a growl. His arms wrapped around my waist, pulling me closer.

"Kiss me," I replied breathily.

CHAPTER
Nineteen

"Is this a kissing book?"

MARK LOWERED HIS head toward me but paused half-way. "Who are you kissing?" he asked. "Me or Mr. Darcy?"

"Shut up, Mark," I reached up and put my hand at the nape of his neck, running my fingers through his soft curls. "I'm kissing you, you idiot," I said as I pulled his head down the rest of the way. I stood on tiptoe again and captured his mouth with mine.

The warmth that shot through me was pure bliss. It felt so right to kiss him. Exciting and thrilling, but somehow comfortable at the same time.

His mouth moved over mine. I may have started the kiss, but within just a few seconds he was fully in control of it, teasing me with his tongue and nipping my bottom lip. I pressed against him, my hand still around his neck holding him as if I was afraid his lips would leave mine. Mark didn't seem inclined to stop kissing me, though. After a moment I relaxed my hold, playing with the strands of hair curling over his collar as my other hand ran up the front of his vest and over his shirt and started loosening his cravat. It was very intricately tied. I tugged at it fruitlessly for a few seconds before he made a low sound in the back of his throat and let go of my waist long enough to reach up, push my hand out of the way, and untie his cravat.

I sighed in happiness as I ran my fingers over the strong column of his throat. Mark took advantage of my sigh to deepen the kiss and my brain came to a stuttering halt. Time ceased to exist and all I could do was hang on for dear life and kiss Mark back for all I was worth.

There was small sound to our left and we both jumped back. I stumbled over my long gown, nearly losing my balance and Mark hit his head on the tree trunk directly behind him.

"Ow!" he grunted rubbing the back of his head as we both turned to look toward the offending sound. A small fox stared at us curiously before turning and slinking off in the direction he'd come from.

We stared at each other in silence for a long minute before I dissolved into laughter. By Regency standards I'd just been thoroughly compromised. However, I doubt the fox was going to tell anyone.

After a moment I heard Mark's rich, baritone laugh join me. I was so wound up with desire for him that the sounds sent shivers up my spine. For some reason that made me laugh even harder.

I stumbled forward to place my hand against the

tree for support. I was doubled over with laughter, tears starting to form in my eyes. The action made me brush up against Mark once again—my shoulder against his chest—and I suddenly found myself being lifted almost off my feet, his large hands wrapped around my upper arms. The laughter died in my throat, replaced by roaring desire, when he kissed me firmly on the mouth.

It was a short, hard kiss. When he took his lips off mine I made a small, protesting sound and tried to recapture his mouth.

"Kelsey," he said urgently. My eyelids fluttered open—I hadn't even realized I'd closed them—and I looked into his serious eyes. "Tell me you want to get out of here. To go home with me."

I swallowed, my mouth was dry and my throat suddenly felt constricted. I felt like my whole world hinged on this one answer. "Yes," my voice cracked and I tried again. "Yes, Mark. I want to go back home with you."

The look on his face was equal measures of pleasure and relief. I think at that point my heart may have actually stopped beating, and then restarted itself with an entirely new rhythm.

He set me down letting go of my arms. I wished he hadn't. "What should we try next?"

I thought about it. Mark had been right, he hadn't come into the novel the same way I had. Instead of falling asleep reading the book, he'd been effectively pulled in by me. What if I got out the same way I usually did and could somehow pull him out with me.

"Writing myself out seems to work for me," I said. "What if I wrote myself out and tried to take you with me?"

"How would you do that?"

"Well, what if I wrote my story, fell asleep on it like I usually do, but like, we could hold hands or something while I fall asleep and then maybe you'd come with me when I go."

Mark thought about it for a moment. "What happens if you get out, but you don't pull me with you?"

"Then I come right back in. Right back to the drawing room at Rosings."

"Can you do it with that much precision?" He looked impressed in spite of himself.

"I'm getting better at it. You know I'd come back for you, I wouldn't just leave you here, right?"

He chuckled. "Of course you would come back. God forbid I stayed around screwing up the dashing Mr. Darcy."

I frowned. "That's not why."

He looked down at me and gave me a half smile. "I know. I was just teasing you."

I relaxed a little. "Well, we could try tonight. I don't know quite how we are going to pull this off. We might cause a little bit of a drama if we are caught."

"Would they march us off to the parson first thing in the morning? Although, I suppose you are already living at the parson's. Convenient."

"Usually if I mess up a scene or do something really reckless and out of character the scene resets.

But we are so far off the storyline track—I mean we are almost a week past anything that was supposed to happen actually happening—so I honestly don't know what would happen."

"Reckless and out of character?" Mark was looking at me with a wicked gleam in his eyes. "I think I want to hear more about this. How reckless are we talking about?"

"But I don't think we can just fall asleep together at the parsonage. That might be frowned upon," I continued on as if I hadn't heard him, but I felt the hot blush creeping up my face at the thought of confessing to him that I'd kissed George Wickham. Even the thought of it made me slightly ill and ashamed. Although, truth be told, what I did with Wickham couldn't really be called kissing when compared to what I had just shared with Mark. The two experiences were not even in the same realm.

"I suppose I could sneak you into Rosings," Mark said thoughtfully. "But if that Lady Catherine person found out she might actually kill you before we have a chance to try to jump out of the book." He looked around the little grove of trees. "How do you feel about camping?"

I looked around in shock. "Here? Won't it be cold?"

Mark shrugged. "I can bring blankets and stuff. Hopefully we won't be out here long. Just however long it takes for you to fall asleep, right?"

"Um, that is the hope." I wasn't sure if I would be able to fall asleep very easily. Being outside was the least of my worries. Laying there holding Mark's hand was more likely going to keep me awake then a chill in the air. "So then, I just sneak out of the parsonage and meet you here?"

"No, I don't want you walking all that way in the dark by yourself. I'll meet you outside the parsonage tonight. Down at the end of the walk before it goes into the lane?"

I nodded.

"What time do Mr. and Mrs. Collins go to bed?"

"Not too late, Mr. Collins is a morning person. So if we aren't at Rosings, which I don't think we are tonight, everyone should be in bed by midnight."

"All right, let's meet at 12:30 then. I'll be there earlier, just in case. But don't worry about it if you have to make me wait."

"Okay, will, um, will you walk me back?"

"Sure, let me try to retie this thing," he indicated his cravat and I snorted in laughter.

"If anyone sees you with me like that, I suppose we won't have to be worried about creating a scandal tonight. You'll already be in hot water."

We walked, hand in hand, as far as the small lane that led down toward the parsonage. He squeezed my hand right before I left. "Write a good story."

"Oh, I will."

I walked through the front door the parsonage, swinging my bonnet in my hand. There was a row of pegs in the front hall where we could keep bonnets and our spencers, but I preferred to take mine up to my room. It was only a few extra minutes out of the day, and I didn't have to worry about Mr. Collins accidentally knocking them down on his way in or out.

I passed the row of pegs and then stopped dead in my tracks. I retraced my steps and examined them. I could swear that they'd been slightly above shoulder height, and now they only came up to my chest. I hung my bonnet up. I definitely didn't have to lift my arm at all to hang it up. What the heck?

It was still a little early for breakfast so I walked into the little room where the family took their breakfast room and measured myself against the sideboard. The top of it, instead of coming up to my waist, instead bumped against my hip as I leaned against it and tried to catch my breath.

Could I actually be growing? Returning to something closer to my normal Kelsey height? In the real world I was 5'9. Elizabeth Bennet was significantly shorter than that. There had to be a good five to six inch difference between us. Could I have made up that difference in one morning? I didn't feel any different. I'd never changed how a character looked before, but Mark had certainly altered Mr. Darcy's appearance. Maybe it rubbed off on me?

I nearly tripped over my own feet as I ran up the stairs and knocked on Maria's door.

"Come in," she called.

Maria was sitting in front of the mirror fixing her blonde hair in a simple style that didn't require a maid or any help. I felt bad for not having been here this morning to assist with her hair.

"Oh there you are, Lizzy!" she said as I came through the door. "Did you enjoy another early morning walk?"

It took me a moment to realize she had spoken to me because I had caught sight of myself in the mirror. Not only was I significantly taller—the very top of my head was being cut off in my reflection—but Lizzy's dark chestnut hair was now a soft light brown color. It had been dark brown when I'd left the house just an hour or so ago. At this rate, it would be my normal Kelsey-colored medium blonde within another few hours.

"Wh-what?" I finally asked, still not able to take my eyes off the reflection in the mirror. I didn't look like myself the way Mark looked like himself, but I certainly was starting to not look entirely like Lizzy. I looked like I could be Lizzy's much taller and lighter haired sister...

"Did you go for a walk? It is a lovely day." Maria didn't seem to notice anything different about my appearance, and she was looking right at my reflection in the mirror as she returned to fussing with her hair.

"Um, yes, I went for a walk. Maria, do you, um, do you notice anything different about me?"

Maria twisted in her seat to look directly at me. She

narrowed her eyes in consideration. "Not that I can tell. You look just as you always have."

"Just as I always have?"

"Yes. I am sorry, did you try a new hairstyle which I am not noticing?"

"No, my hairstyle is the same. Thank you Maria, I did not mean to bother you."

"It is not a bother, Lizzy." She turned back around and added a few finishing touches to her hair. "Do you think we shall see the gentlemen from Rosings today?"

"I should think we might," I answered as I sat slowly down on her bed, my brain spinning. What could I have done to effect this change in Lizzy's appearance, and why did no one but me notice it?

The only thing that I'd done drastically different this morning than I had yesterday or the days before was kiss Mark in the grove. Could that be it?

But if that had started the change and my appearance had been altering on the walk back from the grove, then wouldn't have Mark have said something? Assuming he noticed. But as I could notice his transformation from Darcy, it stood to reason that he should be able to notice the changes in Lizzy's appearance. Stood to reason—ha! I almost laughed out loud at the thought of reason having any place in this mess.

We did not, in fact, see the gentlemen from Rosings during the day. Neither Mark nor Colonel Fitzwilliam came to call. I could tell that Maria was disappointed. I suspected she was harboring a *tendre* for Colonel

Fitzwilliam. Unfortunately for her, he needed to marry a woman of fortune. I knew this because I'd read the book, but poor Maria had no clue. She was really young: hopefully she'd have more chance at some dashing beaux. Although if she followed in Charlotte's steps at all, someone like Mr. Collins would be the most dashing she could hope for. The thought was depressing.

I was disappointed as well. I wanted to see Mark's reaction to my transformation. If he hadn't noticed it before it would be hard to miss now. By mid-afternoon I was most definitely blonde and my hair had lost of all Lizzy's lovely curl, returning instead to the stick straight locks I was cursed with in real life. I still had all of Lizzy's features. So, here I was a tall, blonde, Elizabeth Bennet waiting for everyone to go to bed so I could sneak out in the middle of the night with a muscle-bound, red-headed Mr. Darcy. Something was most definitely wrong with the world.

It seemed to take forever for everyone to settle down for the evening and the house to grow quiet. I had told Charlotte and Maria when they retired for the night that I had wanted to finish a letter to Jane and had stayed up writing in the sitting room. I hadn't been writing to Jane, of course, but writing my life story in as much detail as I could possibly manage. I remember how hard it had been to get out of Caroline, and I figured it would be even harder to get out of Lizzy because she was such a strong character.

My pen had faltered when I got to the part about

Mark. At first I just stuck with facts—our meeting, our blind date, the coffee shop, our first real date, the baseball game, telling him about the book jumping. I explained how he had shown up as Mr. Darcy—how I had pulled him in—and how he had begun to change Mr. Darcy, to remake him in his own image. About our kissing against the tree. But somehow the facts seemed too dry. I was afraid of it not working. Hadn't I told Mark that details and feelings were important?

I am not entirely sure what I feel for Mark. I really like him. A lot. I think I am more attracted to him than I have ever been to any other guy. Which is kind of funny, because if you asked Tori or really any one of my friends, they would probably say he wasn't my type. Honestly, though, he's incredibly smart, and nice, and really secure in himself. I wish I could be like that. And he's incredibly handsome. Just thinking about him makes me feel warm and tingly. I really like him and I am pretty certain he likes me. I'm too scared to say much more than that though. That fits well. Kelsey Edmundson, coward.

Kelsey Edmundson woke up in her own bed, in her own apartment in Anaheim, California. No time had passed. She brought Mark Barnes with her out of Pride and Prejudice. He woke up with her.

I finished it and reread what I had written before

folding the pages neatly and tucking them into the pocket in my skirt. I sincerely hoped Mark never had an opportunity to read this.

CHAPTER
Twenty

*"I am having a bit of a strange
post-modern moment here."*

I DONNED MY pelisse and my bonnet. It seemed kind of silly to wear a bonnet out in the middle of the night, but I was hoping it would help keep my head warm. Doubtful as it was so light and frilly.

I considered taking a candle with me, but I felt bad pilfering even a single candle from Charlotte.

I let myself out of the front door, closing it as quietly as I could, and made my way down the front walk. It was dark, but some light was provided by the moon. It wasn't until I had come here, so far away from the modern city that I was used to, that I'd noticed how much light the moon really gave off. I'd always thought it was funny in stories when people found their way anywhere by the light of the moon. But here, away from the miles and miles of modern electric lights I was used to, I'd discovered that the moon, especially when it was overhead and the sky was clear, could provide a shocking amount of light.

The amount of moonlight was a good thing because otherwise I likely would have turned my ankle on my way down the path. But because of the soft, silvery light, I was able to skirt the offending dips and ruts in the dirt path as it wound its way down the little hill and toward the main lane. I slowed as I reached the end of the walk, my eyes searching the semi-darkness for Mark. He'd said he'd be waiting for me, and when I didn't see him right away I felt the strangest piercing sadness in my chest. I barely had time to even register the feeling, let alone examine it in any detail, when he stepped quietly out from the dark shadows beneath a tree on the side of the lane.

"Evening," his low-pitched voice carried the few feet that separated us and caused a delicious shiver to shimmy up my spine.

"Mark." I replied.

He covered the remaining distance and reached for my hand which I gave to him freely. He tucked it into the crook of his arm, bringing me up so I was standing next to him. "Hey, you're taller!"

"Wasn't I earlier?"

"No, you were Lizzy height when I saw you last at the end of the lane, and here you are Kelsey height." He squinted at me in the dark. "And your hair."

"Yeah, it's back blonde. And straight, unfortunately. I kind of wish the curl hadn't gone," I ran a self-conscious hand over my loose bun.

He made a small, exasperated sound. "You've got

gorgeous hair, and you know it. Kazza spends a small fortune trying to make her hair look like yours."

I was secretly pleased that he thought I had gorgeous hair. "Does she?"

"Yeah, be careful, though. When she meets you she might try to scalp you for it. I don't know how to tell her that no matter what she does she will always be stuck with this out of control mop. She considers it some sort of genetic curse."

If I'd been pleased by his complimenting my hair, I was over the moon at the casual reference to me meeting his sister. I tried to tell myself to slow down and just worry about getting us out of the book first and about other stuff later, but it still made me happy.

We walked arm in arm toward the little grove of trees on the far side of the park where we'd met the previous two days. It was much slower going than it was during a morning walk, but the moon still guided our way, and there were worse things than walking next to Mark with my arm wrapped around his much stronger one. Even though our heights were similar, he still made me feel small and petite because of his strength. Touching him like this as we walked, I could tell that he kept most of that strength in check. It was interesting, he was so casual and so laid back, and he walked with an incredibly easy, loping stride, but I could feel his corded muscles under my fingers, and knew that if he wanted to turn that raw power on in a flash he could. I kind of desperately wanted to see it happen.

Focus on getting out, I reminded myself. *Just focus.*

We finally made it to the stand of trees. I could make out several dark shapes under one of the trees. I am pretty sure it was the tree we were leaning against earlier this morning when we kissed, and I hoped that it wasn't light enough that he could see my quick blush.

"What's that?" I asked in a low voice. I suppose this far out from either of the two houses we could speak in normal voices, but the intimacy of the soft darkness made me keep my voice lowered.

"I brought some stuff from Rosings," he answered, his voice also still low. "Blankets and stuff so we won't freeze. There hasn't been any frost these last few days, but you never know." He let go of my arm and walked over to the tree. He knelt down and rummaged around. A moment later I heard a match strike and a flame sputtered to life as Mark lit a candle. He turned back toward me and held the candle out so I could see the ground in front of me as I walked toward him.

"Oh, a candle! I thought about bringing one, but I didn't want to take one from Charlotte," I said as I reached the tree.

"Here sit down." He held his hand up to me and I took it as I sank down on the blanket he'd spread out picnic-style. "I think Lady Catherine can spare a few candles," he laughed as he turned to light the candle in a small lantern placed to the side of the blanket. He set the first candle carefully down in a holder and leaned back settling against a roll of blankets he'd propped against the tree trunk. "Come here," he gestured for me to join him and I scooted over, sitting next to him and snuggling into the crook of his arm. "Warm enough?"

I nodded against his chest.

"I've got a few more blankets we can put over us as it gets colder," he said nodding to a small stack of neatly folded blankets. "I'll blow that candle out in awhile too, once we get sleepy. I think the one in the lantern should be okay."

"You're certainly prepared," I teased softly. I was actually really touched by how much effort he'd gone to. But was afraid if I said anything that everything I was thinking and feeling about Mark—or pretending I wasn't thinking and feeling—would come tumbling out of me of its own volition.

I felt the laugh rumble in his chest. "You don't think I'd invite a girl out to the woods in the middle of the night and not bring some creature comforts with me, do you?"

I grinned into the dark, but tried to make my voice sounds as scandalized and severe as possible. "Do you often take young maidens out into the woods in the middle of the night, then?"

"It would be ungentlemanly of me to say," he sighed dramatically. I poked him in the ribs and he laughed again. "I can safely say that I've never done anything like this before."

"Yeah, it's a little bit unique," I said.

"A bit," he agreed.

"Thank you for making it so nice."

"You're welcome." We settled into a comfortable silence.

After a few minutes it was Mark who broke the silence. "Are you sleepy?"

"No."

"Me neither. You have your story, right?"

"Yup, it's in my pocket."

"How do you usually do this?"

"I usually fall asleep with my face smushed on it, 'cause that's how I got in. I fell asleep with the books smashed into my face. Really attractive, I'm sure."

I could feel him smile. I'm not sure how, my head was resting in the crook of his arm, but somehow I could just tell he was smiling down at the top of my head.

"Not everyone has to be attractive one hundred percent of the time. We're all allowed a few book face-smashings in our lives. I fall asleep reading all the time."

"Do you? What do you read?"

"Mostly incredibly dry historians rattling on about things they know very little about, but are very sure they are experts on. And I like a lot of detective fiction."

"Really?" I turned my head up to look at him. "Don't tell anyone 'cause it might ruin my rep as a classical lit girl, but my undergrad undergrad thesis was on Raymond Chandler."

"Kelsey Edmundson, are you a closet lover of the hard-boiled detective novel?" he asked with mock shock dripping from his voice.

"I admit nothing," I sniffed delicately. Mark dropped a kiss on the top of my hair. I froze, torn between acting casual and between turning my face up to his and begging him to kiss me for real. "How is it living with Lady Catherine de Bourgh?"

"That woman is a menace."

I snorted in laughter. "So I've heard."

"I basically just avoid her. At the moment it's pretty easy because she's angry at me."

"Oh really?" Now this was interesting. "What could you have possibly have done to make her angry? Darcy is her golden boy."

"Well, the first day or so I was here I didn't react...well...to the whole valet thing so apparently I wasn't properly attired for dinner."

I nodded against his chest. "Yeah, that having someone help you get dressed thing is weird. I'm guessing those cravats are hard to tie by yourself."

"But then my ultimate transgression was that I told her in no uncertain terms that Mr. Darcy wasn't going to marry his cousin. I may have used 'words not fit for delicate ears.' Honestly, I didn't mean to curse, she just took me by surprise."

"Oh my god, Mark. Did you 'bloody hell' Lady Catherine de Bourgh?" I was both horrified and delighted.

"Uh, yeah, that and a few other...descriptive terms. And she's right, they're not fit for delicate ears, so I won't repeat them."

"How gentlemanly of you." I grinned at the thought of Lady C's expression. "I'm surprised that none of your little un-Darcy outbursts have sent you back in the timeline. But on the other hand, I guess

I'm not. If not following the timeline hasn't then I guess it makes sense you could behave however you want and we'd keep chugging along time wise."

"There were really only the two. I've been trying to keep a low profile. Fitz keeps suggesting we go riding, but I'm not about to get on a horse. I mostly just spend time playing billiards or hiding out in the library."

I tilted my head up and stared at him. "Did you just call the Colonel 'Fitz?'"

Mark shrugged. "That's what Darcy calls him apparently."

"Seriously? What's his first name? Austen never tells us."

"I have no idea. I didn't really want to ask. He already thinks there's something wrong with my head."

"There is. It has curly read hair on it." I smiled so he knew I was teasing.

Mark laughed and wrapped his arm more tightly around my waist. We fell back into an easy silence. I'm not sure how long we sat there, but the night started growing colder and eventually I felt my eyelids getting heavier. I was surprised because I thought I'd be so wired that I wouldn't ever be able to fall asleep. But somehow, being here with Mark, half-sitting and half-lying here in the crook of his arm had helped melt away all of my stress and tension.

"Getting sleepy?" Mark asked when I stifled a yawn.

"Yeah. We should get covered up so we don't freeze."

Mark reached over and pulled a few blankets from the stack to the side of us and used his free arm to arrange two of them over us. I snuggled further into his side. He was like my own personal heater and with the blankets over us I was starting to get nice and toasty.

"Is your arm falling asleep?" I asked, yawning for real this time.

"You're fine," he answered, tightening his arm around my waist.

"That's not really an answer," I pointed out.

"My arm is not currently asleep," he laughed softly down at me. "Don't forget your story."

"Oh, yeah." I pulled it out of my pocket, opened the folded pages and debated what to do with them. I was really comfortable where I was. Mark solved the problem for me by gently taking them out of my hands and laying the open pages on his chest. I looked up at him and smiled.

"Goodnight, Mark," I said as I lay my head down on his chest, my cheek firmly pressed onto the pages. I reached across his chest and grabbed his other hand, lacing my fingers through his. "Don't let go," I reminded him.

"I won't. Goodnight, Kelsey."

As I drifted off to sleep I thought I felt him press another kiss to my head, but I was too far gone to be sure.

It was the light that eventually woke me up, and the warmth on my face. I could still feel Mark's warm body pressed into mine. I was laying half in the crook of his arm and half draped across his chest, our fingers still interlaced. I could feel his chest rising and falling steadily under me. I lay there for a few minutes, not willing to open my eyes and see if our attempt at getting out of the novel had worked. I figured we could just as easily be sprawled out on the bed in my room at the apartment as in the little grove in Rosings Park. There was a part of me that just didn't want to know. Lying here feeling Mark's chest move under my cheek was so close to heaven I didn't want to ruin it by opening my eyes.

A breeze blew across my face. I sighed and cracked my lids open. We were under the tree at Rosings. The sun had risen and was chasing off the last bits of pearly grey fog from between the trees. We were still very much stuck in *Pride and Prejudice*.

I made an unhappy little sound in the back of my throat. I'm not sure exactly what it was, some combination of a sigh and a sob I suppose. At the sound I felt Mark stir under me, and I tilted my head to look up into his face.

His was already looking down at me. I momentarily lost track of where I was and what I'd been thinking. His eyes always did me in. I couldn't quite make out the expression in them, so I offered him a small smile.

"Morning," I said in a small voice.

"Morning," he replied as a smile broke across his face. I noticed that his dimple had reappeared with a vengeance. That and—

"Oh, the bump on your nose is back!" I sat up and looked more closely at his face.

Mark grimaced. "Wonderful, the day's news just keeps getting better, doesn't it?"

"I like it." In a moment of uncharacteristic boldness, I reached out and ran my finger down his nose. He caught my hand, brought it to his lips and kissed it. I am pretty sure I blushed an unbecoming shade of bright red. "Do you not like your nose?" I asked. "You don't seem to have any image issues to me at all."

He shrugged, "I don't mind it. Everyone has some feature they wish was different, I guess. It's my dad's nose, but his never got broken like mine."

"It adds character," I informed him gravely and he laughed at me. "I suppose we should discuss the fact that we are still in *Pride and Prejudice*," I said after a moment.

"I suppose we should," he agreed. "Though, actually, I've got a more interesting topic I'd like to touch on."

"Do you? What could possibly be more interesting than us still being trapped in a book as fictional characters? More interesting that my best, and honestly my *only*, theory for getting us back home has failed spectacularly."

"Well," he paused, considering. "It might really be of more interest only to me, but I'm actually quite pleased with at least some of today's developments."

I looked at him, completely at a loss.

He sat up and reached over to the lantern and held it up in front of my face. I stared at it in confusion, the candle inside had long since burned down. I looked at it harder, and that is when I saw my reflection in the glass.

My reflection.

The wide set hazel eyes, the high cheekbones and mobile mouth, and that damn too-square jaw that was the bane of my existence. Kelsey Edmundson stared out at me from the glass on the lantern. I couldn't see a single trace of Lizzy Bennet.

CHAPTER
Twenty-One

*"I'm in a real identity
crisis here, Al!"*

WELL, THAT IS interesting," I admitted as stared at my reflection. And that is when I realized that this whole time I'd been speaking in my own voice. Gone was Lizzy's light soprano with its crisp British accent, back in full force was Kelsey's brash, American alto.

"I think it's awesome. I'd rather you looked like you." Mark set the lantern down and I attempted to school my features into a neutral expression.

"Thanks," I said. "I wonder if this means we've completely erased Lizzy and Darcy, or what?"

Mark eyed me speculatively and I shifted uncomfortably under his gaze. "Is that the only thing that's upset you?"

"I'm not upset."

He raised an eyebrow.

"Well, I'm not any more upset than a person who is stuck in a work of classical literature and has likely just destroyed the two main characters of said work has any right to be," I amended huffily.

"Uh huh," he grunted looking highly unconvinced.

"It's true," I insisted.

"You didn't seem this upset a few minutes ago."

"Well, that was before..." I trailed off and glanced away.

"Kels, are you upset that you look like yourself?"

"No, I'm upset that I've erased Elizabeth Bennet somehow." I thought I sounded pretty convincing, but he didn't look convinced and somehow my next words came out without my permission. "She's prettier than me."

To his credit Mark didn't laugh, but he did cross his arms as he leaned back on the tree trunk and studied me. "I guess it's just a matter of taste," he commented drily.

"Yeah? Well, I'd prefer to look like Lizzy," I bit out.

"I prefer you to look like you," Mark responded. "By a large margin."

I glared at his crossed arms and generally closed-off body language. "I can tell," I said sarcastically. It was probably not the smartest thing to say, it left me wide open to a whole world of hurt, but I couldn't help myself.

Mark ran his eyes over me before looking heavenward as if praying for patience.

"Kelsey, I am trying to keep myself from showing you—physically and explicitly—how much I like how you look. We happen to have serious things to discuss. And as much as I'd enjoy taking advantage of you here in the grass, they're going to miss you at the parsonage and we need to come up with a plan of action."

I don't think Crayola has yet invented color name that could adequately describe the bright red that infused my face. I have to admit, that only a part of me was flustered by what Mark had just said. The other part of me wanted to lean forward and kiss the section of collarbone the neckline of his shirt had gaped open to reveal just to see what would happen.

I couldn't think of anything to say in return that wouldn't sound horribly stupid and naïve, so I settled for whispering, "I don't have another plan of action."

"Well then, why don't we each think about it for awhile and maybe one of us will have a stroke of genius."

I nodded silently. Neither of us spoke for a moment. "I'm sorry, Mark," I said eventually.

He looked surprised. "For what?"

"That it didn't work. I really wanted it to work." I found myself fighting back tears. I'd wanted to wake up with Mark at home. Where we could have a chance together. Where we could be ourselves. I realized with a start that this was the first time in months that I'd wanted to be myself over someone else. Of course I'd wanted to get out of Caroline rather desperately, but it wasn't so I could stay myself so much as so I could try again to get into Lizzy. It was a cruel irony that now that I was finally looking forward to just being me I couldn't seem to figure it out.

"It's not your fault. For all we know you could still be here because you were holding on so tight to me and I held you back from jumping somehow. It might be better if you tried on your own to get out."

I shook my head violently.

"You could come back for me, like you said," he pointed out. "I mean, we could test the theory. If you can jump back out, then it's me holding you back."

"I'd rather not leave without you," I sniffed. "I don't know what will happen to the storyline or if I'll be able to get back to you."

"I appreciate it, but we might have to explore it as an option at some point."

"I'll come up with something better. I just need some time to think about it."

"Sure," he grinned at me. "Don't cry. It will work out."

"I'm not crying," I insisted as a tear slipped down my face.

"Why don't we get you back to the parsonage. Don't want to mess up your favorite book more than we already have, right?" He rose swiftly to his feet.

"Okay," I agreed half-heartedly. I was quickly losing interest in trying to preserve as much of the storyline as possible. We'd already screwed it up completely beyond repair as far as I could tell. What would it matter if anyone found Lizzy and Darcy traipsing in from having obviously spent the night together? At this point I was beginning to wonder if anyone would even notice. They didn't seem to be noticing other obvious physical changes going on around them.

"Darcy's valet is going to have a heart attack and die when he sees what you've done with this shirt." I shook my head sadly at the dirt and grass stains on Mark's back.

"I'm planning to hide it," he grinned at me mischievously. "Actually," he reached into the picnic basket and pulled out a neatly folded lawn shirt. "I should just bury it out here where he will never find it."

"You brought a change of clothes?" I'm sure I sounded as disappointed as I felt. "Did you know it wasn't going to work?"

"No. I just thought it was best to prepare for all contingencies." He pulled his shirt over his head, and I forgot what I was about to say.

Oh my gosh. I knew Mark worked out—I'd spent the better part of the night lying on top of his chest—but nothing had prepared me for the reality of Mark shirtless. I seriously almost cried. Angels may have sung. I made all sorts of promises to myself that I was going to start going to the gym when we got back.

"I—I—" I stuttered.

"I'm sorry. I didn't mean to make you upset." He looked over at me contritely, his arms halfway into the clean shirt.

I swallowed hard. "I'm going to need you to put your shirt on. Now."

I saw comprehension dawn in his eyes as he realized I wasn't melting into a Kelsey puddle because he'd prepared for my novel-jumping not to work. A slow grin spread across his face, but he obliged me by pulling the shirt over his head.

I gasped in a breath. I hadn't realized I'd been holding it. I felt lightheaded.

Mark walked over and offered me his hand. As I stood, Mark pulled me against himself and covered my mouth hungrily with his. I felt as if my entire body was bursting into flame. I kissed him back eagerly, running my hands up under his still untucked shirt, trailing my fingers across his corded abs. Before I could even settle into the kiss he broke it off and stepped away from me.

"Wha?" I slurred in confusion, my brain struggling to catch up.

"Sorry, I couldn't resist just one," Mark smiled in chagrin as he offered me his arm, "May I escort you home, Miss Edmundson? I promise I won't maul you again."

"That's unfortunate." I pouted at him for a moment before accepting his arm. "I'm not averse to being mauled, you know."

His smile widened. "I noticed, but somehow these Regency manners are rubbing off on me."

"Annoyingly bad timing for that to happen," I responded as we started walking back toward the lane. It was really later in the morning than I'd originally thought. We'd be lucky not to run into Mr. Collins on his morning walk. "Although, I suspect, even in the twenty-first century you've got rather old-fashioned manners."

"Hmm, this may be true. I admit nothing," he winked at me as he repeated my expression from the night before.

We walked the rest of the way in silence. Right before we got to the juncture of the lane with the walk that led up the little hill to the parsonage, Mark suddenly came to a halt. I took another step or two before I was pulled up short and realized he had stopped.

"Kelsey, will you go out with me again?"

"Go out with you?" I repeated, confused.

"Yes, like on a date."

I looked at him in shock. "Like right now?"

He smiled. "No, not right now, when we get home. A real date with dinner and everything, just you and me. I want to make up for our last one."

Something about the fact that Mark was making plans post *Pride and Prejudice* was comforting to me. It meant that he still thought we could get out of the book and also that he wanted to be involved with me post-book. I suppose I could have assumed that based on the last twenty-four hours or so, but I've learned that assumptions aren't always a good thing in relationships.

"Yes, of course I will go out with you."

He leaned forward and brushed a kiss across my forehead. "See you later today. Try not to freak out."

"Easier said than done," I responded darkly as I turned and made my way up the walk to the parsonage. I turned around halfway and waved back at Mark who returned my wave and then started back in the direction of Rosings.

I grinned as I watched him go. He really did wear breeches well. It probably was horrible of me to stand there and ogle him as he walked away. I found that I was completely unrepentant, however, and I watched until he was out of sight and then I turned and let myself in through the front door of the parsonage as quietly as I could.

It was apparently even later than I thought, because the family was already in the small breakfast room. Silently cursing whatever architect had decided to put the breakfast room so near the front of the house (my money was on Lady Catherine being behind it) I made a valiant attempt to walk past the open door without making any noise.

Charlotte looked up as I walked by and called out, "Lizzy, there you are. We thought you must be out on a walk but were wondering if you were ever going to get back."

I froze in place, but there was no getting out of it now. I reluctantly turned and entered the breakfast room.

"Yes. I am sorry to see I have missed the start of breakfast. I had quite a long walk and was going to just, um, freshen up a bit before coming back down."

Both Charlotte and Maria took in my rumpled clothes and mussed hair with widened eyes. Mr. Collins did not deign to look up from his sausage and eggs, which was just as well. I knew he had a moralizing streak hidden somewhere in that rotund body of his that I kind of wished to avoid.

Charlotte looked from me to her husband and then quickly back to me. "I am sure we would not mind if you took a moment to freshen up, Lizzy." Mr. Collins, still plowing through his breakfast, made an assenting noise without looking up from his plate.

I sent her a grateful look. "Thank you, Charlotte. I'll be right back."

I turned and left the room and nearly ran up the stairs. Once I got to my room and looked at myself in the mirror I almost collapsed in laughter. Mark may not have had his way with me outside under the trees but it certainly looked like he had. My hair was a complete mess, my clothes were creased, there was a rather large grass stain on my skirt, and a smear of ink on my chin from pressing my face into my story. I can't believe Mark didn't say anything before he let me walk into the parsonage. I was going to have to read him the riot act. Although, there wasn't much I could have done about it if I had known I suppose, maybe run my hands over my hair and try to make it look a bit more decent.

God knows what Charlotte thought I'd been doing. I was so glad Mr. Collins hadn't seen my state of dishabille. He likely would have carried the tale to Lady Catherine. It turned out he was a bit of a gossip about his poor parishioners. He considered it his duty to report all of their failings to Lady Catherine, and Lady Catherine in turn, thought it her duty to correct all of their bad behavior.

I sorted myself out as best I could, put on a new dress, and went down to breakfast. To her credit, Charlotte never asked me what had wreaked such havoc with my appearance, even after Mr. Collins went out to visit in the village and we were all assembled together in the sitting room. I could tell

Maria was dying of curiosity, but she seemed wise enough to follow her older sister's lead in social situations. Neither of them seemed to notice my complete physical transformation either. It was weird, yesterday when it had been just my height and my hair, Maria had said I looked as I always had. And much like Mark had found with Darcy's clothes, mine fit even though there was a height difference. For my part, I was more than willing not to bring either topic up, so we conversed on typical daily topics and whether or not we might see the two gentlemen from Rosings later.

I knew for a fact that they would call, but I couldn't exactly say that to either lady. Behind my polite conversation I was trying to figure out another possible option for getting out of the book. A new theory to present Mark with when he came that afternoon.

Mr. Darcy and Colonel Fitzwilliam came by the parsonage later that afternoon. Unfortunately, Mark and I didn't get much chance to speak privately. Charlotte must have been beginning to suspect something because she watched us like a hawk; conveniently placing herself where she could see both our faces and abandoning her sister to Colonel Fitzwilliam's flirtations.

When they finally got up to leave, Mark bowed in my direction. "Good afternoon, Miss Bennet, Mrs. Collins, Miss Lucas."

"Mr. Darcy." Charlotte and I curtsied in response, but I delayed my curtsy long enough to see Mark mouth "Trees. Morning." over Charlotte's head.

CHAPTER
Twenty-Two

*"Till this moment, I never
knew myself."*

WE MET BACK at the little copse of trees I was starting to think of as "our spot." We were going to have to stop meeting here. Eventually we would get caught. There were just too many opportunities for discovery; too many risks. I suppose if we got caught, Darcy and Elizabeth would be forced to marry. I'd briefly considered what would happen if Mark and I just sped up the timeline by announcing Darcy's and Lizzy's engagement and heading off to the altar. Would the book finally kick us out because we'd achieved happiness for literature's most beloved couple? I somehow doubted that. If there was one thing I'd discovered about *Pride and Prejudice* while I'd been here, it was that it wanted to be played like it was written.

I'd already done enough damage by bringing Mark here. He wasn't like me. He was stronger than me and being with him made me stronger. I was convinced that's why he was changing Darcy. And why I'd started changing Lizzy once I'd kissed him.

But I think the book still wanted to be played correctly.

"What's the new theory?" Mark asked me after a quick kiss hello.

"You're not going to like it," I warned.

"Try me."

"You remember how I said that if I played a scene wrong, I'd get bumped back until I did it right?"

"Yeah, but that's stopped happening."

"Yes, ever since I pulled you in. And we've changed the main characters. But I think the book isn't letting us out because we need to fix it. We need to proceed forward with the timeline of the novel and let it play itself out. When I've left before I was leaving the storyline undamaged, but we've broken it and we have to repair it."

Mark nodded. "I guess that makes sense in a way. But isn't there a lot of time left in the book?"

I glanced up at him through my lowered lashes, trying to gauge his reaction as I answered. "A little over eight months."

"Eight months?" Mark ran his hand through his unruly curls. "Seriously?"

"Well, it's the beginning of April now. Lizzy and Darcy won't see each other again until the start of August. Then they don't see each other again until September. Then they finally get engaged in October and married some time in December."

"So you want us to not see each other, at all, for four months?" He still looked shocked, and something else I couldn't quite put my finger on.

"No. I think it sucks. But I think it's best chance we have." I fought the tears I felt prickng behind my eyes.

"Kels, babe, don't cry." Mark pulled me closer and wrapped his arms around my waist. I rested my head on his shoulder, my face buried in his neck. How was I going to go four whole months without even seeing him? And then even more months before we could be together? We were talking about staying almost two thirds of a year here, most of it apart.

"There's gotta be another way," he muttered as he stroked my hair. "What if we got married now? I mean isn't that the point of the book—Darcy and Elizabeth get married? We just take a shorter route to the end of the book."

"I don't think it will work," I said sadly into his neck. "Too many things have to happen to other characters that wouldn't happen if we did that. Bingley and Jane wouldn't get together, Lydia wouldn't end up with Wickham—that'd be an improvement actually, but I think it has to happen how Austen wrote it."

"And how she wrote it is?"

"You propose, and I reject you, and you go off and become a better person, and then I see your house and fall in love with you."

Mark laughed. I snuggled closer, trying to savor every second of his laughter. I was going to have a very long, lonely, road ahead of me. And so was he.

And it was all my fault.

"I'm so sorry, Mark. I'm sure spending eight months in Regency England wasn't really on your bucket list."

"Not really. But we'll survive it if we have to, right? If you think it's our best shot, we have to try it."

"Yeah. It's the best I can come up."

Mark continued to stroke my hair. I wished that we could just stay like that forever. "You're going to have to tell me everything I have to do."

"I wrote down everything I could think of. Where you're supposed to be and when. The good thing is once we get the timeline moving again I think it will just sort of sweep us along with it." I reluctantly stood back from him and handed him a sealed letter. "It's all in here."

Mark took it. "Is this my *Pride and Prejudice* instruction manual?"

I nodded. "The first thing is we have to get the first proposal out of the way. I put it in there for you to memorize. I...I say some pretty nasty stuff. So does Darcy."

"I think I can handle it."

"Okay." I stared at him. "The Collins's are supposed to dine at Rosings, then you come over and propose."

"I'll tell Lady Catherine I want to have you all over for dinner tonight then."

I swallowed. Tonight. God, that seemed soon. I knew it was best to get it over with, like pulling a Band Aid off. Then we could get on with the rest of the story. The sooner we parted the sooner we'd be together. That made sense to my head, but oh my god, it didn't make sense to my heart.

"Oh, I almost forgot. I brought you something," Mark smiled at me, his dimple winking. He pulled a few sheets of folded paper out of his jacket and handed them to me. "Read it later, though. It'd be weird if you read it in front of me."

"What is it?"

"My story, the second one. The one I didn't show you."

"Oh." I was suddenly dying to read it. But reading it meant leaving Mark and going back to the parsonage.

"So this is goodbye as Kels and Mark, huh?" He asked. "When I see you tonight it's just Darcy and Lizzy."

I nodded. "I'm so sorry."

"Stop." He pulled me back into his arms. "No more sorries. Let me say goodbye to you properly."

Mark's kiss was full of everything I wished I could somehow say to him. Full of longing, desire, and just a hint of desperation. His mouth moved over mine, sometimes soft and worshipful like a prayer, sometimes hard and rough like a there was a fire raging between us.

The tears were streaming down my face, completely unheeded. His lips left mine just long enough to kiss the tears away and then returned with a passion that left me breathless. My arms wrapped around his neck, my fingers tangling in his hair, trying somehow to bring him even closer to me.

I wasn't going to be able to let him go.

He did it for me. Because he'd always made things easier for me, even when I didn't deserve it. He untangled my arms from his neck then leant forward, cupping my face in his hands, dropping a kiss on each of my closed eyelids.

"Goodbye, Kelsey." He whispered in my ear. I felt him move away. I couldn't open my eyes as I heard him start to walk back toward Rosings.

"Goodbye, Mark." I whispered.

I ran all the way back to the parsonage clutching the papers he'd given me to my chest. I didn't stop to say hello to anyone, just sprinted up the stairs to my room and slammed the door behind me. I sat down in the chair by the window and opened Mark's pages with shaky hands. It was pretty much the same as the story he'd written originally. Until the end.

Kelsey. She's the reason I'm here. I don't know how or why she pulled me into this novel, but I'm kind of glad she did. That might sound weird, but if she is here, I'd rather be here with her.

She fascinates me. I know she thinks that the Lizzy character is prettier than her, but she's so wrong. I could watch Kelsey's face for hours, everything she thinks shows up in her expressions.

She reminds me of the ocean. She's got undertow...in a good way. In a 'pull you down and drown you in the love of a good woman' way. In the 'it will seep into you and sink into your pores and immerse you way.' But also in the 'it will challenge and push you and pull you apart and help put you back together better than you were before' way.

I cried until the tears ran out.

That night Mark stood before me, wearing Darcy's best jacket, his cravat tied in an intricate pattern that must have taken at least an hour. He didn't let on that we were playing a scene at all—no smile or reassuring wink. He'd fully committed to the role, and those famous words were uttered with absolute perfection. Who knew Mark was such a good actor?

"In vain have I struggled. It will not do. My feelings will not be repressed. You must allow me to tell you how ardently I admire and love you."

He continued on, expressing Darcy's opinions of the inferiority of Lizzy's connections, of her family's manners, of his own pride. Jane hadn't given us an actual script here, so I'd written him a hybrid of the proposal scenes from the two most famous movies. He'd memorized it well.

I stared at him. Which was probably good because that was what Lizzy was supposed to do. There was an almost audible breaking sound coming from the vicinity of my heart. I wanted him to be saying those words for real. Or maybe not those words exactly, because Mark wasn't Darcy and, thank God, could never really *be* Darcy. He wasn't proud, self-conscious, or arrogant. He wasn't any of the things that Darcy was up until this point—up until he came up hard against Lizzy's vivacious, open, and honest spirit and found himself lacking.

I was the Darcy. I was the one trying to hide my own insecurities behind stupid bravado. The one quick to jump to conclusions, the one who retreated inside a wall of silence and secretly coveted Mark's ease and openness. And Mark saw straight through it all.

He was waiting for me to reply, to play the scene like we'd decided—straight to Austen. I opened my mouth but the words wouldn't come.

Elizabeth may have rejected Darcy, but I couldn't bring myself to reject Mark, even if it was fake.

"I...I can't," I finally managed. He looked at me in surprise, one eyebrow raised, wondering why I'd just veered off track. "Mark, I don't think I can do this." I stood up, and took a tentative step toward him. "I'm sorry, it might be the only way, but I can't just say no to you and not see you for months and months."

Mark reached out his hand and I took it gratefully, closing the last few steps between us.

"Why, Kelsey?" he asked, looking into my eyes.

I had to say it. I couldn't be a coward anymore.

"I can't have you say those things—that you love

and admire me—and not have them be *to* me. I can't have you say someone else's words like that, it breaks my heart. I won't sit here and listen to it because—" I swallowed; my throat was painfully dry. "Because I love you. I love *you*. Mark Barnes, not Mr. Darcy or —"

I think I would have kept blabbering on for goodness knows how long except that Mark cut me off with a kiss that took my world apart. Took it apart and then rebuilt it, piece by piece, with his kiss at the center.

I kissed him back with everything that was in me. I didn't care anymore about anything but me and Mark. I didn't care if we destroyed *Pride and Prejudice*. I didn't care if Lizzy ended up with Darcy. I didn't care about anything but us. Our story.

I don't know how long we stood there, Mark re-writing my life's story with his lips, but when he finally lifted his head from mine it felt like it had been forever and somehow not long enough.

"Darcy did make a rather poor job out of it the first time," he brushed a strand of hair off my neck with his thumb. At some point his hand had found its way up to the back of my neck, cradling the back of my head. "I'd rather not be stuck with his words. I love you, Kelsey Edmundson, the end. No qualifications, no struggling with anything at all."

There wasn't any way to respond to that other than to wrap my arms around his neck and pull his head closer to mine. You know, sometimes reality really is better than fiction.

As Mark's lips settled onto mine again I gasped against them, pulling away slightly.

"Kels?" He asked, concern etching his brow.

"Wait! Wait!" I jerked out of his arms and ran to the small writing table in the corner of the room, scrabbling around for a quill and ink. "Just a sec!" I grabbed a piece of paper and wrote frantically on it. I threw down the quill and waved the sheet of paper in the air, hoping the ink would dry quickly. I tested it delicately with my finger. It didn't smudge so I folded it up and held it in the palm of my hand.

I ran back to Mark. "Sorry," I said, a little out of breath. "I just had to do something."

"No problem. Not quite the reaction I was expecting after declaring undying love and all that—"

"Shut up and kiss me," I instructed.

He laughed that deep, delicious laugh that always turned my insides out. He drew me close, his strong arms wrapped around my waist, "No more running away," he whispered as he leaned forward.

"No more running," I agreed as I brought my hand up resting my palm and that folded piece of paper against his strong, broad chest. He captured my mouth with his and I whispered against his lips "Let's wake up, Mark."

A rushing sound, like waves crashing inside my head, filled my ears. I could feel the familiar pull and push that I'd experienced so many times when popping back into a scene. I ignored it all, keeping my eyes tightly closed as I focused on the sensation of Mark's arms around me, on the feel of his lips on mine.

I felt the bright, warm light on my face. I cracked an eyelid open and glanced up. I'd left the blinds open again and the brilliant Californian sun was streaming cheerfully through the window.

I was in my own bed, in my own apartment. The bright face of my bedside alarm clock had the right date on it. It was as if no time had passed and nothing had changed.

Except for the warm, strong, male body that was sprawled out under me, his large hands still gripping my waist.

I took a moment to study Mark's face, he still had his eyes closed, his sandy colored lashes resting against his cheek. I thought for a moment my heart might actually burst with happiness. I reached up and ran a finger across his cheekbone as if to make sure he was really there.

Mark's eyes opened. He took in the popcorn ceiling of my bedroom before his gaze centered onto my face, hovering a few inches above his. A slow smile spread across his face as he reached up and pulled me down for a kiss. It was long, slow, and completely brain-melting. At some point he rolled me to the side, our legs tangling together. I lay there in the crook of his arm as I kissed him back with everything I had.

I could feel laughter rumbling in his chest as he finally broke the kiss. "Well, I'll be damned," he laughed. "How did you manage that?"

I smiled, feeling suddenly shy. I was still clutching the sheet of paper in a death grip against his chest. I managed to pry it out of my hand and hand it to him.

Mark unfolded the wrinkled paper and read what I'd written.

"I know you love *Pride and Prejudice*," he said as he grinned at me. "But I like this better."

I took the paper from him and looked down at the simple phrase:

Kelsey Edmundson loves Mark Barnes.

The End.

"So do I," I answered.

~ The End ~

CHAPTER
Quotes

ACKNOWLEDGEMENTS

Attempting Elizabeth would not have been possible without the amazing work of Jane Austen. I owe her a debt of gratitude both as a reader and a writer.

Thank you to my husband, Edward, and my children, Maddie and James, for your love and support, and for letting me "go writing."

The Austen community, especially the readers and contributors at IndieJane.org have been so supportive of this project. Kelsey's story would never have been told without your encouragement. Thank you to Nancy Kelley, my Indie Jane partner in crime, for always believing in this story.

Attempting Elizabeth was originally written as a short story for the Jane Austen Made Me Do It contest hosted by Laurel Ann Nattress. Many thanks to Laurel Ann for providing such a great opportunity and for supporting all of the writers involved.

I have the best beta readers, story editors, and editors without whom I would be lost: Kimberly Truesdale, Patricia Marquez, Rebecca Nyenhuis, Jacqueline Maxman, C. Allyn Pierson, Amanda Beaty Chambers, and Mark House.

The writing community on Twitter is such a valuable resource. I would like to thank Jennie Kohl Austin for responding to my desperate plot tweet with a suggestion that changed the course of this novel for the better.

Special thanks to my Australian dialect coach and editor Rob Austen.

To the Starbucks on Prospect in Helena, thanks for never getting tired of me taking up the back table with a wall outlet and for providing me with lots of caffeine in delicious and fattening delivery systems.

As always, a huge thank you to Jennifer Becton for inspiring me to self-publish and for being such a wonderful and giving colleague.

A huge thank you to my amazing cover designer and biggest cheerleader Victoria Austen-Young. Thank you for always talking me down off the ledge, spending countless hours looking at pictures of rugby players with me for "name research," never laughing at my crazy ideas, making sense of my ramblings, correcting my Aussie speak, and generally being awesome.

ABOUT THE AUTHOR

Jessica Grey is an author, Janeite, fairytale believer, baseball lover, and recovering Star Wars fangirl. A life-long Californian, she now lives in Montana with her husband and two children, where she spend her time writing, perfecting the fine art of preschooler-wrangling, and drinking way too much caffeine.

You can follow Jessica on Twitter @_JessicaGrey or read her blog at www.authorjessicagrey.com

Also by Jessica Grey...

a fairytale

Alexandra Martin didn't believe in fairytales...

Alex has always been more interested in rocks and science than stories about princesses and magic. Now she's far too busy with her summer internship at the Gem and Mineral Museum to think about children's stories. Between avoiding her former best friend and high school baseball star, Luke Reed, and trying to hide her unrequited crush on her mentor at the museum, the real world is occupying all of her time.

...Until she walked into one.

It turns out fairytales aren't all fun and games. A curse has turned her neat and orderly world upside down, and to break it, she bands together with a fellow intern and a recently awakened princess who's been asleep for 900 years. Can this trio of unlikely heroines put an end to an ominous enchantment, discover true love, and keep an ancient and evil magic from being unleashed on modern-day Los Angeles?

THE TOWER

After spending her whole life isolated in a tower, Rapunzel's salvation is finally at hand, but she may have merely traded one form of captivity for another...

Special Agent Alice Harrison of the Office of Narrative Order should know better than anyone not to follow a suspicious (and suspiciously good-looking) man in a white rabbit suit down a hole...

Miss Lucinda Beacham is bored. The endless balls and dances she must endure as a debutante hold no enjoyment for her—that is until she finds a frog sitting on the edge of a fountain, a frog who just so happens to know her name...

Being a fairy godmother isn't all it's cracked up to be, especially when you're a junior in high school and your next assignment is your former crush...

Views from the Tower is a collection of short stories that offers new perspectives on some of your favorite fairy tales, including a trio of different takes on Rapunzel. Each story offers a unique foray into the exciting world of fantasy, as well as a golden opportunity to see some well-known legends in a whole new light.

Made in the USA
Charleston, SC
28 September 2013